THIRST

A NOVEL

THIRST

A NOVEL

K.L. BARRON

SEA CROW PRESS
AMPLIFYING VOICES
www.seacrowpress.com

to Greg
and to my mothers, daughters, and fathers

"To survive in the desert is to dominate destiny."
—Mano Dayak

CONTENTS

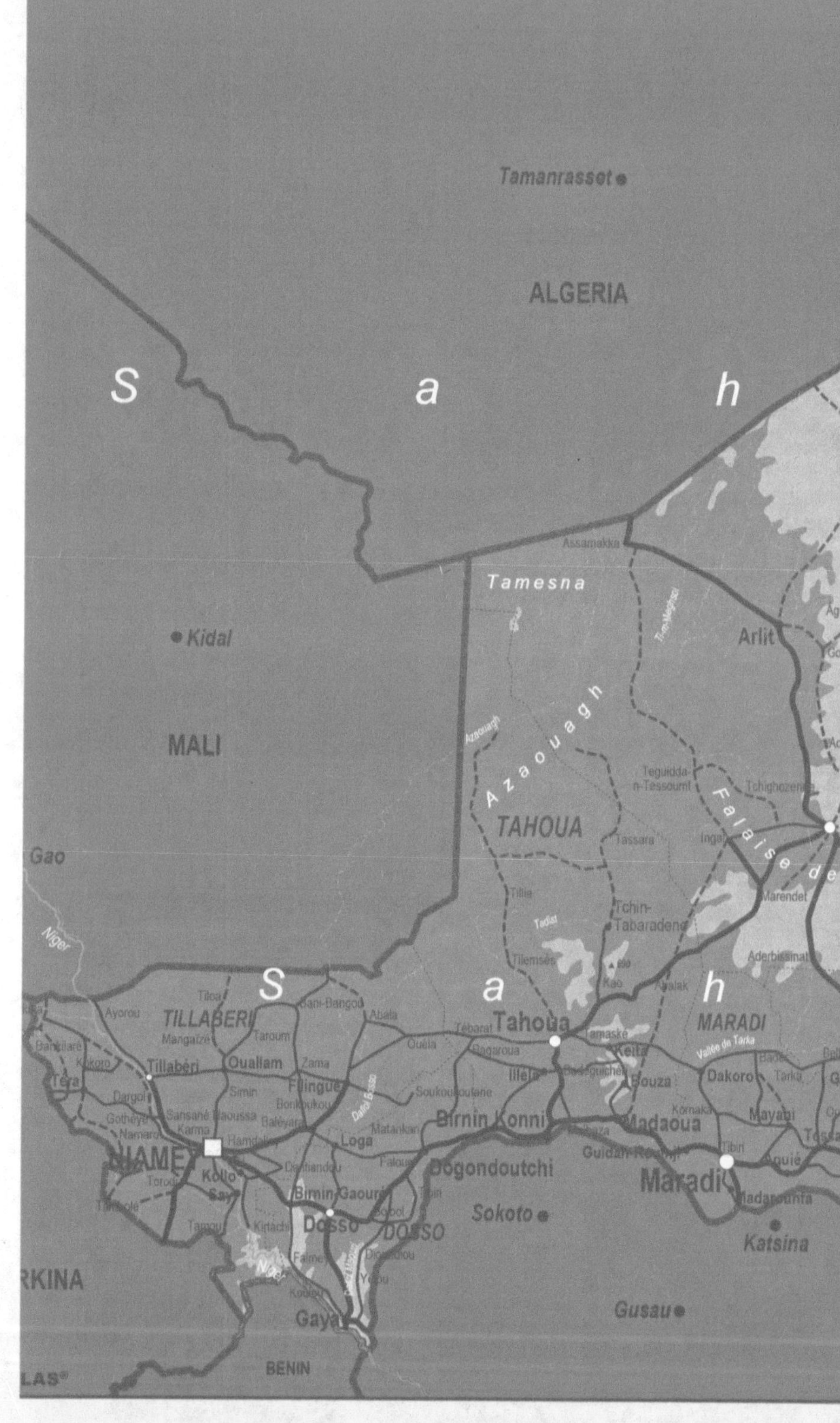

ALGERIA
Tamanrasset
S   a   h
Assamakka
Tamesna
Kidal
Arlit
Azaouagh
MALI
Teguidda-n-Tessoumt
Tchighozerine
Azouagh
Falaise de
TAHOUA
Tassara
Ingal
Gao
Tillia
Marendet
Niger
Tadist
Tchin-Tabaradene
Tilemsès
Aderbissinat
Kao
S   a   h
Tiloa
Bani-Bangou
Abala
Teguey
Balak
Ayorou
TILLABERI
Taroum
Tébarat
Tahoua
Tamaské
MARADI
Bankilaré
Mangaïzé
Oualla
Baguroua
Keita
Vallée de Tarka
Kokoro
Tillabéri
Ouallam
Zama
Illéla
Badeguicheri
Bouza
Dakoro
Tarka
Ga
Téra
Filingué
Bonkoukou
Soukoukoutane
Komaka
Dargol
Simin
Dalla Bosso
Mayahi
Gothèye
Sansané Haoussa
Baléyara
Matankari
Birnin Konni
Madaoua
Tessao
Namaro
Karma
Hamdallay
Loga
Falou
Guidan-Roumji
Tibiri
Aguié
NIAME
Dallandou
Dogondoutchi
Maradi
Torodi
Kollo
Say
Madaraunfa
Tillole
Birnin Gaouri
Sokoto
Sokoto
Tamou
Kirtachi
DOSSO
DOSSO
Diokouchou
Katsina
Falmey
Yélou
Namé
RKINA
Koulou
Gusau
Gaya
LAS
BENIN

Plateau du Mangueni
▲1120 Pic d'Ahoh
▲1054
Enneri Achelouma
▲1176 Eni Lulu
Madama
Plateau du Djado
Erg du Bouma
▲878
Djado
Chirfa
Ténéré du
Dao Timmi
Tafassâsset
Séguédine
AGADEZ
577
Aney
Dirkou
Bilma
Grand Erg de Bilma
Tchighazérine
Kaouar
▲1635
1635
Fachi
Erg du Ténéré
ZINDER
Termit-Kaoboul
DIFFA
Tégouma
Ngourti
Tasker
Dilia
Manga
Koufey
Boultoum
▲615
Mao
Nguigmi
Damagaram Takaya
Gouré
Kellé
Lac Tchad
(Lake Chad)
Bol
Goudoumaria
Kabélawa
Bossa
Kalguéri
Alkaman
Diffa
Bené
Maïné-Soroa
Dengas
Ndjamena
CHAD
NIGERIA
Maiduguri
CAMEROON
0 km

INTRODUCTION

This is a work of fiction. The characters are fictitious, though some historical figures are mentioned. The places and historical political events are real.

It is a perspective, from a Western point of view, of life on the Sahel in Niger, the edge of the Sahara, in the 80s and 90s. I only lived among the nomads in this place a short time. The Tuaregs have always lived there it seems, at least since the 15th century, as a part of the desert landscape, the desert landscape as part of them, time and boundaries, a Western construct. The chapters are arranged by Sahelian season: hot season, rainy season, and cold season with the year and location included for clarity. Any expression of the political situation from the Tuareg perspective is my interpretation of Tuareg leader, poet, and negotiator Mano Dayak's thoughts in his books *Touareg, la Tragedie,* and *Je Suis Né Avec Sable Dans Les Yeux.*

Readers may have seen images of Tuaregs astride camels, the indigo dye of their diaphanous clothes staining their faces blue, may have heard their music, attended their concerts where they are dressed in desert garb, playing their local drums and western guitars, and listened to the lyrics in their language, Tamasheq. Readers may recognize the Tuaregs from the news over the years, and if they believe many governments' perspectives including that of the United States' (global war on terror), they may see Tuaregs as terrorists, but that is not true, and that truth is the inspiration for this novel. Fiction's power is the ability to speak the truth—or at least a truth.

This novel is about love, about personal and cultural identity, and what it takes to survive in a brutal landscape, personally, geographically, and politically. It is a blend of memory, research, and imagination. I hope it honors the Tuaregs who have been surviving on the margins their entire lives despite the odds.

PROLOGUE

HOT SEASON, TCHIN-TABARADEN, NIGER 1990

A deep roar startled the camels and goats. They shied away from the trough, water dripping from their mouths. Nomads drawing the water from the well dropped their black rubber buckets on the sand. The sound came not from a predator stalking their animals from the surrounding dunes but from above. They shaded their eyes against the sun. "Avions," airplanes, a shirtless schoolboy shouted, his friends jumping and waving their arms.

Nearby, women pounding millet paused, the sudden sound and shadows of the planes interrupting the steady rhythm of their wooden pestles. Business at the market stopped mid-transaction as the traders turned from the piles of spices and silver bracelets and looked up. Along the sand roads in the village and in the dunes beyond, the Tuaregs stopped and turned their faces toward the sky, then hurried along when someone saw the first armored cars.

Clouds of dust from the vehicles hung in the air. No one knew what was happening. Traders peered from their doorways unsure of why the military was there but knowing the gendarmes, military police, would be thirsty and hungry from the journey. One vendor quickly rewrapped his turban and arranged some orange Fanta under damp burlap bags on a table in front of his shop. A soldier got out of a car, opened a bottle with his teeth, and drank it without paying.

The feral dogs ran wild when paratroopers started dropping to the ground. The students and teachers, the families in their encampments, even those in the refugee camps were taken by surprise—all except a handful of young Tuaregs running for their lives.

CHAPTER ONE

SUMMER, GAIA COMMUNE, CENTRAL VALLEY, CALIFORNIA, 1989

The commune dogs loped after us through the garden, past the yellow heads of sunflowers, over the ripe strawberries we didn't pick to sell at the market but left for the birds, cutting sharp turns against the sea-colored herbs, their fragrance clinging to our skin, to our destination: a concrete statue in a cemetery, an unnamed young girl holding a flower basket. She called to us, splitting us from what we knew of time, waiting for us, binding us together.

I slowed, waiting for Gita to catch up.

"Lark," she said out of breath. "It's not a race."

I'd thought it was, but the entire moon of her face lit up against her dark hair, her cheeks flushed, her water-colored eyes glinting, and I realized it wasn't.

We were fifteen, showered excessively and smelled of soap, lightly floral scented with hints of sage and honey rather than the heavy patchouli our mothers favored. I was still growing into myself like the others our age. Gita was physically fragile but already fully herself, and I loved her more than anyone. We'd written our goals on handmade paper rolled into scrolls and bound with narrow blades of grass. Every year, Gita and I took them to our private place, the concrete girl, to read aloud five

3

goals to her and to ourselves, promising to help each other attain them, then we burnt the evidence so it flew into the ether. No one else's business.

She handed me hers to read:

- To go once a month to the hardware store in town to study faucets (she liked design)
- To weave some window blinds out of slump grass
- To climb to the top of the sycamore
- To go to at least one high school party in town
- To reveal myself to my true love

"Who is your true love?"

Her expression reminded me of the Mona Lisa. "I could be more help if I knew."

"Pay attention and maybe you'll figure it out." She lit a clove cigarette and unrolled my scroll. "Now yours."

I breathed in the smoky herbal scent and tried to relax but felt restless. I knew I wanted something, but I couldn't say what. Still, I'd made a list:

- To drive the truck to market (so we can drive around town)
- To find a rookery
- To get my own camera
- To learn to sing opera (ha-ha)
- To start a beehive
- To read 52 poets and write 52 poems of my own

"That's two."

"The opera one was a joke."

"I know. The poet/poetry one."

"Do you think the little girl cares?"

Gita puffed on her cigarette. "She's just glad we're here."

I nodded, a bead of sweat tickling my neck.

Gita handed me a hairband, then drew hard on her cigarette and lit my scroll, handing her cigarette to me.

"Lighter," I said snapping my fingers and holding out my hand. I did not have her patience. She had to constantly blow on the charred edges to get them to ignite, but gradually all our goals disappeared from our grip as smoke and ash, and we walked, Gita completely spent from her exertion, back to the commune.

When we passed the barn converted into a garage, a guy from our Montessori days glanced up from the truck he was working on. A saffron limbal ring around his hazel eyes matched the paint smudged on his white t-shirt. Any sense of solid ground fell away beneath my feet. All my senses not only acute but vibrating, as if I were able to exist on multiple planes at once, pure positive energy.

"Your aura is sparkling," Gita whispered

He extracted himself from under the hood. Dark stubble on his chin, several shades of blonde hair grazing his shoulders.

"Is it going to make it?" I asked. The truck had been running rough, missing, the topic of our last group meeting.

"You driving it to market?"

I'd only practiced driving in the field. "Yes."

"I replaced the spark plug. Should be good to go." Then glanced directly at me. "For you."

He looked down at his feet—white Converse high-tops—and picked up a marble the same color of mottled hazel as his eyes. A child must have lost it. Maybe me when I was younger, maybe Gita, maybe him. He rubbed it clean, turning it between his fingers and thumb. When he placed the marble in my palm, it turned into a tiny sea with white caps.

I kissed him. Eyes closed, lips touching, tasting. Hormones and pheromones firing in all directions like time-lapsed complex root systems racing through the earth's current, bolting like underground lightning, mooring us deep into the earth before bursting into the light.

When I came back to myself, Gita had disappeared.

We were raised to accept biology, not fight it, and to be

responsible. I went to the midwife for protection. She suggested an IUD. "No need to add unnecessary chemicals to your system."

I met Roy at my tree. I spread out a batik, thin as breath in shades and patterns of green. We lay on it, looking up at the stars until I turned into him. The contours of his body, the sensual curves of a familiar landscape, heavy buds opening, blossoming. It seemed as divine as sensual, simultaneous and inextricable.

Every week, we took the commune truck to the market, sold out of the veggies, eggs, and flowers, and then explored. He gave me a Roelli 35S camera he'd found at the flea market, and we came up with the idea to sell vintage black and white photos to pay for gas and an excuse to take the truck on longer excursions away from the commune. We took turns driving, but I chose the destination: a rookery, bird sanctuary, wildlife refuge, a tree, a field, a view of the sky, a car show where he peered under the hoods, and I captured the lines, the curves, the light of the vehicles, the stance, the expressions of the owners, the onlookers. We drove to Death Valley, Mt. Whitney, to the Bonneville Salt Flats to watch the races, the desolate landscape one of my most powerful photographs.

We watched the Dakar off road race on the commune TV. I photographed Roy watching, tried to see what he saw. He built me hive boxes and we captured a swarm of wild bees on one of our camping trips, adding more photographs, honey, and beeswax candles to the market produce. I wrote him poems. We made love in every place we ever went.

"Put your camera down and dance with me," Roy said. In the blind, waiting for the light to see the cranes pausing at that place on their migration. The sensation of his breath on my neck, the leathery scent of his skin. Dancing so slowly, so blindly. We held each other up, breathed for each other. We flew as we stepped from our bodies. After the car show, during the road race, under the tree, the stars, in the grass, in the back seat. Like thirst.

I saw Gita only rarely now. While she wove her grass blinds, I sat next to her weaving a rag rug from Roy's old jeans.

"You look like a goddess," she said.

I felt like one. I glanced over and met her gaze. The fibers stung our eyes. "I miss seeing you," I said, but I never once went to the hardware store with her.

I saw her try to scale the sycamore, but she lacked the strength or balance to make it to the top, or maybe she changed her mind halfway, the commune dogs barking at the base, pawing the trunk. They split their time now between Roy and me, and Gita, their own equal visitation.

Sometimes our names aligned on the chore list, and we prepared the evening meal together or weeded the garden. We went to one town party.

"You're always so distracted," she said with her little laugh as if amused rather than mad or hurt. Her porcelain face always composed. She had the best manners of anyone on the commune. We no longer met at the concrete girl, but I knew she understood, or she would when she revealed herself to her true love.

Roy and I remained inseparable for a thousand days. One hundred thousand moments if you calculate moments as 90 seconds as some do. But such moments have nothing to do with time. Those moments are immeasurable, richer, more complex than any linear measurement.

When I saw Roy holding hands with Gita, their arms intertwined as they murmured together, heads inclined, the air got knocked out of my lungs as if I'd fallen from the top of the sycamore. I remained somehow vertical, trying to learn the language for that moment, but I didn't know what it was. Not as if the fragments could be gathered up and formed into something comprehensible.

"Lark," Roy called.

"Lark," Gita echoed.

Our eyes sparked as we passed. I kept walking.

Everything whirled together in my mind: Roy is Gita's true

love. Gita is passive aggressive. Roy's an idiot. Roy played me. I'm an idiot. I tried to separate it all out, to regain my balance, so I could function. We knew the intense attraction we would never fight. Why would we? Within the commune, we shared everything: economy, property rights, gender and power, common child-rearing, voluntary division of labor, a relationship with nature, each other.

At first, I acted as if I didn't care that Roy and I had split up. With Gita, all my parents, every single person who lived on the commune. Especially Roy. I upheld the code.

But this is the truth: Amputation. With no anesthesia. I had to fight myself to the death to let Roy go. I split from my body and watched it happen from a distance.

When the resident psych asked how I was feeling, I told him. "I could light myself on fire and burst into flames and not feel anything." No pain. No ecstasy either.

He acted surprised. "Our commune is based on the dissolution of one-on-one relationships," he said.

I thought I knew what that meant, but that was before Roy and me. Now, I not only had to break up with Roy and Gita but with the entire commune, the landscape, the dogs, Oblio, my favorite, everything I'd known.

"May I make an observation?"

His voice sounded smoky or sharp, my senses ashes. "What."

"It seems you seek emotional excess. For example, the sometimes violent, sometimes pure sublimity you find in nature, in weather."

"Ions."

"Maybe."

He leaned forward in his chair. "The euphoria of falling in love and now the desolation of falling out."

He paused for emphasis. "Everything else is flat by comparison."

This is before I tell him I feel sorry he has lived such a shallow life. After I hold on to Roy's and my relationship like a pit bull because I don't know how to let go. After what the psych refers to as suppressed denial and depression. After my entire emotional state drifts aloft like a cumulus cloud suspended over an Ansel Adams landscape, leaving my empty and lighter body with only its brain to figure out how to stay aloft.

After so many such days, when I turn completely numb and finally let go of Roy, he grabs hold of me as if he is drowning. This is before I don't save him. After I drop the marble on the ground. After he dies in my mind as if there's been a tragic accident.

I had to get away, far away. Gita, the psych, my mothers, you, anyone else might have handled it differently.

My first thought: Peace Corps. The returned volunteer at the commune recommended Africa, West Africa specifically, if I had a choice.

"It'd be perfect. You already speak some French."

As I waited for the "but," I could hear an ibis calling in the distance. My name could have been Ibis.

"But you're 18. They like people who have stuck through college. Better odds they'll commit to two years."

"I can commit to two years." Maybe permanently.

"I know. I'll be your reference."

Everyone at the commune loved the idea, the concept: Peace, a common outward-directed political and creative activity. I called the Peace Corps regional office from a phone at the library and interviewed with a female voice for a couple of hours. I answered her questions, gave no additional details that she might read into. She said 18 was young but I sounded resourceful, my experience with French and the returned Peace Corp volunteer reference a plus. They needed someone in West Africa, Mauritania or Niger: a nutritionist, someone to start a fisheries program, design pedal-powered machinery, an English teacher.

"We provide training," she added.

"An English teacher?"

"The President of Niger wants all children to be educated in math, French, and since Niger borders Nigeria, English."

The initial volunteer meeting in L.A. included details about the countries and the jobs the national officials requested. I was the youngest there; everyone else had just graduated from college. Maybe they had no idea what to do next either. I didn't ask, just listened to the information about health concerns and required immunizations, but the meeting seemed mostly designed to weed out the weak, those in serious relationships, to eliminate having to send people back across the world. I couldn't get there fast enough. Kept that to myself.

I got immunized against Yellow Fever and Hepatitis before returning to the commune where we practiced homeopathy using native plants; if the body is healthy, it can take care of itself naturally. But I no longer trusted my body.

Almost everyone in the commune pooled together money for airfare and supplies to send with me: a flashlight, Swiss Army knife, the tip of the blade broken off but still sharp, Rescue Remedy, a journal and pen, two mid-calf length gauze skirts, a pair of naturally dyed cotton socks, bulk organic cotton tampons, Nivea, Tom's fennel toothpaste and a new natural bristle tooth-brush, a wooden comb, some clove chewing gum, a mineral salt natural deodorant crystal, an orange, white, and green embroidery floss bracelet, and a worn deck of cards featuring cats dressed in vintage clothes.

When I saw Gita working in the garden, I gestured to her and ran to the concrete little girl. I didn't know what I was going to tell her exactly: That I was sorry. Demand an apology. That I might be pregnant. At least goodbye. But Gita never came.

No one acknowledged the schism between Roy and me, Gita and me, the commune and me. They saw my leaving the country as a worthy cause, an adventure. Except Roy. Too late.

In less than a month, I left Gaia to be an English teacher in

Niger, a developing country the size of a large state. The guidebook described the southern landscape as savanna, grassland; the northern as Sahel, Aïr Mountains, Sahara. A similar varied landscape as the Central Valley. I would find a school in the desert. Poets recommended it. Byron wrote that he preferred sand to human flesh; Auden wrote that you couldn't be healed until you went to the desert. Step one.

CHAPTER TWO

HOT SEASON, NIAMEY 1989

The plane landed in the dark. Scant light rimmed the runway; a feeble red bulb blinked on a tower. Inside the plane, locals stirred; a couple dozen volunteers tittered in English, excited, anxious. All of us curious. I held my pack close and slowly filed down the dimly lit aisle wedged between a sleeping baby bound to its mother's back with cloth and a guy from our group hidden deep inside a hoody. A step forward. Stop. The passengers ahead must have stowed a lot of baggage. Forward, stop. Everything I owned fit into my pack. I held it tighter. Maybe I should have brought more. Eventually, I reached the exit and stepped into the dense cloud of sweat and spices, the hot breath of Niamey. The shock of it slowed us all down.

I remembered then. Only sporadic electricity in Niger's two larger cities, one on each end. Here in Niamey, the actual capitol of the country in the south along the Niger River, the source of the humidity, and in Agadez, nearer where I hoped to live, the nomadic Tuareg capitol in the north along the edge of the Sahara.

"Bienvenue! Corps de la Paix!"

Subdued light in the empty concourse amplified sound. I recognized them immediately, a ragged crowd of established Peace Corps volunteers gathered near the baggage claim to welcome us.

All natural. They could have lived on the commune. Dressed in embroidered local garb, some of the women had shaved heads.

"Oh, shit," a guy from our group of recruits mumbled. "Don't tell me I'm going to look like that in a year." Another, "Run, Jane, run!" Then a wordless high-pitched, hysterical sound.

We greeted them: a few with bravado, most of us cautious.

"Toughest job you'll ever love," one of them actually said.

They checked us out, too. Speculating with their darting eyes who would stay and who would go, who might want a relationship. I kept to myself.

Daylight revealed a kaleidoscope of images: camels and loaded donkeys weaving in and out of shiny jet-black Mercedes, rusted Toyotas, and bulky American trucks on red, dusty roads. Women wrapped in colorful batiks walking along the Route Nationale—the narrow, paved road that connected south to north—balancing baskets on their heads and babies on their backs; old people and children with various afflictions begging on corners. I took it all in, this new world, nothing like I expected and with no idea what it meant.

We lived on the school grounds: simple concrete structures built on red dirt, first, for two weeks of French immersion—I worried my unstructured French lessons with the guy at our commune would be inadequate. An additional two months of cultural sensitivity training—don't look directly into someone's eyes, no shorts or form-fitting clothing, avoid talking religion or politics—and job-specific training. The grounds included several cinderblock classrooms, sleeping dorms oddly segregated by gender, and a common building for communal meals. This part familiar. Our instructors, the first and second-year volunteers we'd met at the airport, encouraged exploration of the city between required sessions. We ventured out in groups, to split cab fare and so we wouldn't be alone. Local Hausa males, wearing a variation of western t-shirts with packs of cigarettes rolled up in their sleeves and beltless synthetic slacks drove the dented, dingy white Toyota taxis. Some drivers added a matching suit jacket and a pair of heavy black glasses frames with no lenses. You had to know the typical fare ahead of time and even then, it required hard bargaining to reach it; every group included at least one person reasonably proficient in French and someone else comfortable with bartering.

The taxi swerved toward us and stopped, the driver looking over the top of his fake glasses. "Bonjour! Où allez-vous?" Where to?

"Le Grand Marché," I said, the serviceable French speaker in the group compared with some who didn't speak any language other than English.

"You are not French," the cab driver said, taking us in, a half-smile on his face.

The flirtatious blonde from Berkeley bartered for the fare, and I helped translate. A shiver shot up my spine remembering when I'd first glimpsed her hair from across the compound and thought it was Roy. The driver countered with an offer twice the going rate. The fragile guy in our group was digging a bill out of his pocket. The blonde slapped his hand down.

"It's not that much," the quiet guy added in English, pulling out a cigarette the guy in the hoody bummed and pulling out another in one fluid motion.

"Let's go." The blonde turned her back on the driver and motioned for us to follow.

Even doubled, the price was minimal, but the point was to try to see things from the local perspective. I locked arms with her.

"Mademoiselles!" he called after us.

"Come! For you, cheap," he said, waving us back. The going price.

The driver's eyes shifted from the blonde to me in his rearview as we headed for the large open-air market. I looked into my own eyes, the out of place green reflecting what were you thinking? My damp red curls frizzing and matted to my forehead, neck, and chest. I sat sandwiched between the blonde and the vulnerable-looking boy as pale as he seemed fragile—the one who sounded hysterical when we landed? I needed a hairband. The guy in the hoody from the plane took the other back window seat because he was even hotter than the rest of us, and the attractive, quiet guy sat beside the driver. He and the guy in the hoody spoke no French. Maybe they too were running away and didn't have time to learn it.

The driver sped through the lane-less congested traffic, maneuvering and breaking like a racecar driver. No seatbelts. I looked straight ahead, gripping the front of my seat for balance, wondering if the fragile boy was feeling even more motion sickness than me.

"Tout ce que vous voulez!" the driver exclaimed, still looking at me and the blonde. Everything you want! The air inside the cab felt damp, thick with dust, but we got there quickly.

"Voila!" the driver said.

We moved as a group among local boys pedaling rickety bicycles, a blend of locals, tourists, and expatriates perusing stacks of mattresses, piles of men's rubber wingtip shoes, and tables filled with richly patterned Belgian batiks. Some of us browsed for souvenirs, the silver cross of Agadez, earrings etched with symbols we didn't know the meaning of. Before we knew what we would remember, souvenir, what we would want to revisit in our minds. The smell of people trapped in intense heat crowding the narrow passages between piles of yellow turmeric, red pepper, tainting the otherwise rich scent of spices reminded me of home. I tucked my chin and sniffed myself, hoping I wasn't adding to it. The food section included some of the same produce as our market but more limited: dates, groundnuts/peanuts, mangoes, wilted lettuce, and suspended carcasses crawling with flies.

The fragile guy covered his mouth and nose with his bare arm that reeked of insect repellant. "I can't," he said.

We all had the same horrified reaction to the defiled meat, a collective Western perspective, the only one we knew.

Another taxi took us to the La Grande Mosquée. The famous mosque was nearby, but no one suggested walking. The shortest distance required so much of us. But seeing the sprawling adobe structure with latticed archways and a brilliant green tiled dome was both stunning and calming. We got out of the taxi and stared at it.

"Allah 'akbar," the driver said.

God is great. I recognized it from the Muslim prayers.

"It was financed by Ghaddafi ten years ago," the guy in the hoody said.

A loudspeaker from the minaret called everyone to prayer in Arabic five times a day. I don't know if anyone else heard it at 4 in the morning, but I did and opened my palms, asking for peace, love, and even though my IUD was 99% effective, that I wasn't pregnant.

"Four o'clock every morning, like an alarm," the guy in the hoody.

"Beautiful," the blonde. "Expensive."

The fragile boy stood in the shade beside the quiet guy silently smoking.

We briefly toured Le Petit Marché. The smaller outdoor market along the Niger River offered only food items that none of us could buy after seeing the meat carcasses. Nearby, at Score, the French boutique, we all purchased something: chocolate, Galouise cigarettes, liquor, pears. Way over-priced but we all needed something familiar. We divided everything and ate, drank, and smoked our way to La Musée Nationale, the national museum. The taxi driver, the only one who saved his share.

Life-size statues represented the major ethnic groups that inhabit Niger. Most of the sedentary people (Hausa and Djerma) lived in the cities in the south, and the nomads (Tuaregs, Fulani, Wodaabé) lived in the north. My future neighbors if I could arrange it. Dressed in their particular culture's clothing, figures stood beside a variety of dwellings: banco structures, mud and straw huts, and animal skin or palm fiber tents depending on region and ethnicity. The female nomad's hair was elaborately braided, and some wore multiple large aluminum earrings in piercings the entire perimeter of their ears. The blonde elbowed me. "Love that look. Like windchimes in your ear." The Tuareg men draped entirely in cloth, the Fulani men wore stiff straw hats woven with bands of color. Many of the faces were scarred and darkened with ash, or coal rather than the tattoo ink we were familiar with.

"I'm staying in a city," the fragile guy said. "Near to services, civilization."

"Need to see for myself what's out there before I decide," the blonde.

"I'll go wherever they send me," the quiet guy. The guy in the hoody and I said nothing, aloud.

An artisan area featured representatives from different cultures crafting their wares: a Tuareg blacksmith wearing a turban and flowing robes squatted, tending the coals in his wire brazier. Using a small hammer, he tapped yellow-tinged pieces of metal he called Tuareg gold. Another Hausa man wearing an embroidered tunic, matching pants, and a fez wove multiple colors of thread into a four-inch-wide strip of cloth, then sewed the strips together to make it wide enough for a table or bed. "No female artists," I said to the blonde.

Our group clustered at the hundred-million-year-old Iguanodon dinosaur skeleton—an American childhood touchstone as Gita once observed—discovered near Agadez in the north of the country, the placard read, before it became a desert. She would love this museum—seeing how other people live on this planet.

The last exhibit was a dead tree, "the remnants of an acacia, common to both savannah and desert environments." The inscription read that it had once been famous in the Ténéré, the great sand desert east of Agadez. For 300 years, it had been the only tree for hundreds of kilometers in any direction until 1973, when a Libyan truck driver collided with it.

"Fool must a been smoking a sherm," the guy in the hoody mumbled.

So we could make it to the post office before it closed, I suggested we skip the American Cultural Center featuring a swimming pool and weekly movies in English. Exactly the kind of thing I was distancing myself from in preparation for when I didn't have a choice. We all wanted to stop at the post office to mail our postcards and aerogrammes. The simple transactions we all understood, the exchange of money for stamps with no bartering.

As we waited in line, I reread my postcard to the commune: "Made it! Will be living in the desert among the nomads—Tuaregs! You can use this general address; they will forward it. More later. Love you all, Lark." I added a stylized smiling sun, so it took up all the space. The other side featured the skyline of Niamey—a couple of European high-rise hotels amid single story mud houses joined together like paper dolls—against a red sunset lining the murky Niger River.

I looked up and saw a slight woman with dark hair at the front of the line and stopped breathing. "Gita!" I yelled from the back of the line, everyone turning at once to look. A dark-eyed woman who looked nothing like Gita raised her hand above her brow, squinting in my direction. "Ça va?" I glanced around for the source of the outburst like everyone else. A hand on my shoulder, my elbows, the small of my back connected us all.

When the dark-haired woman passed me on her way out, she paused, squeezed my hand, and disappeared.

Everyone wanted to take a pirogue ride on the river, but we'd heard stories about people contracting schistosomiasis, snail worms, acquired from standing in water. One of the new nurse volunteers read a description of the disease from a journal article: "...a chronic illness that can damage organs... the second most socioeconomically devastating parasitic disease after malaria... symptoms include abdominal pain, cough, diarrhea, fever, fatigue, enlargement of the liver and the spleen." She was older, retired, wiser probably. When she passed me the article, I continued reading aloud: "Over several weeks, the parasites migrate through the host tissue and develop into adult worms inside the blood vessels of the body. Once mature, the worms mate and females produce eggs." The guy in the hoody puked, the fragile boy already outside. The second years shrugged. "Don't stand in the water."

Another reason to live in the north, at least on the edge of the desert. No standing water to worry about, no humidity and frizzy hair. The stark simplicity of a desert landscape, what I needed.

They also told us that some of the people begging on the corners had self-harmed or relatives had disfigured them to earn money for the family. "You'll have to toughen up."

On weekends, we traveled by bush taxi to nearby villages with names like Téra, Filingué, Dosso, Gaya, Tillabéri, some of us to scope out potential living situations. My favorite, the Sunday livestock market in Ayorou: 200 kilometers from Niamey on the Niger River near the border of Mali. Dozens of cattle swimming across the Niger River, driven not by cowboys on horses but by nomads on camels. I recognized the Tuaregs wrapped in indigo cloth, their faces stained blue from the rich dye. Some of the Fulanis wore straw hats like those in the museum display, laughing, joking, herding cattle, and sheep or goats. All of them, excluding the Tuareg men, ornamented with beads, shells, or silver around their necks, wrists, ankles or woven into their elaborate braids. A Tuareg man invited me to ride his camel. He made some sounds, and the camel folded its knees in a forward and then backward movement. I sat on a Tuareg saddle in front of the camel's hump, my feet crossed and braced against its neck. In the picture someone took that I see later, I am smiling, waving, the wind blowing my hair before it has broken off. I am barefoot. I have no idea what happened to my sandals.

We teachers trained at the model school studying from an orange paperback TEFL manual. Teaching English as a Foreign Language. The idea, to speak only English in the classroom accompanied by images, objects, charades. Experienced volunteers looked over our lesson plans and observed as we taught enthusiastic grade school-aged Hausa and Djerma students, boys in Western shirts and trousers, girls in pagnes, the traditional dark or patterned cloth they wrapped around their bodies like a long skirt, with a matching top. They came by the dozens. Free lunch.

On the map of locations requesting English teachers, I chose Tchin-Tabaraden, a nomadic village in the Sahel, the edge of the Sahara. Too far to travel to ahead of time, our trainers unfamiliar with it. An unknown community. No expectations from them or me.

"The bus only travels the main route," the trainer with the shaved head said. She traced her finger north on the map along the Route Nationale, then stopped at a place called Tahoua. "You'll have to take a bush taxi from here."

I nodded as if I knew exactly what I was getting into and how, but I only knew why: to forget, to be healed, to prefer sand to human flesh, at least to Roy's. To begin again.

We learned basic phrases to communicate information in Hausa, the predominant local language. The trainer said most people in the north could speak some French or Hausa. The training made us feel prepared.

Later that evening, I sat on a warm plastic chair at a searing, unbalanced aluminum table in an open-air neighborhood bar and ordered a beer, Flag, a local brew. Joel, the quiet guy from the taxi, sat across. We talked as if we were sitting in a bar in the States except for the subject. Joel said his job was to teach local youth to play basketball in Dosso.

"Did President Saibou request that?"

He shrugged. "Someone did." Taking a swallow of beer, he grimaced. "Warm."

I preferred room temperature wine with our evening meals at the commune and was not a fan of beer generally because of the bitter, stale after-taste. I drank with an open mind, but the warmth exaggerated the dank flavors. I practiced not showing it, while Joel lit a cigarette—a Marlboro—exhaling the smoke like a sigh.

"Honestly? I just went through a divorce," he said. "This opportunity came up, so."

He took another drag.

I nodded and asked the server for ice. She hesitated, tilting her head wrapped in a turquoise scarf with yellow ibis but returned minutes later and dumped cubes into both our beers.

Joel gave a half nod and drank. "Better."

Much. We ordered another with ice, Bière Niger, the other local brand to compare, concluding that cold bad beer is better than warm bad beer.

When Joel came to my window in the middle of the night because he couldn't sleep, I waved him in. The two retired nurse volunteers lay motionless in the other bunks. I invited him into my bed, closed my eyes and held him. I finally relaxed, could breathe. His hair smelled of sweet shampoo and smoke. I cupped his face and kissed him slow like I meant it. We pulled each other in from that place we had been and then slept, still entangled despite the heat. I barely stirred when he got up. Glimpsing him through the haze of half-sleep, he slipped out the window, then turned and held eye contact like we'd been practicing not to.

I awoke some hours later shivering, my teeth chattering, the sheets soaked.

"Lie back," one of the nurses said. "You're burning up."

The other brought damp cotton balls and rubbed them on my limbs, my forehead, and neck. The smell of rubbing alcohol burned my nose.

"To bring the fever down," she said.

It felt fantastic. I closed my eyes again, vaguely heard them say something about malaria and Aralen, the pink preventative pills we took once a month. A finger parted my lips and poked in the pills. I may have kissed it.

"Here now," one of them said, cradling me into a semi seated position, encouraging me to drink the iodized water and wash down the meds.

"...the recommended treatment... drink the sterilized water... rest."

She shook me awake.

"Lark, can you hear me?" She poured pills onto a tissue on the table. "We have to go now. If we're not here, be sure to take the next dose in 12 hours."

The cracked clock she set beside the pills read 10:02, the last thing I remembered.

I resurfaced from somewhere deep, below sound, a vague sense of muted color. Still shaky, I blinked a few times and squinted at the numbers on the clock: 10:05—I must have slept twenty-four hours straight. Swallowing the other pills with several gulps of the bitter treated water, I turned on my side and fell right back to sleep but this time it was fitful and exhausting.

A giant screen covered an entire wall of my mind, filled with oblong capsule shapes containing different colors and widths of stripes, all moving. The objective: to make sure the hundreds of capsules had the same pattern of stripes, accomplished by moving them around with my eyes. As soon as I got several of them to match, the stripes would switch places, jumping from one pulsating shape to another. I focused and refocused, such concentration exhausting. Perseverance, futile.

When the violent churning of my stomach woke me, it was a relief.

I stumbled to the communal toilets and stayed, my body in a perpetual state of purging. I was so weak that had I consciously wanted to drink some water or go back to bed, it would have been impossible. When the nurses found me, I was semiconscious.

"Lark, we came back to check on you." She may have touched my shoulder.

I opened my eyes trying to get their faces to come into focus.

"You weren't supposed to take the next dose of Aralen for another ten hours."

I may have nodded my head.

"I'll call a taxi to take you to the Peace Corps doctor," the other voice said.

I roused when they washed my face with cool water and was able to stand and move forward with their assistance.

The taxi driver opened the rear door. As the two nurses were pushing me into the back seat, someone else was pushing Joel in from the opposite side. We sprawled next to each other, too out of it to speak.

Tests showed that we did not have malaria but amoebic dysentery. It would have to run its course through our systems along with the antibiotic metronidazole, and water.

"Treated water," the doctor exhorted after determining that the ice in the beer had been the contaminant. "With time, warm beer will be the least of your worries," he said. "Welcome to Niger."

Had I been cognizant at the doctor's office, I'd have asked for a pregnancy test to ease my mind. I was late, getting later, but there could be so many reasons for that. The change of situation, food, the stress. The meds I'd taken, the megadose of Aralen followed by the powerful antibiotic. Toxins, my mothers would say. The temple of my body was not used to any of it and now as slight and fragile as Gita's. I needed to talk to her.

After weeks, on the last night of training, we partied. Cigarettes, beer, and music mostly, mangos and dates. Someone had weed but wasn't sharing. The wine at Score too expensive, I contributed a cold bottle of Perrier, brie, and a baguette cut in small, ragged chunks with my Swiss Army knife. We danced to someone's mixed tape, the volume cranked high on a trainer's shortwave radio/cassette player. The fragile guy pulled me away from the brie to dance to "Jammin." Maybe because after dropping ten pounds from dysentery, he thought I looked fragile too. He said he was recovering from a bout of malaria. "Reggae immunizes us all," I said.

The music played on: "Happy Birthday to MLK"; "Free Falling"; "Bette Davis Eyes"; "Dark Side of the Moon"; "American Woman."

Dance partners:

The 2nd year trainer with the shaved head going back to the States the next day. "The North is different, Lark. The landscape, the people because of the landscape. Better get a gris-gris to protect you from the djinn, the evil spirits in the desert. And another one for health."

She might have been joking, but I noticed a leather bundle on a string around her neck. "What's yours for?"

"That's personal."

Both retired nurses at the same time. "You look anemic." Roz.

"Anorexic. Be sure to take the vitamins we gave you for lactating mothers and take advantage of canned goods. You should be able to get tomato sauce and sardines, maybe pineapple." Stacia.

"We'll be just three hours away in Tahoua. See you for your gamma globulin shots." Roz.

Nick, the guy in the hoody, who excelled at moving but didn't talk, the reason we danced three songs in a row.

By the time we took a break, the food was gone. I drank the rest of the Perrier while waiting for more Reggae.

Joel. Marley's "Coming in from the Cold." We danced a while before speaking.

I started. "You sturdy?"

He winked and pulled me in for the goodbye kiss. Smoky with warm hints of brie and beer.

Three guys dressed like women. No idea where they got fishnet stockings. Last song, a sort of group hug, swaying to "Imagine."

We were all there for our own reasons. I only knew my own and Joel's, the retired nurses', the only ones who seemed to have their lives already worked out, and maybe the fragile boy's.

CHAPTER THREE

HOT SEASON, EN ROUTE TO TCHIN-TABARADEN 1989

Before sunrise, before the hung-over promises to be in touch from the party the previous night, I caught a ride to Niamey's autogare, a bustling terminal where the taxi de brousse, bush taxis, transported people and goods across the country. I thought getting there early would save time and avoid Niamey's full-on humidity. I'd get in the first taxi going north and be on my way to my final destination. I'd miscalculated.

After bargaining with a middle-aged driver with three passengers who said he could take me as far as Tahoua and paying him more than necessary to make sure, he took my money, gestured me toward a shade tree, and said we'd go soon. He wore a button-down short-sleeve, leisure pants, plastic jelly wingtips, and a watch. "What time?" I asked. I didn't wear a watch myself, my sense of time internal. He shrugged. I tried again. "What time?" pointing to the imaginary watch on my wrist. Again, he shrugged and waved me on. Was his watch broken? Maybe he didn't know how to tell time.

I waited under the tree for hours, observing. Nothing seemed regulated. The drivers sold the seats but still didn't leave. The trainer with the bald head said we would have to figure things out for ourselves. I figured out that the notion of Western time didn't exist here.

By mid-morning, the air smelled of piss. I looked around for the public toilet. None. The lot filled with tourists, locals, volunteers, and vendors catering to those of us suspended in limbo. Air temperature bottles of soda, peanuts, fried bread, brochettes, and mangoes. Some peddled cheap silver bracelets and necklaces. Mostly the people from other parts of the country passing through and ragged-looking Western tourists bartered for it. Peanuts appealed to me for the salt, protein, and their protective shell, but I was afraid to move from my spot in case the driver, now dozing against the driver's door, decided it was time to leave. I refocused my attention on the other vehicles. Peugeots and Toyotas bought second hand from European tourists, Mitsubishis, Hondas, Renaults, and a couple of worn Mercedes. I could name them because of Roy. Most had dents, bald tires, and rust spots. Few had windows. It reminded me of a junkyard. I saw young boys lugging tools, nuts, bolts, miscellaneous parts of cars. Were these cars even safe? But people were clamoring to ride in them. The only other option, the weekly SNTN bus not leaving for days. I was anxious to get to my desert village, to begin my job, to reconstruct my life, tired of anticipating it. So far, I'd been wrong about everything I thought I knew. I closed my eyes against the dusty air and opened my palms.

I woke to the smell of dough sizzling over a fire and an elderly woman staring at me. Her eyes darted to my chin when we made eye contact. Her lined face appeared kind or amused, a faded batik of delft blue flowers, wrapped around her head, a muted blue top, and a pagne wrapped around her lower body in the same patterned cloth. I practiced some Hausa. "Ina kwana?" a tentative good morning.

The old woman smiled broadly. No teeth. "Lahiya lau."

In good health. The stock response, "fine," but more specific. And she might have been, besides her teeth.

"Nescafé?"

Concerned for my own health, I confirmed the water was boiling over the fire beside some beignets. "Oui."

The woman spooned instant coffee into a blue enamel cup, dropped in nine sugar cubes, and added sweetened condensed milk as I stood there in shock, unable to find the words to stop her. I hadn't eaten processed sugar in my entire life. I took a small sip and thanked her. "Na gode."

She made a clucking noise from the back of her throat that sounded positive.

Good. I'd miscommunicated before when trying to speak the local language. Once I asked where I could find water. "Ina ruwa?" The direct translation of the words, "where is water?" The meaning more complex. Water, a metaphor for someone else's business as in "What business of it is yours?" or "It's none of your business." When possible, I stuck with cognates. "Toilette?" I had to pee and discretely get rid of the sugared Nescafe.

"Babu bayan gida."

"Babu" meant "not any" and context suggested, no toilet in the autogare. People must plan ahead. I set down the cup and pulled out my playing cards for a distraction. The jokers featured one cat dressed in a top hat with a green ribbon and a shamrock. The other wore John Lennon glasses and a hat topped with fresh flowers. Both sported silk neck scarves and some kind of fancy clothing hidden by the table where they sat. I started laughing so hard I was crying, and then I was just crying.

"Lark, are you all right?"

Roz and Stacia, the two retired nurses. "Oh, hi. Fine." I stood up. "Couldn't stop laughing." I held up a card. "The heat." I touched my wrist to the corners of my eyes. "Good to see you." That part, true. "Have you seen a restroom?"

"No, but the hospital will have one."

They were going to Tahoua, too, to work in the hospital there.

"We're sharing a car with Nick, the young man who wears the

hoody even in this heat, though he's continuing on to Agadez. Your taxi already has seven passengers," Stacia said.

In a Toyota? That couldn't be right; there was only room for five adults counting the driver. Nick and the nurses would be my nearest neighbors. Roz touched my forehead with the back of her hand. Stacia handed me some peanuts and reminded me to drink treated water.

The driver called me over.

I turned back to them. "Thanks for the peanuts. Maybe I'll see you later at the autogare in Tahoua."

The driver said he'd seen my cards and we should play and then he'd be ready to go.

By the time I'd shuffled the mathematically recommended seven times on the hood of his car, someone had spread a cloth on the ground and now five passengers and the driver settled down to play. Stacia was right. "Poker?" It seemed appropriate. He took the deck, shaking his head at the well-dressed cats.

"Huits."

"Eights?" I said it in English.

He dealt seven cards to everyone, put the deck in the middle of the blanket, turned over a card and went first, the other players followed, ending with me. Crazy Eights. Something in common. I played as if I didn't know the game in case winning could delay departure. Next round, he only shuffled twice.

"Donc," the driver said after several boisterous rounds. He stretched and hoisted himself on top of the Toyota's roof.

The passengers immediately got up and started throwing their baggage to him to tie on top. I tossed him my pack and he made a show, groaning as if it were heavy. Everyone laughed. I'd added more books besides my *Teaching English as a Foreign Language* manual: *Where There is No Doctor*, a partial copy of Thurston Clark's *The Last Caravan*, and a leather-bound copy of the Quran someone had left in the sleeping dorm.

"Allons-y," the driver said, let's go.

I glanced at the people already jammed in the backseat. Unless they could scoot even closer together, I'd have to sit on someone's lap. "Excusez-moi, sorry."

They all shifted slightly, and I ended up sitting halfway on the door. Another guy motioned me out of the way and took a seat on the windowsill like the passenger in the front. Someone else took the other back passenger window. No glass in the window frames. No seatbelts. This is before I find out there is a gris-gris for safe travels.

We bounced along, the car without shocks, the paved road uneven. Was I the only one who needed to pee? I focused on trying not to touch the man's thigh next to me, trying to adhere to the community rules, but every time we bumped, we touched. I avoided eye contact and looked out the window at the passing red landscape interrupted with scrubby trees and local pedestrians, maybe the same women I'd seen balancing baskets on their heads and babies on their backs my first day here, still walking.

After an hour or so, the driver suddenly pulled over. I surveyed the area for an outpost of some sort. Nothing. The men piled out of the car on one side, the women on the other. They rinsed their hands and feet with water and began praying. I was calculating whether I could reach the scrubby bush in the distance and relieve myself before they concluded. I walked as fast as I could while trying to hold it. It took all my concentration. After the release, the unburdening. I sprinted back.

It turned out I needn't have hurried. Everyone had gathered on the shady side of the car to eat some dates while the driver enjoyed a leisurely smoke.

We drove on for hours through the shifting landscape interrupted by fewer trees and two more prayer breaks.

By the time we arrived in Tahoua, it was dark. The passengers looked wrinkled and damp from the ordeal, but they all retrieved their belongings and dispersed. Either Tahoua was their destination, or they'd made arrangements to spend the night.

It felt good to stand as I waited for Roz and Stacia's taxi. I would help them settle in for a place to sleep. Ate some dates, drank some iodized water from my canteen, moved to the far edge of the lot to brush my teeth, and resumed watching the autogare traffic. Several vehicles came and went with no one I recognized. Did the nurses arrive before me? After a couple of hours, I moved to a cinderblock building to lean against. I slid down and closed my eyes. They burned from the glare, the wind, the dust. I opened them again and looked around. I was completely alone. Was it safe to stay here? I moved to a more obscure spot, hidden from the street, and tucked my Swiss Army knife in the waistband of my skirt.

The wind picked up at some point. Miscellaneous bits of garbage kept pelting my face. Moving to the other side of the building helped some, I tucked my gauzy skirt under my legs and started to relax but then jolted to full alert from the moon staring at me. I didn't recognize it. Calm. Down. In my mind, I sang all the Rastafarian songs I could remember. Same theme: Every little thing's going to be all right. The light became hazy, eerie as the wind picked up the surface layer of dusty sand and never set it down. I pulled a t-shirt from my pack and put it over my head as a filter for the dust, debris, and the light and dreamt and woke in fragments: *Gita and I eating strawberries ripe and warm from the sun. Waiting for Gita at our private place, I looked up at the concrete girl and saw it was Gita. The little girl ran across the field with her basket of owers to Roy, who bent down and picked her up, turning in circles, the two of them laughing. A poetry reading at the commune where everyone spoke in tongues. The dogs barking at the cats dressed in vintage clothing. Roy staring right at me like a still photograph.*

I woke up tired, with a stiff neck. It took a moment to orient. Niger. Tahoua. The autogare. I needed a ride to Tchin-Tabaraden. Even without the filter of my t-shirt covering my face, the light remained hazy, sounds of vendors starting their fires, setting out their wares. But besides the pain in my neck, I passed the night in health, lahiya lau. I felt safer in the daylight when I could see people around me. According to my map only three plus hours away from Tchin-Tabaraden, the desert village where I'd be working, living, healing. My final destination.

For now, I needed protein, caffeine, some relief. Again, no public toilet. When the trainers had warned us about watching where we stepped in public places, I'd thought, exaggeration. I washed my hands and face with some floral-scented glycerin soap from Score and brushed my teeth. Tahoua felt less humid than Niamey, but the temp already seemed high. I ran my fingers through my hair, a rough estimate of a part, reached through my shirt and applied the honeysuckle deodorant, also from Score, so I didn't have to worry if it worked. This time, after greeting the vendor I ordered black coffee, sans sucre. Beignets, no thanks. Peanuts/groundnuts, yes, but none around. Even a goat meat brochette sounded good. Too early. Tahoua smelled different than Niamey, less spicy. Less populated, the skyline close to the sandy ground, a maze of banco, mud, structures.

The first car pulled into the autogare early. I walked over to see if it would travel west. The people piling out looking rough, haggard even from a distance. Maybe they'd traveled from a different country. Two Tuareg men draped in their traditional cloth got out first, then another man in a hoody. I started running toward him. "Nick!"

He looked at me as if I cursed at him. The nurses got out on the other side just as I reached the vehicle.

"You made it! Welcome home," I said, breathless from the sprint. They looked exhausted. "Are you all right?"

A bead of sweat dripped from Roz's gray bangs. "It took fourteen hours to get here."

I handed her some water. "I wondered where you were."

"Car trouble the whole way." Stacia.

"I'll get a taxi to take you to your house."

"We need to check in with the hospital director first."

"Right." I turned to Nick looking at the smoldering bush taxi. "Will it make it to Agadez?"

"Eventually." He seemed in no hurry.

"Got a cigarette?"

He almost looked me in the eye. "No, but the vendor with the coffee and beignets sells Rothmans."

I started toward the street to wave down a city taxi just as a driver likely saw the foreign nurses standing beside their luggage and pulled in.

I helped them into the taxi and wished them well while the driver loaded their luggage, and lingered before closing the door. "Do you mind if I come with you?"

Roz patted the seat beside her.

I knew they thought I was weak or homesick or scared. "That way I'll know exactly where to go for my immunization boosters."

"And they have a restroom." Stacia. "It may be a long wait to find a taxi going to the bush."

"We'll check back." Roz. "If you don't get a ride by this evening, you can stay with us."

The hospital was small, spare, concrete. The staff a mix of locals and expatriates. Roz and Stacia connected with the director, and I located a bathroom. The mirror over the sink reflected a rough version of myself. A lack of sleep and balanced diet. I washed my hands and face again, applying a thick coat of Nivea from my shopping spree at Score and continued with a sponge bath, stripping my t-shirt to use as the sponge. I'd worked down to my legs before someone knocked on the door.

"Excusez-moi."

I quickly finished washing, pulled on a fresh t-shirt, slipped back into my Birkenstocks, refilled my canteen, and swallowed a vitamin for lactating mothers. I opened the door, "Pardon," to an expatriate.

"Pas de problème," she said. No problem. I caught a taxi back to the autogare.

Nick was sitting in a patch of shade, the hood of the taxi

opened before a crowd of men in animated discussion. I gave him the side-eye. His head remained hooded; the long sleeves of his sweatshirt covered his arms in 95-degree plus weather. Maybe the rumor was true that he was on the run from illegal activity in the States. I'd dismissed it at first, but he was definitely protective, defensive. Maybe why he didn't want me drawing attention to him. I left him alone and made my way through the line of taxis that had arrived in my absence. The first Toyota beater was headed south. The driver said that there might be one traveling west if Allah saw fit.

"Do you mean today?"

He laughed as if I were telling a joke.

Four more battered vehicles pulled in. Back to Niamey. South to Birnin Konni, Maradi, Zinder. The lunch vendors turned brochettes over the fire. I bought one, tearing into it like a carnivore. It tasted unbelievably good, spicy, rubbery in texture. Some sort of organ?

"Good?" Nick.

I pulled the last two bites off the stick with my teeth and left him standing there to check my vehicle situation.

One driver seemed promising but indecisive. He needed to drop something off at Kao, the nearest village to Tchin-Tabaraden, but no other passengers wanted to go that way.

"Come back later," he said.

He was dressed similarly to the Tuaregs but his turban more relaxed, the end blowing in the breeze. I understood that he needed the trip to be economically viable and considered offering him twice as much to ensure a ride, but after splurging at Score, and not knowing exactly what to expect expense-wise, I resisted.

Raised voices caught my attention—Nick engaged with two gendarmes, military police, Niger's normal police. I still hadn't gotten used to them. They wore drab green uniforms, typically fatigues, with Kalashnikovs slung on their shoulders. Disconcerting. Frightening. What would require that kind of firepower? The men talking to Nick dressed Tuareg style, faded green turbans, flowing tunics, and what I'd heard called bouzou pants—drapey to the ankle—and sandals. They wore the traditional desert garb of the Tuaregs. Only the Kalashnikovs gave them away as MP. They were hassling Nick about his passport. Interrogating him. He gave it to them but wasn't saying much. Did he have something to hide? Maybe he didn't understand the language, what they were asking. Passeport, a cognate, but the rest?

"Nick," I said, smiling at him, as if we were friends, and at the gendarmes. "Is there a problem?"

"You speak French." The shorter one. "This passport photo doesn't look like him."

"Can I see?" The photo appeared to be someone else entirely. This may have shown on my face. "Terrible likeness," I said. "Poor quality. Cheap."

Nick lit a cigarette and sucked it till sparks flew.

"We trained together in Niamey the last several months. We're teachers, he in Agadez, and I'm in Tchin-Tabaraden."

"What can he teach?" the taller one said. "He doesn't know the language."

"English. We're teaching English to the children of the nomads. President Saibou wants all the children to be educated." My French was more staccato than fluid but serviceable. I understood better than I spoke. "Since Niger borders Nigeria, he requested some English teachers." I'd said this phrase repeatedly to everyone who wasn't teaching English during training.

"Oui," Nick said.

"Donc," the taller one said, holding out his open palm.

I looked at Nick. "Give him something." I may have hissed.

"I don't have any money until we get paid next month."

"Your pack of cigarettes."

"Bummed only the one."

I pulled the cat cards out of my pack and placed them in the gendarme's hand.

He shook his head.

"Allez," go, the shorter one said.

"When the car is ready." The other.

Nick said, almost inaudibly, "I owe you."

I nodded, possibly imperceptively, and returned to my own transportation problem.

"Where have you been?" the driver said, both hands in the air. "Let's go!" I'm making a roundtrip. Drop off, pick up. You can ride."

I noticed another passenger in the front seat. Good. A woman. Better. She was dressed similarly to him with some markings on her face, her hair in a knot at the front of her head and shells woven in some lose braids that worked into another bun midway from the base of her skull. Along the perimeter of her ear, she wore multiple sets of the thick, lightweight earrings. Around her neck, a bundle of gris-gris with occasional red beads I'd never seen before along the strand of leather. A beautiful woman, older, 30ish?

The driver laughed at my meager cash offer but put it in a decorative dyed leather pouch-type wallet hanging from his neck.

"You can pick up firewood along the way."

"Oui," I said. "Bien sur," of course. Whatever it took.

"Allons-y."

I got in, the backseat to myself, smiling at my luck. According to my map, a two-hour drive to Kao, only an hour from Tchin-Tabaraden. I changed my expression to impassive as I made eye contact with Nick, still waiting, on the way out.

The driver and the woman passenger spoke in another language I didn't know. They seemed friendly. Laughed a lot. Possibly at my expense, but it didn't feel that way. The car needed a muffler, so I didn't bother trying to talk to them. Just watched them and the passing landscape.

Soon, we were beyond any sort of civilization, in the bush, and it did have some bush-like vegetation and sporadic thorny acacia trees, but mostly sand and no road that I could see. A stake pounded into the ground appeared occasionally along vast stretches of sand like a trail that wasn't well marked. The type you had to guess if you were even going the right direction the entire way. I turned and looked out the back window. How did people orient themselves? Maybe because they knew the place. To me, everything looked the same in every direction. The sand we were driving on appeared to have a reddish cast, but it might have been the angle of the sun.

When we stopped the first time, I thought maybe they had to relieve themselves as there was nothing but the stark landscape we had been traveling through.

"Voila," the man said, gesturing out the window with his chin.

There, what is? I looked hard, squinting against the afternoon light. A bush, a tree, some divots in the sand, and two twigs. Was that what he meant by wood? I recalibrated. The fires the vendors used to cook on were small and there wouldn't be much wood in the Sahel, the edge of the desert. I got out to pick up the sticks. "Don't leave me."

He laughed as if I were joking.

I handed the paltry sticks to him through the window, resisting letting go of my end.

He revved the motor and laughed. "Tanamert."

Possibly that meant got you, thank you, or maybe it was a type of wood.

I resumed my place in the back, relaxed then, and observed. Everything as far as I could see looked the same, wave after wave of sand, then a series of sand hills where the wind must have turned sharply, carving contours into the landscape. I figured out it was best to avoid an expansive view; the glare and the unending repetition of so much open space made me dizzy and disoriented, carsick. I fixated on what would fit in the immediate frame of my window trying to spy a bit of wood the driver might have missed. It was a tedious process. My eyes burned from the dry heat, or bright light, or whipping sand even at such a slow speed. This journey would take more than two hours. The car belched every now and then maybe from cheap gas, but I was glad, extremely glad, to be moving at all.

By the time we reached Kao mid-afternoon, I had gathered a scant armload of kindling. The driver said we were even.

Kao was a smaller village than Tchin-Tabaraden but probably similar architecture and layout. Banco dwellings dotting inter-woven sand paths. A few nomads on their way to draw water, to the market, or back home. Most hidden from the heat of the day. I could adjust to anything.

The driver stopped at a shop to deliver the bundle of firewood and a burlap bag of something heavy.

"Fanta?" he asked.

I didn't normally drink soda. My mothers at the commune referred to it as poison, and I hadn't acquired the taste for sweet liquid, but I knew it was rude to refuse. "Yes, thank you," I said, hoping for grape. Maybe less sweet and would dye my lips a more natural darker shade rather than the radioactive orange. I stood out as it was. Anasara, Western foreigner. The trainers said to get used to being called anasara, and espion, spy. I should have asked for details.

Orange Fanta. Even warm, it tasted cool but made me thirsty. I chased it with some iodized water from my canteen.

The woman said something, and the man left again, this time returning with some rice and sauce from a woman selling it at a nearby table protected from the wind.

"Pas de sable," he said.

No sand in it. This is before I understand the extreme odds of that.

White rice with a red pepper tomato sauce. The woman in the front seat handed me what looked like a wooden serving spoon. I ate from the side of it. She used her middle and index fingers.

We drove further down the sand road and stopped, I thought for another business transaction.

"Autogare," the driver said.

An abandoned solitary bench on the sand surrounded by a

windbreak woven out of brittle grass. I waited for him to laugh. He didn't. I grabbed my pack, got out of the car, and just stood there.

"Allah 'akbar," he said. God is great.

He extended his hand and I started to shake it, but he pulled his palm across mine, slow, his hands rough like he usually gathered the wood himself, then snapped his fingers one at a time starting with the pinky. This somehow made me feel better. The touch probably, human flesh. I still preferred it. I watched as the car disappeared into the distance, a moving smudge on the landscape, then nothing but desert. I dropped my backpack on the sand.

The sky appeared colorless, the sun a bright spot burnt into it. I squinted against the violent light. I had never seen a white sky that wasn't filled with snow. It made me shiver. I felt small, alone, at the mercy of the landscape. Out of range of civilization as I knew it. But this was what I wanted. To begin again. A single blade of grass in the unending desert. Was I a single? I still hadn't started my period but since there were no other signs or symptoms, and the science pointed against it, I tried not to dwell on it and just take care of myself.

"But if I had a girl," I said to no one. "I'd name her Gita."

I took measured sips from my canteen alternating between closing my eyes for relief and taking in my surroundings. Blinding bright sand interrupted by occasional scarred plant life extending to the horizon in every direction. I dug in my pack and engraved with my sandy pen tip, Dear Gita, on the back of a postcard of a smiling hippo raising its dripping head from the Niger River. I tried not to think about the dryness in my throat, which made me swallow, sounding bizarrely loud. Could it be possible that I was already dehydrating? I took another drink.

Dear Gita,
*   I hope you're feeling well.*

Please forgive me for not realizing your true love is Roy. I honestly did not know until that day. I wanted to tell you I'm sorry for not getting it and for how you must have felt for years.

(here I drew a basket of flowers)

I love you always and miss you like crazy.

xo, Lark

P.S. Tell the dogs I miss them, too, especially Oblio.

I knew that anyone from Tchin-Tabaraden to Gaia could read a postcard, but since the ink didn't come through, it took effort to make out the words. Like the invisible writing Gita and I used in the secret notes we wrote to each other as children. Only time and distance let me write this one at all. I realized I missed her more than I felt betrayed. Once I arrived in my village, I would mail it, and when she forgave me, we would correspond.

A sudden wind blew the postcard from my hands, and I chased it as it cartwheeled through the sand, "Stop!" I yelled, and the wind seemed to listen before carrying it away again, toying with me. When I accidently kicked sand on my toes, the skin blistered immediately. My throat felt like I'd swallowed fiberglass by the time I captured the postcard. I zipped it into my pack, drank some more water, and tried to breathe and think like a normal person, like a normal local person, and rest until the sun backed down the sky to a less intense level. The bench was too short to lie on, the fiber windbreak too lightweight to lean against. I arranged my pack to serve as a pillow and gingerly stretched out on the hot sand making sure no bare skin touched the surface. The air temperature was hot, yet there was no sweat on my skin; any moisture evaporated on contact with the parched air. My own body felt foreign. Anasara. I lay there in a sort of a trance, willing myself to meditate on the rhythm of my breath, letting go of any doubts, any negative thoughts until soothing darkness calmed everything down. In the desert landscape, I felt safer once the sun, the danger, was gone.

The night lit with an intoxicating number of stars, pinpricks of dazzling light across the vast dark plane that a person could look at directly. In the measureless space of silence, I could hear the stars breathing. Then low drumming, faint singing somewhere far away.

A flicker of light in my periphery. I raised up on my elbow and looked without squinting. What I first thought might be headlights in the distance became a flat opaque disc illuminating the sky, the earth. I didn't recognize this moon, but it knew me. It loomed close, breathing my breath.

I hadn't realized I'd been sleeping when I woke to someone kicking my Birkenstock. Brightness burned through the slits of my eyes. Morning. I squinted up at a person in a conical hat with a wide brim who was speaking another unfamiliar language. I took him in as I maneuvered slow motion into a standing position. Striking to look at, delicately featured with swimming brown eyes and incredibly white teeth, tall, lithe; I could easily have mistaken him for a woman, a model, had his chest not been bare. I responded with greeting phrases in Hausa, Djerma, and French, but the man didn't seem to understand. I tried English on a whim, and when that failed, opted for charades to convey that I needed a ride west.

His hat suggested he might be a Fulani nomad, some loose-fitting drawstring pants, and paper-thin leather sandals. Leather strands threaded through two small, stitched bundles hung from his neck. Another dangled from his right bicep. He gestured for me to follow him to a huge faded red truck parked on the other side of the windbreak. How did I miss hearing that?

"Tchin-Tabaraden?" he asked.

"Oui."

I climbed onto a pipe that served as a running board, creaking open the heavy door to a stunning Tuareg woman dressed in rich indigo cloth, her skin stained bluish from the dye in the fabric.

Intricate long braids framed her lined face, a plug of tobacco rested on her lower lip. She flashed a smile, the tobacco perfectly balanced.

"Salaam alaykum," she said.

Arabic. The Muslim greeting. I knew this. Peace be upon you. "Alaykum a salaam." And upon you be peace.

The extent of our conversation.

I looked out the passenger window. The sand reflected the sun, bright pale rather than golden. So much light eclipsed color. How did people survive in such an environment? The closer we got, the more I realized how out of place I was. The sparse scrub trees and thorny plants coated in dust, more sepia than green, like a vintage photograph. Looking through the windshield, I could see the village up ahead.

When the truck driver slowed, I told him to stop, gestured that I wanted to be let off on the sandy plain just short of Tchin-Tabaraden. None of us spoke French well enough for me to explain that I wanted to arrive on my own, that my mothers said, "You see so much more of a place with the soles of your feet." The woman in the passenger seat sounded hysterical. She and the driver argued in a raucous guttural language for a good five minutes. I recognized anasara, Allah, and djinn.

They continued arguing as we drove a few hundred more feet to a windbreak. Finally, the driver made a clicking noise with his lips, ground the gears to a stop, and gestured with his chin to the passenger door. I grabbed my pack and jumped down, still standing in the same place when the truck disappeared into the distance. I felt woozy, almost seasick. Maybe from residual effects of dysentery. Maybe from the endless desolation. I took a long drink from my canteen. I recognized this desert from poetry, a sand ocean. Waves of heat undulated above the vast plain. I swallowed, concentrating on calming my stomach, and forced a deep breath of the searing air. A faded woven mat, attached to three branches pounded deep into the desert floor by someone, provided shade—but there was no one. I walked alone into the light, the sand, the intersecting planes of land and sky far from where I'd ever been.

I tried to orient myself. Figure direction from location of the sun. Though still at that moment, I knew the wind could alter this landscape and obliterate any landmarks I could use for navigation. This place had its own language I would need to learn. Some called the desert a wasteland; it looked exactly like I felt.

CHAPTER FOUR

The sand became the village. First, a haphazard pattern of crude tents slung low to the ground, then rows of mud structures that formed a spare civilization. Everyone turned to watch as I passed on my way to locate the school for nomadic children. The Tuareg men's billowing cloth swirling about them as they tended camels or traded, sheathed swords slung over the shoulders of those with turbans. The women wearing loose suggestions of black, blue, or white tops and wrapped in cloth from the waist down but otherwise unveiled, revealing long and intricate patterns of braids and the signature plug of tobacco balanced on their lips, the children, half-clad, playing with tin cans or bones, or kicking what resembled a ball. The Fulani men, women, and children with their top knots and buns, their bronzed bare chests displaying bundles of leather gris-gris and shells maybe from seven million years ago when the desert used to be the Tethys Sea. Goats, an occasional slip of a dog.

An old man fully swathed in desert clothing ran up to me looking directly into my eyes, a gesture I knew was unusual for adults in the culture. He grasped my arm with an ecstatic expression, urging me along the road through the locals, whose eyes all wandered with me. No traditional sword at his side, but he spoke excitedly, gibberish to me. At first, I thought he might be the government official, the fonctionnaire, who would show me the school, but when we came to a herd of camels, the man dropped my arm and nudged me toward a camel with green eyes like my own. He left me standing there, disappearing into the amused crowd.

This is before I learn that he is an anebzeg, a madman, and wherever he wanders, people feed him, give him water, a place to rest. After he was a rich man, and his relatives, friends, and acquaintances always asked him for money or anything they thought they needed more than he did. After he gave and gave until he ran out of possessions, including his sword and his mind, then he started giving other people's belongings to whomever he thought deserved them.

Maybe the nomads thought I was a madwoman, wandering into their village, their lives, speaking a French-Hausa blend that came out as nonsense, red haired with pale skin and green eyes with which the madman immediately connected. They might understand me traveling in search of something I needed, but they wouldn't understand why, if I wasn't married at the advanced age of 18, my mother hadn't accompanied me. I must be crazy, senseless, definitely foolish.

Maybe they were right.

The actual fonctionnaire stepped from the crowd and introduced himself.

"Lark Stevens," I responded.

Both of us playing roles in the wrong scene—a Djerma man from Niamey in his western-style leisure suit and faux glasses, and me, a green-eyed anasara in a t-shirt, gauze skirt, and Birkenstocks.

The school compound where I would live, edged the far side of the village, the fonctionnaire explained.

Too isolated. "Would it be possible to live here in the village?"

"Mademoiselle, teachers live at the school in the cement housing," he said. "Very nice for you. Come, I will introduce you to the director."

Even at a walk, the village was small.

"The French built the primary school including sleeping dorms where the nomadic children stay," the fonctionnaire said.

I knew Niger's previous military president, Kountché, mandated their education. "Do you think President Saibou will improve the Tuaregs' situation?"

The fonctionnaire either didn't understand or chose not to respond. I remembered I wasn't supposed to talk politics.

As we walked, we greeted people along the way. Many offered French greetings, but most, Muslim, salaam alyakum. Everyone seemed friendly or amused, the swords ornamental. The children stared and trailed along after us until the fonctionnaire waved them off. They took off running down the sand road.

The school had its own compound, enclosed with a dried mud, banco, wall. The director, another urban Djerma man, greeted me in formal French with an American handshake. He introduced me to his wife and young daughter who was dressed in a what looked like a plaid dress from Macy's. Said they'd come from Niamey to help with structuring and scheduling, as the school had only been open a couple of years. I introduced myself as Lark. This is before the director insists on a prefix and introduces me to the students as "Miss," and I correct him and reintroduce myself as Ms., before I let that go.

The director, fonctionnaire, and I toured several free-standing classrooms with lights and ceiling fans that couldn't function because the village had no electricity. "A forward-thinking decision," the director explained. Two dormitory buildings, a kitchen, and several residences constructed of concrete for the teachers, who stepped out of their respective buildings on cue, I recognized the Hausa or Djerma men. One, I wasn't sure about. We greeted each other in French except for the man I was unsure of. "Hello," he said. "Welcome." From Nigeria.

I smiled at him but wanted to avoid speaking English outside of the classroom, not wanting to separate myself from the locals any more than I already naturally was. "All male teachers?" I asked the director.

"The woman who teaches French lives in the village."

"Is she a local?"

"No. From Niamey."

I was working up to asking the director himself about living in town and glad for the precedent. I thanked him for the tour and expressed how pleased I was to be living and teaching at the school in Tchin-Tabaraden.

"C'est vrai?" he asked as if he couldn't believe it was true.

I thought I heard the fonctionnaire mumble anasara, but I might have imagined it.

The director continued. "Most teachers are required to serve in the bush for their first couple of years after completing their education."

"Must be a shock," I offered.

"Come." He led me up the concrete stairs to a rectangle porch and a two-room house: a living room space with a table that doubled as a kitchen with a Peace Corps issued mini-fridge and propane gas stove sitting in a corner, a small bathroom, and a made-up twin bed in the bedroom.

"It's very nice," I said looking around the room. "But would it be possible for me to live in the village itself like the other female teacher?"

"She has a husband and a niece already living with her."

"I meant live in another house, if there are any available."

He glanced down at my Birkenstocks.

"By yourself?"

"Yes."

He and the fonctionnaire conversed in what I assumed to be Djerma then switched to French and directed some boys watching the spectacle to move the stove and mini fridge to "the house with the pump." Tchin-Tabaraden had neither propane nor electricity, but I'd heard in training that the fridge made a good bookshelf. I'd seen propane at the market in Tahoua.

"D'accord, okay, Miss." The director and I shook hands again.

The fonctionnaire and I walked back toward the village proper. The students hadn't arrived yet, he said, but once outside the school wall, local children seemed to materialize from the landscape itself. This time, the fonctionnaire said nothing to them, though they kept a safe distance.

About a half mile in, he pointed out an abandoned dispensary.

"Why abandoned?" This is before I break into it and discover the bottles of medicine are labeled in German and take the two I'm sure about from odor and color.

He shrugged, fishing a cola nut from his pocket. I immediately focused elsewhere to avoid an offer of what the volunteer with the shaved head described as solid horseradish. It crunched when he bit off a piece. He chewed it like gum.

The further we walked, the more people. Again, we traded greetings. Whoever initiated, we answered in the response of that language. I felt fluent.

The fonctionnaire pointed to a tiny banco building with a man leaning against the wall, robed like a Tuareg but wearing a striped fez instead of a turban.

He greeted the man, called him Hajji.

I knew that meant he'd made the pilgrimage to Mecca in Saudi Arabia, the birthplace of Mohammed, the place where he received the first revelation of the Quran. The direction everyone faced to pray five times a day. Muslims considered it their obligation to go there once in life, but few could afford it.

"He owns the restaurant," the fonctionnaire explained.

"Restaurant? Where?"

He pointed with his lips to where the hajji leaned against the wall. "You give him money. He cooks you food to take home."

"Does he have a menu?"

"Rice and goat's meat."

Not far from the restaurant, we reached the middle of a bank of connected simple sunbaked mud, banco, buildings and stopped at a crooked aluminum gate. The fonctionnaire pushed it open.

"Voila, chez-vous."

My house: a sand yard with a single spindly acacia tree and a water pump from one of the three wells U.S. AID had dug in the area some years before. The wall skirted the perimeter for privacy or maybe for protection against the blowing sand. A decorative banco railing rimmed a porch area, a rectangle in front of the door. The house itself, also dried mud. The fonctionnaire clapped his hands, then led me inside, the interior white-washed, a simple rectangle with sand floors divided into three rooms, a front doorway and windows but no glass or standard door, rather corrugated aluminum that he said could be closed against the Harmattan winds that caused seasonal sandstorms. He gestured with his chin toward a rolled up woven mat.

"Dormir," he said, resting his cheek on his folded hands.

A mat instead of a bed. I could sleep anywhere.

We spoke in short phrases, but my inner voice ran on unimpeded during the periods of silence.

The thought of severe weather summoned Roy to my brain or maybe it was the closing of the window, or the thought of sleeping by myself, or that everything still reminded me of him.

"Mademoiselle? Ça va?" Everything all right?

"Oui, bien sûr, of course."

The house contained a smaller woven mat on a sand floor and a clay pot, tukunya, filled with cool water, a film of dust floating on top, a kerosene lantern with some gritty kerosene in the base, and an enamel cup. I unzipped the top pouch of my pack for a couple of sterilizing tablets and dropped them in the water sending little ripples of debris like the rings of Saturn. This is after the doctor said I'd become used to the taste of iodine. Before I quit adding it because the water comes from so far below the surface it's pristine. Before I truly taste water.

The fonctionnaire fished three matchsticks from his pocket and set them on the newly delivered stove, then put another one in his mouth, working the plain end like a toothpick. A layer of sand covered everything, outside and in. It crunched between my teeth.

He took the match from his mouth to speak. "The people here don't use propane."

The Tuareg culture appealed to me maybe exactly because they didn't use propane. Resourceful and resilient enough to survive in one of the most brutal landscapes on earth. Nomadic. They traveled for what they needed. The women neither veiled nor oppressed. I spat the grains of sand irritating the raw inside of my lip. The fonctionnaire was staring at me, not directly in my eyes, but staring generally, with a half-smile on his face, which I ignored.

"Do they use the swords?"

"They used to, Miss. They still can be dangerous."

Anyone can be. "But have you seen them use their swords?"

He worked his matchstick as if calculating. "No."

I dabbed my lip with the back of my hand. "Latrine?"

He gestured for me to follow and stepped outside. "La bas," there. He waved his arm, indicating the landscape beyond the village.

The nomads relieved themselves among the sand dunes beyond their tents, not in the market, the autogare, the village itself, an improvement. The desert landscape absorbed everything. I still had some toilet paper I took from the model school in Niamey.

"Donc. Bonne chance," he said, good luck, and left me to myself.

I unpacked the other two mid-calf gauze skirts, the few plain t-shirts, and sweater for the cold season. The Roelli 35S remained wrapped inside my Bowie shirt to protect it from dust and debris but mostly because it reminded me of Roy. At the bottom of the pack in a small pile of sand, assorted toiletries, my Swiss army knife, a compass from one of the guys dressed like a female, a flashlight, and the bottle of vitamins for lactating mothers from the nurses, and something else. I pulled it out of the grit to see and dropped it as if it burned my fingers. The marble. Roy must have somehow put it in my pack before I left. I picked it up and threw it hard over the wall. I took a cleansing breath and drank some iodized water from my canteen since the water in the tukunya still had a film of dust floating on top. With no place to actually put anything, I dumped the sand from my pack, shook out and re-rolled my clothes, stuffing everything back inside except the books. I shelved them in alphabetical order in the fridge, my journal and pen on one end, and stepped outside to get some air and inspect the yard.

A dozen children's faces looking over the wall blinked their eyes at me. They laughed. Some whispered, anasara. Others, mademoiselle. One, Miss. When I spoke, they disappeared.

But others came. A raucous clap at the door. "Entrez, s'il vous plaît," I said, please come in.

Dozens of young Tuareg men poured in tracking my yard in a flurry of goat hide sandals extending their hands to welcome me, looked directly into my eyes, asking if I would be their amie, friend. Roughly half with swords and all of them jovial. "Oui, bien sûr," of course, I said over and over, again surprised at the direct requests and eye contact not typical of the culture. This is before I realize I'd agreed to be everyone's lover, which is after they have gone. The young Tuareg men were joking, knew I didn't understand the nuances of French. This is before I grasp that some had extended their left hands, the hand I, too, would learn to use with water from a teapot after relieving myself. After they left the sand yard tracked with divots like the surface of the moon.

Again, clapping outside the wall. I flung open the gate this time to a familiar face. The stunning Tuareg woman from the truck who'd accompanied me here. I recognized the intricate pattern of braids framing her face, the plug of tobacco resting on her lower lip, her smile, her voice.

"Salaam alaykum."

She was holding a bowl of steaming rice with a bit of stringy meat on top. "Alaykum a salaam."

She touched her heart, said her name was Mariama. I touched mine. "Lark."

"Lark," she repeated and laughed. She handed me the bowl.

"Mangez," eat. She gestured using two fingers as a spoon.

She appeared older, her face lined but her hair pure black and her manner fluid. When Mariama turned to leave, I noticed she was pregnant. Very. I thanked her for her kindness, ate a few bites of rice, and waited a while before I opened the gate again, giving the food to the several children who fell inside.

The mud house absorbed the desert heat so by evening it felt like a solar oven. I picked up the sleeping mat, lantern, and a book of poetry, and moved outside in the open air. Striking the first of the fonctionnaire's matches, I lit the kerosene lamp, moths immediately drawn to the light, the drumming of their wings, its own poetry. I listened for a while, blew out the lamp, and lay down fully clothed to rest a minute. I woke with a start to a sky swarming with stars. I laughed, applauding their dizzying array, took a deep breath of the desert air and turned over.

A strange sound. Eerie and unsettling. I held my breath trying to hear it more clearly. Whatever the sound was, it was deeply disturbing.

I lay there for a long while and listened hard, as when tuning Roy's guitar, striking the key on the piano and plucking the string over the lingering note tilting my ear to hear if they matched, and then to be certain sounding the notes again, and again. Maybe the mating call of a sand cat or the screech of a young wild boar. I followed the sound, a minor key, a repeating fermata with little rest in between. My ear kept wanting it to sound like a coyote— those bizarre haunting staccatos they hurl in the air like prayers— trying to match the sound to one I knew.

It was midnight and the moon had lost its balance in a sky crowded with stars. The mud huts I passed looked luminous, ominous as if I were walking or waking in a dream, or as if the Sahara were dreaming me, my body a mirage rising from the landscape. I didn't hear the sound again before I saw them. The circle of children heard me and turned their faces in my direction. Several of them had what looked like bats, and my first thought was a pick-up game of baseball.

"Anasara!" someone whispered.

I saw then that what they had in their hands were not bats but large sticks. I looked down and saw a hide-less dog in the fetal position. The only thing moving were the dog's eyes, balls of glass that stared at me.

I looked away from the dog and yelled at the children, trying to construct a meaningful philosophy against cruelty out of a handful of foreign words. At the sound of my voice the children ran. The dog and I were alone then, and I moved closer. It was so quiet I could not hear it breathe. I, too, almost drowned in the silence.

I cried walking back to the mud house, realizing that living in this place required something I couldn't even name.

When I returned home, I got the mini-flashlight and holding it with my teeth, wrote an aerogramme to my mothers requesting Levis and sunflower seeds to plant. Something familiar. I wouldn't wear the jeans outright as that would be culturally insensitive but underneath a pagne, the cloth the women wrapped their bodies with like a skirt. Sunflowers preferred full sun. They would add some color. I also decided to get a dog.

When I finally fell back to sleep, I dreamt. *Apples in the full-color language of a place with a growing season. Brilliant red with pale flesh, juice running from my mouth.* I woke up, wiping my chin with the back of my hand and drifted back to sleep.

Roy and I walking beyond the garden. The desert's unrelenting curves, beckoning gold blanket of sensuous contours seducing us to our small deaths with hot breath. Wet seasons appearing, disappearing like mirages. Memory grasping at rain vanishing into sand, evaporating into dust laced air. The moon, waxing, waning,

*keeping the stars' whispering light from the sun. We weren't listen-
ing, but hurtling straight at the searing ball of light, drinking to the
dregs each other.*

I stirred and woke myself up to a boy maybe ten years old, staring
at me with large brown eyes and wearing an oversized faded
Mickey Mouse t-shirt, no pants, no shoes. I'd have offered him an
apple if I had one. He said his name was Oumar.

We recited the litany of greetings. I offered him some water,
then drank from my canteen relieving my parched throat.
"Oumar? I want a dog. "Chien."

He grinned as if I were joking.

"For a companion," I said, "un ami."

"Anasara. Mademoiselle. Miss. Dogs are not friends." Oumar
explained in broken French that a dog had once run across the
Prophet Muhammad's prayer mat. "Peace be upon Him. Only
the Wodaabé herders use dogs, to protect their animals, sometimes to hunt."

"Wodaabé. The dancers in the male beauty contest?" I
remembered seeing their painted faces and elaborate costumes in
National Geographic.

"Only the best-looking ones."

At my insistence, Oumar led me through the hot sand to a
Wodaabé goat herder.

"I know you," I said. The truck driver who'd driven me from
Kao to Tchin-Tabaraden. The one who looked like a model.

Oumar introduced him as Mokao.

He greeted me in French, and I responded.

Then Oumar spoke rapidly in a language I couldn't follow.

The man turned to me. "Vous voulez un chien?" You want
a dog?

"Oui," Oumar and I both said.

He gestured for us to follow and showed me a drowsy puppy
maybe a couple of months old. I paid him a franc, which made

both of us happy. With the brindle puppy in my arms, Oumar and I walked back home.

He shook his head and clicked his lips. "C'est trop," too much. This is before I teach the dog the basic commands, sit, lie down, stay, in French, and the word around the village is that the anasara's dog can speak French, and I don't correct it.

I ignored his assessment. "What should I name him?"

"Patience," Oumar said with a thick French accent.

I lived alone for twenty-four hours. This is before Oumar claps at the gate every evening. Before he comes in and lays his mat near mine and I recognize fear in his eyes. Before I realize someone put him up to it. Before we talk past the usual greetings, which is after we become friends, and I learn Mariama makes him stay with me every evening, to protect me from the djinn, and so I won't be alone.

During the day, Oumar took care of livestock, watering the goats and camel, looking for grass. Not at school. The first year President Kountché mandated education for the nomads, each Tuareg family was required to send one child to school, Ahmed, his older brother. Years later, Oumar's family still followed that rule. Oumar picked up some French on his own and now a little English. He spent his days protecting his family's goats and came back at night to protect me. This is before he tells me his father thinks I'm a government spy and sends him to spy on me.

First day of school, I got up early and walked through the village following the sound of drumming.

"Not drums," Oumar said.

The sound of women and girls pounding millet in large mortars. Some paired up and took turns, each with an over-sized wooden pestle, pounding in an alternating pattern. They raised their arms high above their heads, driving the pestle into the mortar in a drumming rhythm. When they saw us watching, they performed. When one's pestle struck the mortar, the other threw her pestle in the air, clapping, and then plunged it again into the mortar. They alternated, embellishing their moves in the air on the up beats. Each with a fresh plug of tobacco balanced on their lips.

"Manger?" I used one hand as a bowl and the two fingers of my other hand as a spoon and mimed eating. We'd passed the hajji's restaurant. No one. We needed breakfast.

Oumar took me to a woman sitting at a table selling Nescafé and local bread. Like the vendor in Niamey, Oumar dropped nine sugar cubes in his cup, adding condensed milk until the coffee was white. He dipped his small loaf of bread, the sticky liquid dripping from his smile down to his chin where flies were congregating. I plucked gray mealybugs from my loaf until there was only a string of bread left, my coffee thin and black in the blue enamel cup. This is before I become so addicted to Tuareg tea I ache for it.

At the school compound, everyone gathered around the flagpole. I stood at the edge of the crowd as one of the students raised the flag. Orange, white, and green, in equal horizontal bands, a large orange dot in the center against the white band. During training, we'd heard the orange color represents the north and east of Niger, the Sahara encroaching into the Sahel, yes. A tribute to the heroic nomads to survive in such an environment, no. The Tuaregs were not described as heroic in Niamey. The white of the flag said to stand for purity and innocence as well as civic consciousness and the responsibility of citizens to uphold their duties, but it reminded me of the bleached sand, the centered orange disc, the sun. The green suggested the southwest of Niger and its fertile lands along the Niger River, symbolic of agriculture and of hope. That sounded accurate. Everyone stood patiently watching the workings of the pulley. Was I the only one thinking about this? The only sound, creaking as the flag jerked up the pole.

In the few minutes it took to walk to my classroom, the students had already assembled. I hesitated outside, my only training with a small group of young children who attended the model training school in Niamey by choice. The students in Tchin-Tabaraden, required to attend, might be resentful, difficult. I felt jittery, maybe from the coffee, and already hot.

I took a deep breath, entered the room, and automatically flicked on the switch for the ceiling fan. The students laughed as if it were a joke. First impression: anasara. We could have used the air movement, the classroom crowded with upwards of 60 students ranging in age from maybe twelve to around my own age. They sat or leaned on chairs at the rows of tables, thin notebooks, pencils poised. I stood behind a table that functioned as a desk at the front of the room with a blackboard and chalk just behind me. After the fan incident, they surprisingly sat at rapt attention while I gave a lesson on simple objects and verbs. This is before I realize they are afraid of me. After they put on a play reenacting the day the nomads were first required to go to school. Some students acting as gendarmes, military police, carrying simulated guns fashioned from sticks, chasing and capturing the nomadic children running and screaming in terror. The parents and the gendarmes shouting at each other in different languages. The end.

Was it a message to the teachers? But the school had been operating for several years since. The students seemed more adapted than forced against their will now. The audience included nearly everyone in the village, praising the students for their acting. Everyone seemed to accept the arrangement. An historical play. Parents could visit the school whenever they wanted, the students released to travel with their families. The school year was arranged according to European holidays, a month in December and three months in the summer.

My initial thoughts suddenly mixed. My job to teach English

to the children of the nomads questionable but an education would give them options. Another path from struggling to survive in such a brutal landscape plagued by drought. But it also took away their way of life. It would never again be the same. Like Native Americans, like Australian Aborigines. People deeply connected with their landscapes. This is before I learn that many girls in the village aren't in school because they are helping their families survive, and many of the older boys have left the country to fight for Ghaddafi, same reason.

According to the fonctionnaire, there were thousands of people in the village, but that must have included those camped beyond the village and calculated on market day when all the nomads in the area came in for tea, sugar, grain, spices, and other supplies. A few Arabs' boutiques offered canned pineapple, sardines, tomato sauce, toothpaste, though no one knew what it was for, Omo laundry detergent, Bic lighters, and Irish Spring soap. I bought all of these things, dividing my business between the few shops. The locals mostly bought or traded for the tomato sauce, laundry soap, and a bright yellow Vaseline product for plaiting their hair.

Two of the governmental institutions, the school and prison, edged the town in opposite directions, but the post office sat in the center where the majority of the sedentary people lived. I walked there and mailed the postcard to Gita. The postmaster was a hajji and wore a fez. He chewed a kola nut while he worked or maybe waited for work.

"How long does a letter take to get from Tchin-Tabaraden to the U.S.?"

He blew out some air through pursed lips as if calculating, then shrugged his shoulders.

"When Allah wills it."

When I came home from school to rest during the afternoon heat that first day, I opened the gate to a man wearing wrinkled work clothing, standing beside some bags of cement and a bucket of wet concrete, trowel in hand, halfway finished building something. This is before I learn that the director sent a prisoner to build me a latrine. Before I learn that it's a political prison.

Beads of sweat dripped from his temples.

"Salaam alaykum," I said, and he responded, but he didn't understand French or Hausa, and I was limited. I dipped my cup in the tukunya, captured the dust, and poured the murky liquid at the base of the acacia, then offered him a cup of clear water. The earthen jar kept it surprisingly cool or maybe it was the contrast of the air temperature.

He paused from his work and drank it. "Merc," he said, the "c" soft like an abbreviation of "merci." The sand kept refilling the hole as he dug, the sun breathing down his neck. I hoped the director paid him enough. I went inside and left him to his work, dozing to the sound of the shovel, the whispering of the sand. By the time I reemerged, the building stood, appearing almost dry, the man and his tools gone.

Four walls with a doorway, no door. Inside, a deep hole in the ground, the opening reinforced with concrete, still damp. My first thought: I must look like I require a latrine. Soft. Definitely not tough enough for this place. Anasara. This is before I have eaten my first tin of pineapple and use the empty can to pour cool water from the tukunya over my head, drizzle it onto my parched skin, lather up with my triple milled soap, and pour another can of cool water to rinse. And another. After I have emptied the tukunya of water and realize there is no standing water in the desert because the sand absorbs it, so no mosquitoes. This is before I stop taking the antimalarial meds, which is after I realize I require a latrine.

I thought it might be the first public toilet in Tchin-Tabaraden, but no one else showed up to use it. This is before I understand the complexity of the culture and the simple logistics of a latrine designed for limited use.

People came for water though from the pump in the yard. The only time water actually came out of it, around 3 a.m. when the local women paraded through the gate with empty buckets and left with them full and balanced on their heads. They didn't clap at the door as they did during the day or talk when inside, but sometimes I stirred wake from the sound of dripping water and saw them glance over at me through the slits in my eyes. Usually, I slept deeply, as if drugged, until I heard the first call for prayers and opened my palms. My own tukunya I filled once a week, taking great care in drawing water from it. Scorpions, I learned, liked to hide in dark, damp places. The first one I tried to kill before it killed me. I'd read only four species were deadly, but I didn't know how to differentiate. This is before I'd ever attempted to kill anything. Before I learn about scorpions' horses, the even larger insects that race across the sand carrying scorpions on their backs. After I figure out to stay out of their way. After I order my first meal from the restaurant, a bowl of rice with a cooked scorpion on top. Before Oumar tells me it's a joke.

Clapping at the door. Already dark, but not late. Not Oumar. He would just come in. I opened the gate and looked out. One of my students. "Tala?"

Greetings, then "Venez," come. "Mariama is in labor and needs you."

Either Tala or Mariama was mistaken. "Please tell her I'm a teacher, not a doctor. I don't know anything about delivering babies."

"She wants you there, Miss."

Tala's French was perfect, interspersed with some new English words that she pronounced with a thick French accent. "Wait." I went into the house for my copy of *Where There is No Doctor*, the last book in the fridge. It was the first time I'd worn a pagne and Tala walked fast. I tried to keep up as well as the stuttering steps my pagne allowed, but any movement caused the cloth to unwrap, so I held onto it at my waist with my free hand. At first, we didn't converse much—I was breathless—and since the Tuaregs rarely said anything directly, I could concentrate on the awkward rhythm of walking at a brisk pace while bound in a long cloth. Anasara. Still, I decided to try a few sentences.

"I saw you in the play the other night. Very good."

Tala made a clucking sound from her throat that indicated agreement.

"What do the Tuaregs think of school now?"

She shrugged. "Sometimes women have to share some of their children with the desert," she said, completely changing the subject, then grew quiet until we came to a small gathering of Tuareg women.

Mariama reposed on a mat in the center of the tent with another African woman, hands on hips in a short red party dress looking down at her. I understood that this woman wanted Mariama to go to the dispensary, but Mariama insisted with clear gestures that her baby be born in her tent. When she saw me, she waved me in closer. After the Tamasheq greetings, I switched to my brand of French and emphasized that I had no medical training. Everyone seemed to ignore this.

Mariama introduced the woman in the red dress as a midwife from Côte d'Ivoire, the Ivory Coast.

"I'm here for a year. It's required to go to the bush after graduation," the midwife explained.

Tala poured some water in a blue enamel teapot, put in a handful of tea leaves, and set it on a wire brazier over the fire.

"She is having a difficult time. The baby is breach," the midwife said, oddly to me.

"I want her to come to the dispensary where there is at least a table, but she insists that her baby be born in her tent."

Mariama said something in Tamasheq. I glanced at Tala, who translated. "When the music changes, then the rhythm must."

Anything beyond greetings by this time of night made my head throb.

Mariama's labor was interrupted by periodic comments from the midwife that she half-whispered to me.

"These women are lazy. It's almost impossible to get them to push."

Tala picked up the boiling teapot by the handle, lined up several shot glasses, and poured the steaming gold liquid from an impressive height giving each shot a small head of foam.

"Tuareg tea," she said to me, offering everyone a shot glass full.

When the midwife took hers, she winced and snapped her fingers, switching the glass from one hand to the other like a hot potato. I noticed Tala's fingers were thickly calloused, so I took the glass from her with the tail of my pagne and waited a full five minutes before I tasted it. Boiling and bitter.

Even from my brief time here, I already knew the women weren't lazy. The women of Mariama's ethnic group used to have others do physical labor for them, but I'd read things had changed in the last several years, especially after the most recent droughts. Now women of every caste drew the water, pounded the millet with mortar and pestle, prepared the food, and took care of the children and often the animals. It took all day just to survive.

The midwife seemed harsh and condescending. Nothing at all like on the commune. Sometimes she barked orders and pushed on Mariama's stomach, but everyone else seemed unperturbed by her behavior. Did they think this woman knew some better way of giving birth than they had been doing themselves for centuries? They would never say so directly. Did they think the same of me teaching their children?

I crouched down near the dim firelight and opened my book to the chapter titled "Preparing for Birth" and immediately felt queasy. With the lack of a regular diet, regular anything, it was no wonder I'd been irregular, and I had put the idea of being pregnant out of my mind. But it had been three months now, a record. Still, I felt no other symptoms, and the IUD had worked for years. 99% effective. Probably the Tuareg tea. I refocused and resumed reading. "Birth is a natural event." About 1.5% of the time in a typical anasara's case. I'd visited the commune midwife for birth control. Now I wish I'd learned about the birthing process.

Nomadic women had multiple births because one in four would not survive, what Tala meant by women sharing some of their children with the desert.

With one of the shot glasses, Tala hit a foot-high cone of solid sugar wrapped in sky blue paper sending sweet splinters flying. Children suddenly appeared, scattering to pick the sweet bits from the sand, Tala adding a couple of the largest pieces to the teapot along with water. After it boiled, she refilled the shot glasses. I set mine aside to cool.

Further on in bold, the paragraph read, "...the less the birth attendant does, the more likely everything will go well... If there is any reason to think that a birth may be difficult or dangerous, a skilled midwife or experienced doctor should be present."

I closed the book and looked at the midwife, then at Mariama, who was smiling at me. It seemed genuine, meaningful, all the more puzzling. Had she invited me here to see how childbirth is done in the desert? I glanced at Tala, at the ring of patient faces flickering in the firelight and drank my tea. The second round was still hot, still bitter, but tempered by the slivers of sugar and more water.

When Mariama had a contraction, she got quiet. I could see her body relax rather than tense. She ignored the midwife.

Tala whispered to me that Mariama hadn't ask me there for advice or to help deliver the baby. She wanted me there for luck. This is before Mariama tells me that the first day we met, her son Ahmed left the country and that she saw this exchange of places as a sign from Allah.

After adding more water and sugar, Tala served the third round of tea. It tasted like extremely sweet hot water.

Mariama said something else, and Tala translated.

"The first round of tea is bitter like life, the second strong like love, the third sweet like death."

A tea metaphor. I tried not to over-think it, especially the sweet death.

When the baby girl was finally born, the women celebrated,

their voices ululating.

Tala accompanied me home at a slower pace. I felt exhausted, even though I hadn't done anything but try to understand the languages and gestures and worry about things I didn't know. I entered the facts I knew on a page in my journal: healthy female, mother: Mariama, father: Mariama's husband (find out his name), born August 30, 1989, 10:40 pm. I crossed that out and rewrote 30 August 1989 at 22:40. This is before I find out that she is the first child in Tchin-Tabaraden with an actual birthdate.

I dismissed class early, tired from the previous night and not feeling well. If I'd lived at the school compound as the director suggested, my house would be yards, meters, away, but I walked the kilometer along the searing sand road mumbling the ritual greetings to those I passed even though I wasn't feeling in health or at peace.

When I made it home, no dog, good. I didn't feel like talking to anyone, including Patience. Who knew what I was coming down with now? Not dysentery or schistosomiasis, and I'd been vaccinated against the most common diseases. Thinking somehow made me feel worse, or maybe it didn't have to do with thinking. I took my sleeping mat into the room furthest from the door where I felt least likely to be disturbed, unrolled it on the sand floor, closed my eyes, and tried to relax.

My eyes sprung open moments later to violent cramping. My period at last, and with a vengeance. Relief. No wonder I felt so dismal. I rallied at the thought, pushed myself up, and stumbled straight to the latrine, managing to rinse off, pouring tin cans of solar-heated water from the bowl, and lay back down on the sand. Severe cramping turned into something else. Cold with a severe wind-chill, and even though I was shivering in unrelenting, undulating spasms, my insides burned. I felt like I'd eaten broken glass. Was someone trying to kill me? A djinn?

It took all my strength to open the mini-fridge door, but I

managed to pull out *Where There is No Doctor* and looked up delayed menstrual period. I skipped through worry, diet, and emotional upset to "if the bleeding comes later than expected and is more severe, it may be a miscarriage." I turned to "Miscarriage (Spontaneous Abortion): Miscarriages are most frequent in the first three months of pregnancy. A woman who has heavy bleeding after she has missed one or more periods probably is having a miscarriage."

I felt overwhelmed, shattered—"Most women have one or more miscarriages in their lifetime. Many times, they do not realize that they are having a miscarriage. They may think their period was missed or delayed, and then came back in a strange way, with big blood clots"—devastated.

I just wanted to not be pregnant, not to abort Roy's and my baby. I went back to the latrine and stayed there for hours, bleeding and crying in a fetal position, clawing at the sand. When I finally stopped hemorrhaging, it felt like an internal drought where the blood suddenly stills into stagnant pools, then evaporates in time-lapse mode through the pores until even the bones turn to dust.

Eventually, I propped myself on my elbow and read, "A woman should know when she is having a miscarriage because it could be dangerous." I heaved the book as hard as I could against the wall. How was this helpful where there was no doctor, and the woman didn't know? I could seek out the midwife, who would tell me it's already too late. Or maybe too early since I didn't have a husband. Of course I should go to a hospital, but there was none, not even transportation to take me to Tahoua to see the nurses there who would feel my forehead with the back of their palms, "Oh, Lark," tell me I was pregnant with the emphasis on was and adjust my IUD to prevent it from happening again. I needed my mothers, their raspberry tea, cohosh, vervain, their comfort and love. Now came deep gut wrenching sobs. I had just given my first child to the desert. A boy or girl? I would never know.

So much blood. The sand had already absorbed it. Like it never happened. And no one else would ever know except Gita.

In a week's time, my hormones had settled down, and I felt mostly relieved not to be pregnant. I started a letter to Gita but couldn't get the words right. She would tell me there's always a lesson to be learned. I needed her to help me see it.

Mariama invited me to the naming ritual the women performed the evening before the official Quranic naming ceremony at the mosque. She put her baby in my arms, amusing the other women. Had Mariama given some of her other children to the desert? I held the baby close. They moved, carrying their pestles like the men carried their swords, in a circle, the life cycle? A different geometric shape from the typically angular patterns I'd seen on the Tuaregs' embroidered clothing, or the symbols engraved on their silver jewelry. I celebrated with Mariama, with all the women, tried to move to their rhythm as we circled counterclockwise inside the tent. An old woman led the procession carrying a tray with millet, dates, and cheese for good luck, they said. They called the baby Izza, the name she would go by.

The next day when some young Tuareg men invited me to the official naming ceremony at the mosque, I went with them. Baby Izza's head had been shaved for the occasion to disconnect her from the spirit world, I learned. My own hair blew in the breeze like a ragged red flag. This is after the sun dehydrates my hair from wispy curls to straight hair the consistency of straw. Before I leave on break and shear it to my scalp. I was the only woman there. Whether the men were mocking my ignorance or considered me outside the purview of the cultural norm didn't matter.

My presence at the edge of the crowd caused an audible murmuring, "anasara," so I couldn't hear the chosen Quranic name the marabout announced but did hear the simultaneous bleat of the sacrificed ram. Then very clearly, as if directed at me, I heard the word "espion," spy.

I left abruptly and walked home alone, the paper-thin goat-hide sandals I'd bought to better blend in providing little protection from the hot sand or blending in. I'd laughed when the second-year volunteers joked that all foreigners were suspected of spying for the government, but now it didn't seem funny. Spying for the American government and their uranium interest or for Niger's government and its indifference regarding the Tuaregs? I hadn't asked. Only knew that President Kountché first mandated that the nomadic children be educated, that he had ousted Niger's first president in a coup after his mismanagement of the prolonged drought in the sixties and early seventies, when limited sacks of grain and powdered milk from foreign aid sent to the government in Niamey finally arrived in Tchin-Tabaraden but could only be had for a price. This is before I learn that Kountché, himself, was no better. He was also Djerma, sedentary rather than nomadic. Now Ali Saibou was president, also Djerma, sedentary, military.

As I walked along the edge of the sand road past the mud houses and shops, some of the locals acknowledged me from deep in their diaphanous desert clothes. Mademoiselle, Miss, akafar, anasara, espion. Maybe behind my back the children called me the female version of anebzeg or dog lover. My attitude about dogs and my job of teaching English to the children of the nomads now seemed superfluous even to me in a village where many infants died long before reaching school age.

Technically, I worked for both governments. The Peace Corps, JFK's brainchild of a volunteer program run by the United States government. The mission: providing "social and economic development abroad through technical assistance, while promoting mutual understanding between Americans and populations served." I had it memorized.

The Nigerien government requested a Peace Corps volunteer in Tchin-Tabaraden to teach the nomadic children English when the national language was French. Even though Niger bordered English-speaking Nigeria, learning English didn't seem crucial to the nomads' social or economic development or survival, but a spy?

I slowed down, purposely weaving through the locals, attempting some friendly banter in the market, amusing them with my constant mistakes in the languages. "Beautiful full moon last night" translated to beautiful pregnant moon. I didn't laugh.

By midafternoon, Oumar left, and everyone else retreated to shade and dozed. My alone time. I was trying to stay awake because the intense heat caused vivid, almost hallucinatory, dreams I couldn't control, usually about Roy. I stripped down completely, and loosely covered with a pagne, gathered a bowl of water, cup, the bar of Irish Spring, the only soap available in Tchin-Tabaraden, filled the bowl with water from the tukunya, and entered the latrine for a relatively cold shower. Dipping the cup in the water, I poured the cool water over my body, lathered with soap, then rinsed with a second cup of water, goose bumps rising on my dust-free skin. I didn't bother drying off; the moisture evaporated instantly.

The sides of my feet had blistered from the searing sand in contrast to Mariama's feet edged with a faded henna design, her toenails dyed muted red. The crackling dry air felt like sand in my throat, my lungs. I had never lived in a place with zero humidity; the clanging glare of the sun, the arid hiss of the wind, the locals' voices rang in my ears like irregular bells.

'Espion,' I thought while dressing for the staff meeting. People thought what they would; I could only control myself. Even though formal education was now an accepted part of nomadic children's lives, and my classes were full beyond capacity, the students who completed their primary education still couldn't feed their families. The reason many of the older boys left the country to find work as exiles, so their families could survive.

Here I was, at the request of the government, currently on my way back to the school to meet with the Djerma school director from Niamey. At the meeting, I sat across from a Tuareg man dressed in a pale green boubou, his white veil so intact that I could only determine that he had smooth olive skin from his eyelids. Every time our eyes met—a flash of hazel—he readjusted his tagelmust, veil, and looked away. A sign of respect. I found myself fantasizing about holding his face in my hands, hooking my fingers into the cloth, slipping the tagelmust down, and resting my lips against his. It was the heat. A remnant of Roy and his hazel eyes, where my mind still returned when I relaxed even a little, the muscle memory of our bodies. The residual phantom pain. I repositioned my chair away from the man, opened my palms, and drifted back to the meeting.

The director was saying how pleased he was with the students' adjustment to the school schedule, with the teachers and their classes. He wasn't aware that earlier that day during my introduction to the superlative, one of my students stood, snapping his fingers wildly in the back row, waving a Playboy. "Miss! Big, bigger, biggest." The teaching moment suggested objectification, but my TEFL lesson plan wasn't that robust. The entire class riveted on the centerfold; no one looked away. This is before I realize that they gave me their rapt attention not from fear, as I first thought, but from curiosity.

Thoughts walking back: Kountché's call for education, how a Playboy made its way to the edge of the Sahara, the Tuareg man with the hazel eyes, chocolate, fragments of Hausa—strings of soft syllables blending with the harsher tones of Tamasheq.

Interruptions: The muezzin's voice calling for prayer, lyrical Arabic phrases chanted from the mosque on the other side of the village. Even with the loudspeaker cutting in and out or maybe it was the wind, it sounded like poetry. I opened my palms and listened for Allah.

A Tuareg woman, the hatch marks in her face stained blue from her indigo cloth, rode up on a camel. "Bush," she said with a thick French accent. She veered from her quest for water to tell me this. The U.S. President, not the place, I realize after she is gone.

Friday: market day list: henna for Mariama and Tala. Sold out. Two string chairs, a stick broom to sweep out my house. I'd seen women use hand brooms, slender sticks held together at the top with a lidless, bottomless tin can, sweep patterns into their sand yards—on my to-try list—my immediate concern to sweep out debris from the house, a tub to wash clothes, rice, piment, hot pepper, tea, sugar, a guerba, a goat hide canteen like the locals used. Oumar said it kept the water cool. He suddenly appeared and insisted we needed a short-wave radio.

"We hear the news without it though," I said. Again, distancing myself from the west so I could figure out how to live here.

"With a cassette player." Oumar held up a tape of Bob Marley and the Wailers.

Music made more sense.

Interruption: A truck rumbled into the village. I turned at the sound. A white Scout International. The truck pulled to the side of the sand road and parked. I watched as the person got out of the driver's seat. An anasara wearing khakis, a navy-blue polo, and plastic wingtips.

"Hello!"

The voice directed toward me, in English. Maybe a man. Or a woman. S/he could pull off either. Tall, lanky, sparking grey eyes, butched hair the color of tobacco.

I set everything down, extended my hand and drew my palm across hers/his Tuareg style.

S/he held it momentarily, slowing the trajectory. "Pleasure. I'm Frank."

He. "Lark. Are you picking up supplies to go out into the bush?"

"No, I'm here to bring supplies into the bush." He pulled a pack of Rothmans from his pocket and offered a cigarette to me.

"No, thanks."

He quickly doled out several others to the assorted Tuaregs and Fulanis delighted by the offer. He purchased a Bic lighter and tossed it to the crowd like at a rock concert.

"What business?"

"I work for Rothmans." He pointed to the logo on his shirt. "Selling tobacco products. What about you?"

"Education." I wasn't going to say I worked for the government. It was a cognate and everyone listening could interpret it wrong, adding fuel to the spy rumor.

The crowd grew raucous with the free tobacco, and Frank had to calm everyone down to be heard. He encouraged the shop owners to stock his product with a cut of the profits and explained that he would be happy to deliver on a regular basis. He had his audience. He glanced over and again caught me staring at him, perhaps recognizing a look of distain for his contribution to the community.

Someone actually knocked on the aluminum gate. Patience, who now resembled a brindle colored greyhound, jumped up from his spot in the shade. "Restes," stay, I told him. Had to be Frank.

I opened the gate. "Frank," I said. "Come in." Oumar stepped out from behind him.

"Met Oumar milling around the crowd. He insisted I stop by."

I gestured toward the string chairs, but Frank spotted the latrine.

"Here." I dipped a tin can into the tukunya. "Take this with you. There's soap in there and a pagne to dry your hands."

As I gathered the teapot, sugar, and tea from the house, I thought I heard singing.

"You're a fuckin' saint," Frank said, reemerging from the latrine.

"I had nothing to do with the latrine, but you're right; it could be considered a miracle." I waved him to a chair. "Have a seat. I'll make tea."

"Don't bother."

No bother. I turned to Patience, "Assis-toi." He sat.

"Miss," Oumar said, his eyes wide and startled as the first night we met. He picked up the brazier and made a wide berth around Patience to reach the gate.

"I'll get some hot coals for tea."

Patience responded to commands at home, but I doubted he listened to anyone else. He often scaled the wall late in the evening, returning sometimes with a goat's head or a bone with meat on it no doubt stolen from someone somewhere.

Frank and I spent the afternoon talking between the rounds of tea Oumar insisted on making himself, the wind interrupting periodically. After the pleasantries, we argued about his business.

"Maybe it's this landscape, so minimalist and stark, or maybe it's too easy to speak my mind because we share a common language, but I have to ask directly. What are you doing, selling cigarettes, introducing and promoting a dangerous and addictive habit in any society, to one of the poorest countries in the world?" The wind blew my hair into my face. I didn't move to adjust it. Pointless. We were sitting at an angle and my hair immediately blew back out of my face. It sounded rude. I rephrased. "I mean why not offer malnourished people canned vegetables or kits that would filter microbes and feces out of drinking water?"

Frank licked his dry lips. "I appreciate your idealism, but they would not spend what little they have on foreign canned vegetables." He opened his throat and swallowed the cooled shot glass of tea. "What I'm offering these struggling people is a cheap bit of pleasure to carry on through their day, take their minds off the worry for food, give them a little nicotine boost. Six minutes of their lives where they feel they have a little control," Frank said.

I leaned back in the chair considering, suspending the silence a beat or two. "I follow your twisted logic, but what about their health?"

He drew a cigarette from his pocket, cupping his hands against the wind to light it, and took a drag. "These people aren't going to live long enough to develop lung problems."

I stared off into the distance, past the sand road and mud houses to the dunes beyond to the silhouette of a solitary boy herding goats, lit by the sun like a Rembrandt. Most of the people I had met did not seem to be over middle age. They might have been even younger than they appeared. The desert took its toll. I also knew that Tuareg women already used tobacco. Even those half-grown kept a wad balanced on their lower lips throughout the day, discreetly spitting out the door when they came to visit. I accepted it as a natural aspect of their culture.

"They won't die from smoking," Frank said. "They'll die from starvation, from dehydration, from marginalization, from living in this brutal place for too long. The fuckin' desert itself will kill them."

In just a few months, the students picked up English like a card game, Crazy Eights, Huits, while I struggled with trying to become more fluent in French and learn Hausa and Tamasheq. No time to learn the languages separately with a two-year contract, though every day seemed an eternity. Words and phrases blended. Without charades, people other than my students understood nothing I said beyond greetings. Even if I spoke a simple phrase, they appeared puzzled. They always laughed. Was it my accent? Were they distracted by my anasaraness? I tried not to let my frustration show. But sometimes I wondered if they were even trying to understand me. Maybe Patience, but he only knew five words counting his name. I talked to him anyway, which may have been observed by the children peering over the wall to see who had stopped to visit. It did not help me blend in.

The constant struggle did help me forget though. It still took all my concentration to get through a day. Besides the challenges of communicating in different languages, trying to understand different cultural values and perspectives (our differing views on time and dogs for two), the landscape itself demanded attention. I breathed sand, swallowed it, and slept with it like a nomad.

No mirrors made it easier to forget, too. This is long before I glimpse my reflection and am shocked to see an anasara, my own face unfamiliar. My reflection wouldn't be familiar now either and far worse if I actually could see my damaged self. I knew I already looked like the second year volunteers. Same haggard look in the face, the stance, the stare.

I lifted a hank of my straw-like hair from my shoulders and looked at it in the light: my former trademark red curls now straight, splintered, broken.

Oumar looked dismayed.

Too late to cover my head with a scarf, the damage already done.

He pulled me to the nearest shop where he pointed out the glow-in-the-dark yellow pommade the locals used on their hair. I didn't read the label. Whatever chemicals made it that unnatural yellow, irrelevant. It was available. Some sort of petroleum jelly.

"Bonne idée." Oumar, pleased with my purchase.

In the evening, he watched me wash my feet, revealing the deep fissures the sand had etched into my heels, slather the yellow salve on the tender, deep cracks, and put on my pair of socks to lock in moisture overnight.

"No, Miss." Oumar again dismayed that I didn't understand how to use the product, the skin on his heels calloused like hide.

I rationed my Nivea for use on my face and arms, the skin directly exposed to the environment. This is before I become dependent on the desert's sweeping curves that shift like liquid heated by the sun until almost glass. Before my brain, my entire body fills with sand.

After classes, I walked to the post office. My students said I had something. I wasn't sure if everyone knew only my business or if it was like a commune in the way everyone knew everyone else's business.

"Miss!" the postmaster said, waving me over, a letter in hand. "Aux États Unis!"

About time! It'd been months since my first night in Tchin-Tabaraden and the unnerving dog incident when I'd written my mothers requesting jeans to wear under my pagne and some flower seeds to plant, something familiar so I felt more like myself. I'd expected a package. The postmaster handed me an aerogramme with #3 marked on the envelope. Still, my first letter from home! "Are there more?" I asked, thinking I might get three letters at once.

"No, Mademoiselle. Just the one."

I thanked him and hurried back to the house without greeting anyone, the sand roads already empty, everyone resting in shade.

I pulled the aluminum gate open startling Patience awake under the acacia. Too excited to sit, I closed the gate and immediately peeled open the edge of the blue envelope. Again, letter #3 was written at the top. Then the date, April 30, 1989.

Dear Lark,

We carried Gita this morning just as she'd requested, from the spot where she was born, to your tree, where we had a bonfire and drumming before burying her in the cemetery, next to the statue of the little girl.

Buried Gita? Gita was dead?

My body quit functioning. I could not form the words with my mouth, my brain incapable of transmitting. I felt blinded, forgot how to breathe.

I tried to move forward, to where I didn't know. My legs took enormous slow motion steps as if I were under the ocean or a sea of sand, so much resistance, but it could have been the air. It could have been time or the invisible making itself felt. I don't know how long I stood there, if I stood at all.

"Miss." Oumar's voice outside of wherever I was. "Drink this."

I opened my eyes, or maybe they were already open, and slowly focused like Christopher Tyler's autostereograms, the monochromatic pictures that popped out in 3D when you weren't trying to see them.

Oumar nudged my fist with the cup of water. My hand opened in the same slow motion, my palm and fingers as if learning to hold an object for the first time. Two objects. I couldn't let go of the letter, and it took both hands to raise the cup to my lips, the liquid startling, cold. I swallowed and came back to myself or a version of myself.

"I'm going to get my mother," Oumar said. "Stay here. I'll be right back."

I couldn't move, couldn't read. I felt empty but weighted down, my body anchored in the sand. Not like when I'd heard the man who'd trained Roy in mechanics got entangled with a piece of equipment and bled out before someone found him but like when I lost Roy. Now Gita. It was different but felt the same. If I hadn't come here, Gita would still be alive. I should have gone back. Now it was too late.

Clapping at the gate, and then Mariama, Tala, and Oumar squatting down in front of me. Somehow, I had sunk to my knees. I handed Tala the letter.

"Do you want me to read it to you, Miss?"

"Uh, uh huh." The sound the nomads made for the affirmative. It came from my throat. I didn't have to open my mouth or move my lips.

"She was sick, you know, from the first letter."

I never got that letter, but I knew. Gita never wanted to talk about it, so we didn't.

"No idea why she tried to climb that tree, any tree... a tragic accident... Roy found her... beautiful porcelain face turned up to the sky, her hair fanned out as if she were floating in water, posing for one of your photographs. She loved you."

Tala read in fragments or maybe that's all I could hear. I made the clicking sound at the back of my mouth that meant okay, or agreement, or affirmative.

She spoke to Mariama and Oumar in Tamasheq.

Mariama took the cup from Oumar, tipped it, pouring water between my lips. I swallowed, my throat, my entire insides parched. Oumar made tea and we drank the three rounds. If anyone said anything more I couldn't hear it.

The past was beginning to fade except in dreams. Sometimes, exhaustion made me forget even those. But others so vivid, sensual, the shock was to wake to the monochromatic reality of sand and bleached sky. I tried to stay awake in the afternoon, the heat especially dense, intense even in the shade, to avoid the fever dreams that conjured Roy. The heat at that time forced a slowing of the breath, the pulse, the blink of the eyes staring straight ahead at nothing.

At Roy. After noon, we saw palm trees, people reveling knee deep in water, the brain's delirious translation, or a vision either unreliable or believable. A voice. "Salaam alaykum," Peace be with you. Superfluous sounds.

Our words bloomed for each other, our lips, heavy wet heads of fragrance, our touch, the transcendent heaven of General Life, the pool of water reflecting paradise.

A thought bloomed: Gardens without water will drink anything, motor oil, blood, urine before fading, withering.

"Alaykum a salaam." And also with you.

I woke from thirst and drank some water, poured some over my head, my hands, my feet, and opened my palms.

I started asking Oumar to run errands so I could contribute at least money to the family. Once, I asked him to pick up some Omo laundry soap at the market, and he came back with a bottle of Fanta. Maybe the two-syllable rhythm of the words both ending with vowels sounded similar to his ear or maybe he wanted a Fanta. I explained what I'd meant by miming washing a t-shirt in a tub, his smile, huge.

The shop owners stored the clear glass bottles in the shade under damp burlap. Still cool, I handed it back to him. He opened the bottle with his teeth and savored measured sips with his eyes closed. This is before I think of handing him the bottle opener on my Swiss army knife. His smile, orange.

Another time I asked him to bring my flashlight from the house and he brought my camera. Maybe the two items seemed similar because they were both mechanical tools. He smiled then, too, like "Cheese." Not enough light. This is before my camera gets stolen and I visit a marabou who puts a spell in a gris-gris and get it back, before I butch my hair, and my neighbor braids it when it grows in again. It is before the first sandstorm when Patience will come home shiny as a wet rock.

No school on Wednesday afternoons, so after the sieste, some students stopped by my house. Patience sat and stayed on command, only his eyes tracking the students as they moved about the yard, looking into the open windows and door of the house. I offered water and bread—I was out of dates—while they named my objects in French, then English, Tamasheq, and Hausa.

"Come inside." I thought we'd name some kitchen objects.

"Le fourneau."

"Stove," I said. "Tamasheq?"

"Bàrju-tæn."

I tried to repeat it with some accuracy. "Hausa?"

"Kuka."

"Kuka." Cooker.

"Réfrigérateur."

"A cognate. Refrigerator. In this case, mini fridge."

"Asasmad. Firiji in Hausa. Mini frigo," Eduardo said.

"Keeps food cold. But how?"

"Electricity." I held up the cord. Another cognate. "This refrigerator keeps food cold in cities with electricity, but I use it for something else."

"For what, Miss?" Eduardo.

One of my brightest students. "Open it."

"Miss?"

He was checking to see that he understood correctly or maybe he didn't know how to open it. I added a gesture to suggest opening.

There was no handle, but he figured it out. He ran his fingers along the top between the door and the fridge, feeling where the two suctioned together, and pulled the door open. "Livres! Books! The Quran, he recognized, the orange TEFL manual from class. "*Where There is No Doctor,*" he read. "*The Last Caravan.* Yes. But what are these other books?"

"Poetry. Poésie. Do you know it?"

"Miss, all Tuaregs know poetry."

"True. I've heard it in the call to prayers, in your music."

"Yes, Miss. We are fluent in this language."

Another student flipped through some pages of Auden.

"Don't you have a—comme on dit appareil photo—like the French tourists?" Tala, the student who'd first taken me to Mariama's when Izza was born, the one who read to me about Gita's death. Oumar probably told her about my Roelli.

"Camera," I said. It annoyed me to be associated with tourists and spies. "Yes."

"Take our photo," Tala said, and they all gathered together and posed against the railing.

I unbound the camera from my Bowie shirt in the back room and navigated through the small crowd peering through the doorway. "So, you're not afraid, n'ont peur, that it will steal your souls?" I'd read it somewhere.

They laughed. "Ah, Miss," one of the boys said. "That is what our grandparents say, but we don't believe that."

Tala, with her fresh braids, arranged herself in front of the others. I pointed the camera at the green of the acacia to neutralize the light, a practice I'd learned when photographing the salt flats, then focused on the group huddled against the glare and released the shutter. I captured a few different shots, some of students stiff with serious expressions, others of them balancing in odd positions, the moment holding them up, laughing before and after they fell.

"Let's see!" Tala said.

I explained I'd have to send the film off to be processed. It would be months before the prints arrived. Especially slides. "Maybe you've seen a Polaroid that develops photos instantly?"

"Polaroid," Tala said. "I like."

"I'll see if I can get one, but it will be a long time."

Tala shrugged. "Westerners have watches but we have time."

I shifted from something else in common with the French, cameras, pets, and the concept of time, and tried describing Native Americans who'd lived along the Sonoran Desert.

"Past tense," Tala said. "Do they still live there?

"Most were forced out when the Spanish came, to missions to learn to farm." Both camping and missions cognates, something else in common with the French. The students were also forced into boarding schools. Why hadn't I made this connection before? But this school was different, wasn't it, this time? Social and economic development abroad through technical assistance, while promoting mutual understanding between Americans and populations served. The idea to provide options to the nomadic children rather than control them. Like U.S. AID putting in water pumps. Intrusive, yes, but useful to the culture. Options. Still.

"No animals?" someone else asked.

"Not on the farm," I said. "Agriculture." Another cognate.

"Like us but without animals."

"We would die without our animals," Tala said. "Did they die?"

In my mind, I said, "They returned to the earth, where the land still holds them and pieces of the tools they used to hunt or protect themselves, bits of pottery." But my language skills were not as advanced as theirs. With my French, Tamasheq, Hausa, English blend, communication was more like a complicated game or puzzle. I still relied heavily on charades.

The students listened with interest, though I wasn't sure what they understood, until one boy suggested we hunt for arrowheads. He pulled some from his pocket. Stark white, quartz maybe, in contrast to the dark chert, obsidian, or jasper points common in California.

"But the sand is too hot for you, Miss."

"My feet will adjust." Eventually. I opened the gate, and we hiked beyond the town and into the dunes.

Fanning out, we concentrated as we sifted through the sand and our own thoughts until someone found something, usually the bleached bone of an animal, a goat's ribcage or the jawbone of a camel. I saw the tip of something solid sticking out of the sand and set my guerba down to investigate. The boy with the arrowheads picked up the guerba from the ground and handed it to me.

"The desert will drink your water."

First thought: Tuareg metaphor. Second thought: science. "Osmosis. Osmose. Thank you." I slung the water skin over my shoulder. Third thought: at home, the rain revealed what lay beneath. "Did you find those arrowheads after it rained?"

"After a sandstorm, the wind blows the top layer away."

When the sun rested on the horizon, one of the students suggested we walk back. It was nearing dinnertime at the school. I waved them on.

"It's dangerous to walk by yourself in isolated places," Tala said. "The djinn, bad spirits, are watching, waiting to capture you. If you don't wear a gris-gris, you should carry a sword like the men do."

I felt a single bead of sweat traverse my face as I sat in the front of the line of Tuareg women, each braiding the hair of the one in front of her. Maybe I was first in line as a guest or maybe the women assumed I was incapable of their complex system of plaiting. They were right. A fishtail, French, or simple inverted braid, elementary in comparison. I felt sorry for the woman who was trying to ply my hair and then for myself; she pushed into my back with her elbow, maybe her knee for some leverage and tugged another strand excruciatingly taut. When my hair pulled out from the roots or broke off in her hand, she carefully wrapped it in cloth. Was my scalp bleeding? I could already feel a headache coming on from my hair being divided against its natural will. I'd experienced discomfort when even parting my hair in a different spot. This was not that. Another woman was making tea though, and I knew the first strong round would raze the edge off anything.

The woman plaiting my hair was the older woman who carried the straw tray of goat cheese, dates, and millet at Izza's unofficial naming ceremony. Tadeine. Clearly experienced in such matters, she finished my coif in record time and was taking on another head of hair. I looked at the line of women as I returned my tea glass. Mariama's hairstyle: a braid woven down the center of her head divided in two, parting her forehead like a royal browband entwining into a cascade of braids on either side and falling to her waist. She looked up at me with a sympathetic expression. I knew I looked ridiculous with my faded split ends trying to fit into the styles so clearly suited for long, healthy hair, the same geometric designs that decorated their clothing, jewelry, and leather goods. Their hair: smooth, jet-black, tightly braided into triangular shapes, or braids upon braids creating symmetrical patterns outlined with bare scalp. Some middle parts, perfectly halving the sphere of the head and framing the features of their faces. Others wrapped the braids around the head, snaking them, weaving them, sweeping them across the forehead. The parts zigged and zagged with perfect geometrical precision. My hair a sacrifice to the landscape, a loss of a part of myself. It would grow back, but would it be the same? Would I be the same?

The women periodically broke from the routine of preparing food, caring for the animals, tanning and dying skins, working leather into wallets, pouches for gris-gris, bags, and cushions, or weaving grass mats, to braid each other's hair and talk. When I wasn't at school, they invited me to join them. Today, after braiding, we were piercing Izza's ears and then dying our hands and feet with the henna someone brought from Niamey.

Mariama got up and walked around me. "Belle," she said.

I blinked back tears. "Sable," sand, "in my eyes," I said. She lied out of kindness. I felt my head now textured with ridges. One framed my face, and another ran from my forehead to the middle with two smaller braids branching off of either side. The hair under it was smooth, tight to the scalp. I felt a couple of places where bare skin lay exposed to the sun. Behind the center braid, the hair had been parted to create a square shape, the hair from it plaited in small triangles on either side. I was glad for the lack of a mirror and covered my head with a scarf for the benefit of everyone else. "Tafouk," I tried in Tamasheq, directly followed by "Soleil," sun. I didn't want to insult Tadeine's work.

Mariama held Izza while Tadeine pierced her ears with a small diameter stick that had been sharpened like a thorn. The old woman was quick. Izza tried to wriggle out of Mariama's embrace, but she didn't cry. Tadeine broke the twig, so there was about a centimeter or so sticking out from either side of Izza's tiny lobes.

The diameter of the silver earrings much thicker than the twigs, Tala explained that in a few weeks, they would replace the original sticks in Izza's ears with slightly thicker ones, to enlarge the hole so the earrings fit. She described this as Mariama was stirring the chopped henna leaves someone else had pounded the previous day, adding water to moisten them into a paste-like consistency. She added some sugar.

"For the drying process," she said.

Some of the women applied the mixture covering their toenails and then made a solid border along the edges of their feet, repeating on their hands, but after Mariama finished thickly coating my toenails, she applied the henna mixture in sections along the sides of my feet, using a stick to knock off the extra paste and draw a more complex pattern. If my feet hadn't toughened, the stick would have tickled, but the souls and edges of my feet were numb. Other women created their own unique designs. When finished, they covered their feet and mine with damp rags, so the paste would set, wouldn't dry too fast. They wrapped their hands and mine, and then we dozed in the heat of the day. The henna dried by late afternoon. When they removed the rags and brushed the dried leaves away, they set the designs with camel urine, probably for the acidic properties like on the commune when we added vinegar to set our hand-dyed yarn.

Tala translated Mariama's words. "Putting on the henna is not enough; it has to hold."

Mariama's one-liners usually applied beyond the literal. Substance below the surface.

The geometric patterns that had been a challenge with my hair were better replicated in the dark red stain on the borders of my hands and feet. Only the extra cracks along my heels interrupted the pattern, still recognizable as the embroidered designs the tailors added to the Tuareg women's tops and along the edges of their pagnes. The symbols reminded me of the natural environment: sun, stars, constellations, moon, millet, wadis, the valleys said to fill with water in the rainy season like vernal pools.

"It will protect your elem, skin, from the sun."

Mariama raised my hand to eye level. She had made the design especially intricate, and the other women gathered around her. "C'est beau."

I admired her work. The design on my hands and the inch-high miniature art along the edges of my feet, the henna a rich, blood red. She took her time intentionally. I hoped this wasn't for the Cure de Salée.

Most of the Tuaregs in the region would be traveling to the salt cure, Cure de Salée, near In-Gall, in a place called Tegguidda-n-Tessoum. A huge annual fête where the Tuaregs converged with their herds. While the camels rejuvenated with salt and other minerals, the nomads celebrated the rainy season with dancing, music, camel racing, and searching for mates. They wore their finest clothes, hairstyles, jewelry, hennaed designs. I'd seen it in National Geographic. I'd wanted to go but not now. Not the first time I thought myself ugly. Not until my hair grew in.

I looked down at my feet and whispered to Tala. "Is this for the Cure de Salée?"

"No, it will fade by then. The Cure de Salée is at the end of the rainy season."

"You will come."

"Next year," I said.

Another woman entered Mariama's encampment. "Miss," she said. "You have a package at the post."

The brown paper was warm from the heat, their touch. Colorful bird and flower stamps repeated in multiples extended from the right corner. Color. Orioles, Dahlias, and Lilies. I almost took the Swiss army knife from my waistband and opened the package right there but thought the hajji might consider the Levis I was expecting, insulting even though a pagne clearly revealed the curve of the hips. Maybe the suggestion of legs, the danger. I just knew women wearing pants was unacceptable. And he wouldn't understand the sunflower seeds, at least not at first.

I thanked him instead.

"Oh, and this, Miss," he said, handing me a letter from Gita. I burst into tears.

"Ça va?"

"Oui," I said, the tears running down my face. I wondered if she'd ever received my apology letter.

He closed the door behind me for the sieste.

I ran home despite the torrid heat, despite the pagne wrapped around my legs and my goat hide sandals.

Once inside the gate, I put the package on top of the fridge and held the envelope from Gita with both hands like a gift. A muted green color that smelled of sage. Her handwriting appeared different, shaky, as if she'd addressed it while riding in the market truck. The postmark read April 2—lost between Gaia and Tchin-Tabaraden for months. I tore the short end and slipped out the contents: the letter and a hairband that fell onto the sand. She'd touched them in what would have been spring there. I felt my braided hair and put the band on my wrist and decided to wait to read the letter, to savor it, the last letter I would ever get from Gita.

I ripped open the package from my mothers, also postmarked April 2. I looked closer, 3, 6, 8? The ink smudged but a single digit anyway. Almost immediately after I'd written to them, they'd packed my requested Levis and a variety of sunflower seed packets, thinking of me as I did them looking at the moon every night. I cupped the jeans to my face and breathed in the scent of Patchouli, then picked up the seed packets with sticky notes attached.

Hopi Black Dye Sunflowers. *Since you only sent a postcard with minimal information, we did some reading. The Tuaregs remind us of the Native Americans.*

Packet description: "A brilliant obsidian-black seeded sunflower, used for making natural dye. This traditional variety has been saved and used by the Hopi Native American people for dying cotton, wool and other fibers used to make the iconic Hopi basketry. These medium to large sunflower heads are striking in the garden, the simple dye making process will yield stellar shades from dove grey to deep purple depending on the technique and other materials used. A multipurpose variety, the food and fodder merits of this beautiful variety should not be overlooked. Reaches about 8 feet tall."

The wind might destroy them, but not only were the heirloom seeds edible, the dark dye extracted from the shells could be used to line the women's eyes and the Wodaabé male dancers' eyes and lips. Seemed healthier than the local kohl.

Super Snack Sunflowers: "Seeds are especially easy to crack, but one 10-inch head on each plant. Might have to add some support. Annual." Packet description: "Sunflower seeds are ripe when the flower head turns from green to yellow and the seed head begins to brown. To test for ripeness, gently pry out a seed or two and give them a taste. If the sunflower seeds are ready for harvest, cut the flower stem a few inches below the seed head. At this point, the seeds need to dry in a place where they're protected from birds."

No birds. Sprouts out though; they require soil.

Small print: "Flowers pollinate from the outside in, and the seeds underneath will turn from white to black once pollinated. If the plant is under any stress, often, the flowers won't fully pollinate."

Yes, stress. No bees. No insects. But moths?

Velvet Queen Sunflowers: "Self-pollinating a plus." Packet description: "When we grew Velvet Queen in our trial gardens, crowds formed! Velvet Queen really does look like a setting sun, with its play of warm colors and huge size. These flowers arise on 4- to 5-foot stalks—a manageable size for the bed, border, or even vegetable garden, and just right for lining up along a fence or wall! The bloom is heaviest in midsummer, but you will find both early and late comers among Velvet Queen's blooms, keeping your vases full and your garden ablaze for many weeks. Annual." Small print: "Sunflowers are among the easiest of all annuals to grow from seed. Wait until the soil warms in spring, then simply push the large seeds into the earth, water them well, and wait for the thick, Jack-and-the-Beanstalk-like stem to arise! Plant it in plenty of sun and normal to dry soil."

Dry soil—can sand be considered soil? Plenty of sun.

Mothers' final note: *Don't know if any of these varieties will work in the desert climate. Ideas: Self-pollination (homogamy) occurs when the stigma curls within itself—starts the fertilization process and results in a seed. This process could occur even with the varieties that aren't labeled as self-pollinating. How else would sunflowers have thrived in various climates and conditions over 2000 years?*

There are about 190 known moth species in Niger but couldn't find exact info for your location (might pollinate these sunflowers). Though less visible than white flowers at night, the existence of flowers at all may attract them. Then there's artificial pollination by humans. Just dust the pollen from one sunflower to another and see what happens.

Might be best to save back seeds to replant every year. Let us know! Peace & love~

Nothing about Gita. The jeans seemed ridiculous now, too hot to wear by themselves let alone under a pagne. I'd become adept at wrapping the cloth and tucking the end securely, walking like a local woman without it coming undone.

Even though the sunflowers required full sun and were drought tolerant, I planned to wait and plant them in the rainy season. I looked forward to the flowers, to Oumar's and Mariama's reactions to the flowers, to color, to producing enough seeds for the nomads to have access to an immediate and transportable form of protein. I set the packets on the mini fridge, propping them against the wall to provide the only colorful visual art in my house: rich yellow petals with eyes dark as kohl, another, a rich butterscotch color with a deep orange ring, the other crimson, both with dark glittering eyes.

I took a deep breath and picked up the letter from Gita, closed my eyes, and imagined her face, her physically there with me. Already I felt stronger, grounded, peaceful, the essence of her being. I took the letter outside into the light, into the natural world where we'd always spent our time together, and sat in the string chair under the acacia by myself but not alone. I felt her there. Her invisible presence. Patience thumped his tail. "Yeah," I said, reaching down to pet him. "It's Gita."

April 1, 1989

Lark,

I'm sorry I wasn't honest with you. Now you are on the other side of the world because of it.

She'd drawn a world globe as the ripe bud of a plant, squiggly sun rays emanating from the golden band of the Sahara on my side of the world, colorful blooming flowers and green leafy trees on her side.

I wanted to talk to you before you left. But I couldn't. Guilt maybe or fear, but then I remembered there is nothing to fear, and guilt is a waste. I have wasted so much time.

Here she drew Dali's melted watch. "The Persistence of Memory," she'd cited. I hadn't known its title.

You hurt me. But I forgive you. Apparently, you never realized that my true love is you.

I got up from the chair and just stood there, the words echoing in my head. "My true love is you." Not Roy?

I didn't want to have to tell you directly. I still don't, but I have to now. First, know this. The thing with Roy and me didn't mean anything. How could it? I seduced him out of curiosity, like one of our science experiments. It didn't take much effort; he seemed curious too... I mean isn't that how we were raised?

A sketch of a jagged bolt of lightning.

Neither of us thought you would react so extremely to such a meaningless action, but here we are and there you are. None of us together. I couldn't see you truly loved Roy because love distorts our perception. I see that now. And now you see that you have always been my true love. That I have to explain it...

Maybe it's just as well that we are geographically a world apart.

Lark,

Here she drew my namesake bird.

Let's take advantage of this physical space between us and write to each other. I'll even come visit you there if I can. Not feeling the best right now. In the meantime, here are five more realistic goals for the year:
- To manage your beehives
- To apply to architecture school
- To see an allopathic doctor
- To design a treehouse (with steps)
- To climb to the top of the sycamore
Love,
Gita

I was Gita's true love? Why didn't I know that? I had always been attracted to her. Gita and Roy's relationship meaningless? None of it mattered now. Everything had changed. The person I'd been, gone. The relationship Roy and I shared, gone. Our potential child, gone. Gita, my best friend in the world, dead. Maybe the commune's philosophy of the dissolution of one-on-one relationships was right, the commune psychologist right; emotional excess was dangerous. If Gita were here, I'd tell her I learned that I could never put myself in such a relationship again. I'd barely survived. I trusted the poets. I was here now in this place, this community. I burned the letter. And then I wished I had it back. To hold onto.

Oumar came running breathless to the house to tell me my parents had come. Doubtful. It wasn't beyond the realm of possibility but almost. I put some money in the leather pouch that hung from a cord around my neck in case I needed to buy something for dinner and started down the road toward the market where Oumar reported he had seen them. He could hardly contain himself as we recited the ritual greetings with everyone we met. When we were almost there, he grabbed my hand and pulled me to the only other white people there. When we reached the couple, I tried not to laugh. I introduced myself and put my hand Oumar's shoulder. "He's my best friend, so when he told me my parents were here, I believed him."

The man, an anthropologist from Switzerland. "You Americans are crazy," he said by way of a greeting. The woman, a photographer from the States, maybe a dozen years older than me. They were getting supplies before going further into the bush to study the Wodaabé.

"The man that Oumar and I got my dog from is Wodaabé."

"You hunt?" The anthropologist.

"No, I have him for a pet."

"They wouldn't understand that."

"No, but we understand that we don't understand." I invited them for dinner. They wanted to reach the camp before dark but left me with a bottle of wine.

"Gamay," the anthropologist said. "Prost!"

"Cheers." The photographer. "Good luck."

Days later I met another Westerner. He wore typical desert clothing but kept his head uncovered. I was drawn to the braying of his donkey and then to his kind face framed by healthy curly dark hair. "Anthony," he said. A former monk from Italy who traveled with Italian spices in the panniers on his donkey. He left his Order and followed a calling to travel the continent among people who lived in the margins of society.

"Of the earth itself in this case," he said.

"What do you do when you get there?"

"I try to be helpful. If I can."

He was clearly a spiritual man; peace radiated from him like the continuous heat waves above the sand. And he was right. I'd sacrificed Gita to be here. My relationship with Roy. I would not waste this.

That evening, he'd stopped by the house and cooked dinner. I contributed the bottle of Gamay from the Swiss anthropologist and some takomért, local Tuareg cheese. Oumar contributed hot coals. The Tuareg eternal flame. Always a fire burning somewhere, someone brewing Tuareg tea at any moment.

Anthony used my enamel bowl and Mariama's carved wooden spoon to sauté the garlic in olive oil asking about my name as he stirred.

"My mothers heard a lark sing when I was born."

"Not many birds here." He ignored the plural mothers or maybe he wanted to talk about birds.

He crouched beside the fire as he tended the cooking pot.

Oumar sat in a chair, side-eyeing Patience.

"I haven't seen a bird since I arrived in Niger," I said. Anthony added basil leaves. The fragrance hung in the air.

"Why come to such a remote place?" he asked.

I gave him the short version. "To teach English to the nomadic children."

A halo of sepia ringed his head. Maybe his aura protected his hair. Mine had probably burned up, absorbed by the atmosphere. I savored the plummy wine in my mouth. Maybe the sparkles Gita had noticed made it appear like fireworks, at least a sparkler. Gita. "The desert is a place to forget, to be forgotten. To begin again."

"If you came to the wilderness, to the deep solitude of the desert, to search for meaning, you're in good company," he said. "Eckhart, Chuang Tzu, Pascal, Saint Thomas Aquinas, Saint Teresa, Saint John of the Cross."

Maybe he thought my hair and appearance an intentional sacrifice. Anthony talked of love, "the essence of everything," as if it were endless. I wanted to ask him the difference between deep love for a friend and for a lover. Was it sex? But I didn't know if that was a rude question, especially for a monk. Or if he'd know. And I wanted him to come back. When he left, I lay on my mat, starlight pouring from the sky in audible silence, listening to the stars and the whispered breathing of Oumar sleeping near the door. Divine and human love seemed simultaneous and inextricably bound all right, but it couldn't last. After a thousand days with Roy, the love between us couldn't maintain such a convergence over time. In the end, it killed him.

This is before Oumar says there was no man named Anthony, no donkey. After Roy appears in another dream.

We liked the look of leather bundles hung from the neck, braided rawhide thong against the leather skin of tanned torsos, thick hoops drawing attention to the perimeters of ears, jewelry made from bits of broken glass, from occasional cars taking a curve of sand too fast, rolling into oblivion.

We only thought we were divine, mistaking the physical elation of the body's quenching concoction of elements as eternal bliss. After noon, we felt it most when the sand turned to snow.

During the sieste, I tore the house apart as if in a fevered dream. I saw everything happening as I did it, as if observing myself. The refrigerator door gaped open; the contents of my pack lay strewn across the floor. Scorpions scuttled out of my way when I yanked the tukunya away from the wall. I stepped outside to breathe. Patience resumed his post beneath the acacia. He didn't move when Oumar came in.

"Salaam alyakum."

"Alyakum salaam." He cut the litany short. "Qu'est-ce qui ne va pas? What's wrong?"

"My camera is gone."

He made the negative clicking sound with his lips.

"Voleur," I said. "Someone stole it. On purpose." More upsetting because everyone knew me now, recognized me. The anasara teacher. My missing camera felt less a loss than the act itself. A statement. "Someone stole it out of disrespect."

Oumar laughed.

At me?

"Someone thinks he needs it more than you."

"Like the anebzeg, the madman? But no one asked me for it."

"You don't understand. I'll go to the marabout. He'll make a gris-gris."

"You're right, I don't understand."

"When the person who has the camera enters the yard, he will freeze in place."

"Or she. And how does that help?"

"We will know who stole it," Oumar explained. "And he will be shamed."

"What if the thief doesn't return?"

"He will."

More mail at the post office. I could barely breathe. This time, letter #1 from the commune and something from Tahoua.

I opened the letter from home.

#1

April 4, 1989

Dear Lark,

We hope you made it safely and are busy taking everything in. Write when you can; we are all waiting to hear. Peter says the mail in West Africa is irregular, so we're numbering our letters, that way you can read them in order.

This is number 1. It's full on spring here, copious wildflowers woven through the grasses, the colors, petals of stained glass. Your bees must find it hard to fly loaded with so much pollen.

Gita creates the most delicate, beautiful bouquets—they are the first to sell out at the market. She is sick, though, Lark. We don't quite know what it is. We've been treating her immune system with tincture of echinacea. The silica made her think of you, allium cepa, oscillococcinum, gelsemium, arsenicum album. Always in good spirits, and she will feel better soon.

Oblio sleeps under your tree every night guarding you wherever you are.

We all love you.

It felt cruel to read the letter out of order. As if I could still do something, but everything had already happened. Gita had fallen in love without me and died without me, too. I lit the bottom corner and watched the words disappear.

I shifted into automatic and opened the other letter, a reminder to go to Tahoua for the quarterly gamma globulin booster. I didn't want to leave Tchin-Tabaraden. I got out my journal that I should have been writing in but always too tired by the end of the day. On the first page, I wrote down my decision formula. Pros: it'd be good to see Roz and Stacia, hear their stories, get fruits and vegetables we didn't have access to, possibly some good moisturizer, warm beer, maybe wine, probably a good idea to get my IUD checked even though I'd probably never need it. Cons: I didn't want to break my concentration, lose any progress understanding the languages, the cultural mindset, the nomadic value system. I didn't want to start over. I added another pro. Probably should keep up with the hepatitis vaccine, though the odds of a virus, of anything surviving in the desert were probably low. I'd already stopped taking the anti-malarial drug, quit treating my water, given my vitamins for lactating mothers to Mariama.

The two-week window to find transportation and get the shot, necessary in a place like Tchin-Tabaraden. Transportation usually occurred on foot, donkey, or camel. Only occasionally, by Mokao's or someone else's truck. I put the word out and waited.

When I heard the motor, I immediately went to inquire. Frank. I thought about waiting for someone local, Mokao. At least regional, but too risky.

Frank was unloading product to the vendors. Apparently, his business was thriving, though I hadn't noticed many, any, smokers in Tchin-Tabaraden. He'd unloaded a dozen boxes, but his Scout was packed full. They must be selling the cigarettes elsewhere at a profit. I doubted Frank would care. He was making his money.

"Hey, Frank," I said. The simple brevity of the greeting relaxing.

His arms full, the stub of a cigarette on his lip, he tipped his head in recognition.

"Could I get a ride with you to Tahoua?"

He set the box down, crushed the butt with the toe of his fake wingtip.

"Eventually. I'm going to Agadez first to drop off product, but I'll stop there on my way back to Niamey."

It was Friday, market day. Two and a half days before class on Monday. "When are you leaving?"

"Now."

I had to pack a few things, leave a note for Oumar, some food for Patience. "I can be ready in 10 minutes. How long are you staying in Agadez?"

"I see you haven't grasped the African concept of time yet."

"Working on it. Besides you're not African."

Frank half smiled, lit another cigarette. "I thought I'd spend the night in Agadez. It's been a long day of driving. Kilometers to go before I sleep."

"Okay." He knew some poetry. "But Tahoua by tomorrow?"

He blew a smoke ring. "If Allah fuckin' wills it." He fished the keys from his pocket. "Get in."

I changed into a fresh pagne, packed a clean tee, skirt, and underwear, my compass and map, filled my guerba with water, grabbed some dates, left a note, and fed the dog in under ten.

"It's not a race," Frank said.

"I need to be back for class on Monday." The sooner back, the better. I wedged my pack in the back of the truck and climbed in.

"You dress like the locals."

"More comfortable, once you get used to it."

"No matter what you wear it's fuckin' hot. But seriously, a hide canteen?"

"It keeps water cooler here than cloth-covered aluminum. The nomads use the entire goat to store their water. Haven't you seen the headless goat's hides bulging with water tied to their camels?"

"Missed that."

"Even in the sun, the natural goat's hide keeps the water cool."

As we drove past the last cluster of mud houses, I glimpsed a Tuareg, a strand of blonde hair sticking out from his turban. "Did you see that?" I swung around.

"What?"

"A Tuareg with blonde hair." The color of Roy's.

"Tuaregs don't have blonde hair."

"Exactly." I turned back around.

"Probably some tourist gone native."

"Maybe." Someone else that reminded me of Roy. "You know I'm not a tourist."

We passed the tent encampments, driving on the sandy plain.

Frank lit a cigarette. "Yeah, I know."

CHAPTER FIVE

HOT SEASON, EN ROUTE TO
AGADEZ 1989

I was glad the truck was open-air so I wouldn't smell like stale cigarettes. "Can you actually see the road? Oumar says the Tuaregs intuitively know how to read the desert by the stars at night, the sun and the color and texture of the sand by day."

"It took a fuckin' while, but yeah. There's a slight tint, different texture."

Frank took a drag squinting at the landscape ahead.

"For people foreign to the landscape like me, driving across it requires more of a scientific understanding of sand and wind."

Right. "I read that the sand jumps rather than drifts into dunes, and dunes reproduce other dunes." I took a drink from my guerba and let that sit. Felt the need to show off a little. No response. "And at night the larger ones make a hissing sound, though I haven't heard it myself." I offered the guerba to Frank. "Yet."

Poker face. He gulped some water.

I set the guerba on the floor out of the sun and kept on. "Maybe driving on sand is like driving on snow. Not that I've driven much on snow but the textures, you know, the depth, the slickness, the lack of traction."

"I follow your twisted logic," Frank said. "But best to stay on the road. Besides, the desert is not all sand, there are gravel plains, both rounded or sharp, polished boulders, grass plains, salt plains, and mountains. The Aïr Mountains are just beyond Agadez."

"And beyond them, the Ténéré Desert, the Sahara. I've seen pictures of waves of dunes as high and steep as 500 feet straight up. Have you been?"

"I would never intentionally go there."

"Oumar says when the wind blows, the desert trembles."

Frank exhaled smoke like a sigh. I faced the other direction.

"How long have you lived in Niger?"

"Two years. And you've been here what, two months?"

"Four, but I'm staying. At least a couple of years."

He glanced over at me. "You don't seem like the typical college graduate volunteer."

"I'm not. I haven't been to college yet. I'm 18. How old are you?"

"Twenty-two. How'd you get in?"

"Timing, circumstance. I think they needed someone. What about you?"

"Rothmans needed a male supplier for the nomad market. I buzzed my hair, bound my chest, and got the job."

I tried to set my own poker face, but for some reason, I was elated at the news, and it must have shown on my face.

"What," Frank said, his face lighting up with that trademark smile.

"A woman can be anything she wants to be, including a man. But how did you come here to Niger, one of the most impoverished countries in the world, to sell cigarettes?"

"Timing and circumstance. I needed a job and a challenge, and Rothmans needed a male to peddle their product."

"What's it like being a male?"

"Different perspective, mostly from others."

I side-eyed Frank's torso out of respect. "Is your binding excessive or are you built more like a dude?"

"I have to bind. It's fuckin' hot, but cornstarch absorbs the sweat. I've also gotten used to no makeup, wearing a uniform, and the ease of a buzz cut. I'm a woman, regardless. You can call me Frankie."

"Frankie," I said. "Sometimes I feel like a dude. I didn't have a period my first three months here."

"You don't look pregnant."

I hesitated. "No chance of that. A little boy lives with me for one, and I'm ugly." I pulled off my scarf.

She laughed. "You sure you're not a tourist?"

I felt the braided design on my head, glad I couldn't actually see it. "My hair's a wreck, my skin, my feet. Too much sun and heat and not enough fruits and vegetables."

"Your hair will grow out. You'll adjust."

"That's what I keep telling myself. I'm just glad there are no mirrors." Glimpsing my reflection in the side mirror, I squeezed my eyes closed for a full five minutes so I wouldn't be sick.

I refocused on the platinum contours on either side of the route where the dunes rose in geometric shapes, natural Tuareg art. The same shapes and designs they used in the stitching on the edge of their pagnes, engraved on their silver jewelry, the same dyed leather shapes ornamenting the Tuareg saddles I'd seen in the market, the henna designs on the women's hands and feet, variations of the geographic shapes woven into their hair. Now late morning, the sand reflected the eastern sun. I pulled out my map, N22 south to Kao and then east on N25 to Abalak. "72 kilometers, 45 miles."

"Driving on the route adds mileage, Frankie said, "unless you get lost on the fuckin' shortcut."

"Have you taken the shortcut?"

"Hell, no. Heard too many stories of tourists and sometimes locals getting lost in the desert. Even here in the Sahel, the borderland, but it will be the fuckin' Sahara eventually."

She tossed the cigarette butt out the window.

"You should collect those and dispose of them in the trash."

She gestured to the vast expanse of landscape.

"Have you heard if anyone ever makes it out of the desert? Someone lost?"

"Rarely; most of them die there, especially fuckin' tourists."

I was imagining a family of stranded tourists when I saw the mirage of a lake with men casting nets from their boats. It looked so real. "Pull over!"

Frankie cut a sharp right and lurched to a stop. I bent down and dipped my hand, expecting sand. My hand dripped water.

Frankie smiled. One front tooth a little crooked.

"Artificial lake. A seasonal ancient river valley that flows below the sand. Surprised you didn't know that."

My first thought, standing water in the desert. Second, mosquitoes.

"Let's go," Frankie said.

Third, lunch. At least a bathroom break, but Frankie continued driving through the heat of the afternoon, waves rising up from the crumbling asphalt. Up ahead a twisted metal carcass blackened and still smoking mostly on the side of the road but extending into our lane. "What if someone is still in there?"

Frankie slowed down, but the driver behind us laid on his horn.

No one coming from the opposite direction, she did a U-turn and pulled behind the other driver's vehicle.

The driver said something I didn't understand, so I mumbled some greetings taking in the situation. It looked fatal, but no evidence. He mumbled in response, rummaging through the rubble.

Frankie: "I can't tell you how many fuckin' accidents I've seen on this road."

She acted matter of fact, cold.

"You get used to it."

"The bush taxis are in rough shape," I said.

"Yeah, and the local drivers drive like they're in the Dakar."

"The car race?" Roy raved about that.

"It starts in the capitol of Dakar on the Ivory Coast and routes through the Sahara. This year the route is through the Ténéré desert. One of the stops is Agadez."

She lit a cigarette.

I still didn't get the draw of motorized vehicles hurtling through a landscape. I didn't understand the mechanics, but I understood landscapes. "You like car races?"

"Part of the gig."

I spotted a good-sized bush. "Stop; I've got to pee. Where's your teapot?"

"We don't have time to make tea."

"Never mind." I'd become adept with the teapot since I'd run out of toilet paper weeks before. Even had there been a portable toilet, I preferred the nomadic system. I jogged out and back in less than five minutes.

Frankie was eating some dates.

"Hungry?"

"No, thanks." I sucked on a pebble I carried with me. It might have helped.

CHAPTER SIX

HOT SEASON, AGADEZ 1989

We neared Agadez at sunset. Deep crimson along the horizon, Tuaregs draped in the light-colored cloth that protected them from the sand and sun, mounted on or leading their camels or an occasional herd of goats or sheep toward the city. Beyond that stretched the great Ténéré desert bordering Libya and Algeria.

"Agadez was the first stop after crossing the desert along the caravan route," Frankie said. "Used to be a slave market. Now, it trades in animals, salt, tourists, and cigarettes, especially when the Dakar comes through."

"Put that way, peddling tobacco is an improvement."

Frankie lit a cigarette. "According to Rothmans' current market info, the Tuaregs are suffering the consequences of famine and marginalization from the government and struggling to find their place and survive in the current century."

"I've seen some bulk burlap sacks of millet in Tchin-Tabaraden that Oumar said was aid, for sale in the market."

"They're fuckin' used to it."

According to the map, Agadez was located a few kilometers beyond the last checkpoint. Finally. We'd been in the Scout for eight hours straight. I glanced around. Several soldiers playing cards, a line of vehicles ahead and behind us.

Frankie cut the engine. A white guy stepped out of the driver's seat in the car in front of us. Nick? How did he pull off getting a car, a taxi? It was rough—dented, a dusty blue. A local kid got out of the front passenger door and stood beside him. Oumar's age, barefoot, wearing shorts and a ragged oxford button down with the sleeves ripped out.

The gendarmes started hassling them.

"Passeport." the guard demanded.

I'd decided to stay out of Nick's business, especially since I didn't know what it was. He held his palms up emphasizing they were empty.

"I'll have to open the trunk," he explained as if to the LAPD.

His French had improved.

The guard opened the backdoor of the taxi. "Everyone out, s'il vous plaît. I'll need to see everyone's papers."

Nick handed him his passport along with some extra cash, a slight tremor in his hand.

"This isn't you," the guard said in a clipped military tone.

Agadez was a major city in Niger. Maybe they'd communicated with Niamey or Tahoua and suspected something.

"All my documentation is in order. Is there some other problem?" Nick asked.

The guard snapped his fingers and opened his palm.

The kid took the keys from the ignition and put them in the gendarme's hand.

"I'm moving your car out of the way, so others can pass through. Wait over there." The guard waved to the bench beside the small structure that served as the office.

Nick hesitated as his taxi left without him, the other passengers already finding a spot to wait, away from the flow of traffic and the gendarmes. The Tuaregs crouched in the shade of an acacia tree.

Frankie offered Nick a cigarette. "Frank," Frankie mumbled, cupping her hand and lighting Nick's cigarette.

Nick took a drag and noticed me watching him from inside the car.

He stuck his head in the driver's window. "Lark?"

"They think you're a spy," I said.

He almost laughed.

"What else would we be doing here?" Frankie said.

I looked directly at Nick. "What *are* you doing here?"

"Teaching English, like you. This is my side hustle on weekends." He turned to the kid. "And this is my right-hand man."

"Hello," the boy said in English. "How do you do?"

The guard signaled us to drive forward. Frankie tossed the pack of cigarettes to Nick and handed the guard a carton before driving through.

She looked in the cracked rear view. "You know him?"

"Not really."

When we arrived in Agadez, Frankie hung a map in the window for privacy and changed her polo in the back of the Scout. Her round of business stops: various merchants with spaces at the markets, private shops, and some who hawked their wares on the streets. I sat in the Scout and observed. Agadez seemed more familiar than Niamey, a giant Tchin-Tabaraden with sandy roads connecting a maze of banco structures. A Niamey made of sand. We drove by the mosque, La Grande Mosquée, an 80-foot high pyramid-shaped minaret. When we stopped at the Grand Marché, I got out and walked around while Frankie did business: camels, cattle, goats, and sheep penned up for sale on one end, turquoise and red leather saddles and tasseled silver bridles logically displayed next. The Tuaregs' famed indigo cloth, the legendary silver crosses, croix d'Agadez, copious silver rings, earrings, bracelets, Tuareg gold necklaces glinted in the light. I bought some henna for Mariama, Tadeine, and Tala.

Driving further, Frankie pointed out the Vieux Quartier, the old quarter.

"You'll like this. This part of town wasn't laid out in a mathematical pattern but according to where the ancient Tuareg set up their camps. Now its crooked roads are lined with banco houses with the carved doors of Hausa designs. Probably inspired by hallucinations from the fuckin' heat."

All I could think about was food. I stared at the Restaurant Senegalais, willing Frankie to stop. She kept driving.

"I'll deliver the rest in the morning. Let's check into the hotel, then find something to eat."

Yes. Passed the Hôtel Agriboun. Local music drifted from a place called the Bar L'Ombre des Plaisirs. The shady bar of pleasures? The bar of shady pleasures? My head hurt. Passed the Restaurant Islamique, and another called Tafadek near the Hôtel de L'Aïr, where Frankie finally parked.

As we got out of the truck, a Tuareg man strode up wanting to buy several cases of cigarettes. Frankie thought she must have missed stocking one of her customers and tried to place him. He said he didn't live in town but would sell them deeper in the desert where there was demand but no supply.

"Where is this again?" Frankie asked.

"These are remote places in the desert and up in the mountains," he said. "Dangerous for an anasara to go, even if you could find your way. I will buy from you here and deliver them myself."

He wanted a discount for buying in bulk, which made sense, but Frankie either didn't hear him or ignored it.

"I don't carry everything with me," she said. "I can only spare a couple of cases from what's left in my truck."

They negotiated a price for two cases.

He removed the money from the leather pouch hanging from his neck, counted it out, and held it until she unlocked the Scout and pulled out two of the boxes.

"Do you have transportation?"

"No problem," he said, taking the boxes and peering inside her truck. "Bring more next time." He paused then. "Do you have any extra petrol?"

Two jerry cans were strapped in the corner.

"No," she said.

He left then, and we stood outside while Frankie finished her cigarette before entering the Hôtel de l'Aïr to book a room.

"Used to be the first Sultan's palace in the 15th century," Frankie said, watching the man disappear into the crowd.

It advertised single occupancy air-conditioned rooms with private toilets and showers. A popular place for drinks, the sign read. A young guy who was dressed in Western clothes and looked like a student was standing behind the front desk. "Monsieur Frank! We reserved a room with all the amenities."

The 7,000 CFA[1] for the room worked out to less than $15. I took in the lobby, a dusty, old world feel. We walked around the property to our room. The sand/mud construction was arched and carved, a simple, balanced beauty. The bed in the room was draped in white mosquito netting twisted and knotted to reveal a full-sized mattress dressed in light sheets and a patterned blanket with the familiar Tuareg hieroglyphics. I could sleep anywhere. Gita and I slept in the tops of trees when we were younger. Frankie sat down on the couch, her back against an oversized pillow, and kicked off her wingtips onto the sand colored rug.

"Feel the cool air blowing from the vent." She closed her eyes. "Allah came through. Alhamdulillah."

A window overlooked the courtyard with a mix of locals and tourists at scattered tables and a perimeter that brought to mind the flower garden on the commune, plants and trees loaded with pungent blossoms of perennial fuchsia and lilac. My mind drifted to the Alhambra's red gold architecture and the idyllic garden called Generalife I'd imagined through Irving's poetic description. Spain was just across from Africa. I would stop at Granada when/if I went home.

I opened the door to the toilet and was jolted back to the present with the acrid smell of urine. Pulling my shirt up over my nose, I opened the window and tried to fan the stagnant air from the bathroom toward it.

"Here," Frankie said. She got up and lit a cigarette, closing the bathroom door behind her. By the time she opened the door, the smell had either dissipated, or I'd gotten used to it.

"There's a shower," she said. "With running water." She stretched.

I turned on the shower and caught a glance of myself in the mirror. Another version of my face stared back. My eyes startling green. The hair I didn't recognize. When I took out the braids, my hair broke off in my hand. Anasara hair. All the nomadic men and women in Tchin-Tabaraden kept their hair long as mine once was; the Wodaabé parted theirs off into braids or buns, sometimes weaving leather talismans or shells into it like Mokao. The Tuareg men's hair was hidden, but I'd heard they never cut it. I stripped off my clothes and stepped into the shower, still cold.

We entered the courtyard, the low desert sun filtering into the yard.

"Monsieur Frank! Bienvenu! Double Scotch, neat," the waiter said setting down the drink.

"Thank you," Frankie said, then looked at me. "You?"

"I don't care. Anything's fine as long as it's not sweet."

"If you don't care, get a fuckin' beer."

"A beer, please," I told the waiter.

"Do you mind if I order dinner? I'm buying."

"Protein and vegetables? I could eat just about anything."

We dined on steak, couscous, and green beans. I felt the vitamins and minerals traveling through my bloodstream and didn't speak until I'd finished. "Thanks."

Frankie nodded, scooted her chair back and lit an after-dinner cigarette.

I yawned. "Will you cut my hair?"

"I only have an electric razor."

Frankie left a generous tip, nodded to a European woman whose eyes smiled at her as we passed.

"No scissors?"

"Not on me, but I know a barber. Maybe she's still working."

We drove to the market area and parked near a woman shaving a man's head with a straight razor. Flecks of blood dotted the customer's bald head.

"Ciseaux?" Frankie asked. Scissors?

"Oui, Monsieur Frank," the woman said laughing, her own hair hidden by a faded yellow cloth with a turquoise sun pattern. She held up a pair of battered scissors.

Frankie gestured to me and to some European dude with a butch haircut. "Comme ça," like that, she said.

I didn't disagree, the point to start over, but I couldn't stomach the straight razor. Dull scissors the best option.

As the barber cut, she captured my hair and put it in her bag.

"It's supposed to be bad luck or some shit," Frankie said.

Whatever the woman's plans for my hair, I knew it would not go to waste. That comforted me in a vague but necessary way.

The barber held up a tiny square of mirror. I could mostly see my eye. Probably best. I paid and thanked her. Without the weight of hair on my neck and shoulders, I already felt cooler.

"You look even more like an anasara now," Frankie said from the driver's seat.

"Watch the road," I said. "You know you look like an anasara, too."

"Yeah, but I'm not trying to be a Tuareg."

"Right. You're just posing as a dude. And I'm not trying to be a local. I'm trying to not use my old values to understand an entirely different culture. I'll wear a scarf until my hair grows out."

Back at the hotel, I ran my hand through the remains of my hair and looked in the mirror. Frankie was wrong. I looked like an anasara no matter what. Worse, a second-year volunteer who didn't care what she looked like.

I took another shower and washed my stubbles of hair. They dried while I brushed my teeth. When I came out, Frankie was already in the bed.

"Get in," she said, patting the mattress. "I won't bite unless you want me to." She laughed.

I didn't know if she was joking or testing. I thought of Gita. She had once suggested we take a shower together. We didn't touch each other. Had she wanted to? Waiting for me to make the first move? I wish I could hold her now.

"You all right?"

"Yeah," I said. I didn't want to get into it—all those complexities that make up a person. All the things you can't see. "Just tired." And I was.

A boy dressed as a girl ripping my sundress to shreds while climbing a tree in the communal garden. Wind started gusting. The man looked small against the vast landscape. He wore desert clothes, stared directly at me. When he drew nearer, his turban unraveled revealing blonde hair. Roy. When he reached for me, I flew away.

I woke up discombobulated. A body beside me. I sat up in bed and ran my hand through my hair, through nothing, trying to remember exactly who and where I was. The body turned over. Frank. Frankie. I came back to myself slowly. Niger. Agadez. Gamma Globulin shot in Tahoua, my life in Tchin-Tabaraden, my students, Mariama, Oumar, Tala.

Frankie stirred. "What time is it?"

"Seven?"

"Let's go. I need to make some drops before heading to Tahoua, but we should make it there by late afternoon."

She tapped the bell at the front desk. Same young man in the same clothes, now disheveled, handled the bill. "Do you know what time it is?"

He yawned. "Seven," he mumbled.

When I first looked at Frankie's truck, I thought she'd left the window down.

Frankie absorbed the situation immediately. "Shit!"

All her product and the jerry cans of petrol were gone. I figured we'd go to the police and report it and said so.

"Not worth the hassle."

"Do you think it was the Tuareg man who asked about the discount and the petrol?"

"Don't want to talk about it."

We only stopped to fill up the tank, get some coffee from a vendor.

CHAPTER SEVEN

HOT SEASON, EN ROUTE TO TCHIN-TABARADEN 1989

Since Frankie didn't want to talk about the theft of her product and petrol in Agadez, I dozed all the way to Tahoua. We arrived just before 3 pm. She dropped me at the hospital. "Sorry about…"

Frankie held up her hand. "Go get your shot, I'm taking you back to Tchin-Tabaraden tonight."

I asked at the desk for the American nurses. Roz came out first.

We embraced. I held onto her for a while.

"You made it," she said. "Look good."

I pulled off my scarf.

"Except for your hair."

I slipped off a sandal.

"And your feet. Nice henna disguise though. How are you otherwise?"

"Good. Better. Settling in. How about you and Stacia?"

"We're doing well. A simple hospital but we mostly have what we need, and the staff is great. I've fallen in love with a young Egyptian doctor. I should introduce you."

She continued talking as she led me back to a room and prepared the injection. I tried to focus on whatever she was saying.

"The house is nice, we've made friends with the international medical community, our neighbors, we got a parrot." She kept talking. "Just dangle your leg," she said as she changed subjects again and jammed the needle into my thigh.

My muscle spasmed immediately.

"Sorry, I thought you were relaxed. It'll hurt just a couple of days. Nothing you can't handle."

"Roz, can you check that my IUD is in place?"

"Sure. Any chance you're pregnant?"

"No chance."

Stacia stuck her head in the doorway. "Lark? Where's your hair?"

I tied on my scarf.

"Tell me later. I've got a dehydrated child in the next room."

"We don't get off for a couple of hours," Roz said. "But you're welcome to come over for dinner."

"I can't stay. I've got an offer for a ride back to Tchin-Taba-raden right now, and I teach on Monday."

The procedure took less than five minutes.

"You're all set," she said and handed me a box of condoms. "Be safe."

I thanked her and stuffed them deep into my pack. "See you during the holidays!"

Frankie was waiting when I stepped outside. Leaning against the hospital wall smoking a cigarette.

"Picked up some jerry cans and petrol. A cannister of propane for your stove, some beer, a lime and a mango for you, the fruits and vegetables in the market picked over. Let's go."

I stuck a bill in her pocket. "I thought it wasn't a race."

"Only with the sun, before it gets dark. Plus, the odds of your getting a ride to Tchin-Tabaraden aren't good. One less thing I have to worry about."

"You worry?"

Frankie handed me a brochette and I offered her more money. She waved it off.

"At least let me drive, so you can rest."

"No fuckin' way. No offense, but the last thing I need is to get lost in the desert."

"Right. The laterite road. I should have offered when we were on the clearly paved national route."

"Even then. I'm a lousy passenger."

I held the fruit in my lap. The lime, small, hard with a few scratches on the skin would keep for a few days. I'd make Oumar limeade. No ice, but still, tang. I could already smell the ripe mango even with the odor of petrol wafting through the cab. Frankie must have spilled. I saved the brochette meat to add to rice for dinner later since Frankie bought propane. I'd already adjusted to cooking over the fire, wasn't planning on buying propane, but the stove could be a backup. Maybe I'd need it during the rainy season.

I waited until near Kao to peel the mango, saving it as long as I could, anticipating the tangy rich flavor. I took out my knife and sliced the length of the skin, the rich yellow orange flesh, ripe and pungent. Scoring the sides, I lifted the edge of a strip of peel, pulling it away from the meat, pulp clinging to the skin, held it out the window, and let go. "For a desert animal," I said. One of the animals I'd heard come out at night when cooler. "Like the bush cats Oumar told me about with fires in their eyes." Not that a carnivore would eat a mango. Unless hungry enough. Thirsty enough for the juice in the pulp. I scored the flesh then, uniform squares like a grid, tic, tac, toe, trying not to lose any juice. I fed Frankie one small square at a time as she drove. Half a mango lasted all the way to Tchin-Tabaraden.

CHAPTER EIGHT
HOT SEASON, TCHIN-TABARADEN 1989

We arrived at Tchin-Tabaraden at dusk. Oumar already there in the yard with his sleeping mat. Patience elsewhere. Maybe hunting under the cover of night before moonlight.

Oumar's eyes lit up when he saw Frankie, more so when I told him Frankie was staying the night. "Oumar, share this mango with your mother and Izza. Tala, too, if she's there, before you come back for the night."

"Your turn to take the first shower," I told Frankie, who was leaning against the acacia, smoking.

"Go ahead. I'm going to hook up the propane to the stove first."

My milled soap from Score long gone, I'd meant to pick up soap in Agadez or Tahoua to avoid Irish Spring. My aversion to the too sweet smell lessened only because it was available. I filled the basin with the cool water from the tukunya and walked carefully to the enclosure, mindful not to waste any water, a pagne over my shoulder, less as a towel than a cover up.

I stripped down and poured a can of cool water over my body to rinse off the dust, quickly lathering up before the moisture evaporated from my skin, and again dipped the tin into the basin of water. I took my time rinsing, then draped the pagne around myself before stepping out. Movement caught my attention. I glanced up as several children's heads disappeared on the far side of the wall. The aura of the pungent soap dissipated as quickly into the arid air.

I walked into the house just as Frankie pulled the stove away from the corner to access the hook-up.

"I can't see a fuckin' thing." She flicked her lighter. A popping sound. Her entire body instantly ignited in a blue flame. She ran from the house screaming.

"Roll!" I shouted after her.

"Djinn!" someone shrieked.

Frankie dropped to the sand and rolled. I ran to her, stamping at the excess burning cloth as she turned over and over on the ground. Everything seemed in slow motion, her keening cries, the glowing blue of her body against the sand. Then silence.

"It's out," I said. "Are you okay?"

Frankie lay staring at the sky and grimaced as she sat up, her face, flushed. Her hands shook as she turned them slowly, staring at them as if they were foreign objects.

The index finger of her right hand had a blister the same size as her finger, looked surreal, painful.

"Get some water from inside," I instructed a group of children cowering at the door.

Oumar stepped out from among them and brought a bowl of water. Frankie immediately immersed her hands. "Fuck," she finally said.

I shook out my scarf, wetted it, and draped the cool cloth over Frankie's face.

She sighed.

"I'll help you out of your clothes."

"No," came from beneath the wet cloth. "Just help me stand."

I stood firm, as Frankie leaned against me, balancing with her forearms until she was standing.

"Careful."

"Too late," Frankie said. "There must have been a fuckin' leak."

"Everyone else is saying it was djinn. In any case, you're lucky."

"That's one way to look at it."

"Your uniform must have some sort of fire retardant."

"Rothmans to the rescue," Frankie said. "It's a chemical burn, though. Maybe I should stop in the dispensary."

"It's been closed for years, but there might be some medical supplies still in there. Here, sit down and drink some water. I turned to Oumar. "There's brochette wrapped in paper on top of the fridge. You two can share. I'll be right back."

Oumar handed me my flashlight.

It didn't require much effort to jiggle the locked door and put my shoulder into the abandoned building to get in. I shined the flashlight around the room, glinting on some bottles of medicine on the shelves. I opened a cupboard. Empty. No gauze, tape. No bandages of any sort. I picked up several bottles, dark glass, the labels in German. One read Alkohol. Alcohol, not good for burns, but I'd take it for soothing a fever or preventing infection if necessary. I took the lids off the others one by one and quickly smelled. The one that read Jod smelled like my iodized water. I poured some onto my finger—familiar reddish yellow color. I'd add it to some treated water to wash the sand off and provide a little disinfectant for the burns on Frankie's hands. I quickly rifled through the rest of the bottles, took the two I was sure of, and pulled the door closed behind me.

"Iodine," I said coming through the gate. "How are you doing?" Frankie and Oumar were sitting in the chairs, the brochette untouched between them. Unresponsive. I went inside to get *Where There is No Doctor* from the fridge and stepped out flipping to the chapter on first aid. An index of catastrophe: Fever, Shock, Loss of Consciousness, Choking, Drowning, Emergencies Caused by Heat, How to Control Bleeding from a Wound, Nosebleeds, Broken Bones. Bites, Bullet, Knife, and Other Serious

Wounds, I shivered. Burns. Most burns can be prevented. Burns that Cause Blisters, Chemical (2nd degree) "I'll treat some water with my tablets for your hands to soak in, then it says to pour a little tincture directly on the burns. I could also apply some of my pomade—it's petroleum jelly based—but with no gauze, the sand will just stick to it."

Oumar disappeared into the house and returned with the neon pommade.

I took the bowl, dumped the water on the tree, poured fresh water from the tukunya, added two tablets of iodine, and balanced the bowl on the banco railing, stirring with one hand while reading with the other.

"No pommade." Frankie said. "And are you sure that's iodine?"

"Yes." I set the bowl of water in her lap. "Soak."

Oumar made the doubtful sound with his lips. "You should go see Mariama."

"What does she recommend for burns?"

"Something from trees."

Frankie looked doubtful, alarmed.

"Maybe you should see Roz and Stacia at the hospital in Tahoua tomorrow if you think you can manage the steering wheel." I opened the bottle of iodine and poured some on the worst burn.

"Fuck!"

"I was just going to say it might sting a little." I got a fresh cup of water from the tukunya. "Drink."

Frankie downed the water. "Get me the mat; I'm going to sleep."

"No dinner? No shower?"

"Mat."

Oumar lay by the door, far from Frankie.

Frankie still did not want to talk. Sometimes there's nothing to say. When I heard her breathing quiet to the rhythm of sleep, I finally relaxed. It felt good to lie on the sand in the open air under the stars. I'd missed it. I kept my butch head covered partly because it required an explanation to Oumar and because I felt cold. I did not hear Patience return or the women in the night filling their buckets. I did not hear the muezzin's call to prayer. Only the light gradually lifting me out of the depth until the full sun appeared on the horizon. By then Frankie was stirring. She saw me watching.

"Good call on the iodine. I'm leaving for Tahoua."

"Coffee?"

She opened the gate.

I followed, watching her truck rumble away toward the edge of the village. As she left Tchin-Tabaraden, she stopped, got out of the truck, and a Tuareg man got behind the wheel. Not many knew how to drive. Frankie's hands must have hurt more than she said.

CHAPTER NINE
RAINY SEASON, TCHIN-TABARADEN 1989

Clouds blotted the blank horizon, a memory of rain. A frenzied flurry of activity replaced the typically sluggish pace of late afternoon. Restless camels and goats, dogs, usually dodging the locals, ran wild down the middle of the road.

Ordinarily methodical people suddenly rushing, rearranging their affairs. Faded aquamarine and red plastic corded chairs banged the legs of the women as they moved them into banco structures. Empty tin buckets clattered against the chipped white enamel bowls in their arms when they had no more room on their heads. The Tuaregs' tents flapped in the distance. The energy in the atmosphere palpable, exhilarating.

I hurried home to set out my own miscellaneous containers to catch the rainwater, not realizing everyone else was actually gathering them out of the wind. This is before I discover the darkened shapes on the skyline are silica. Before I learn the alchemy of desert clouds. My introduction to the Harmattan that shifted seasons.

By the time I reached the wall around my yard, the sky turned mahogany. The filtered light made everything appear like the negative of a photograph, the apex of a total solar eclipse. The loose edge of my scarf flapping, threatening to come undone. The aluminum gate, blown open, pinned against the cracked mud wall. My camera! I stuck it under my shirt and looked around to spot anyone who might be watching. No one. I called for Patience, my voice absorbed in the wind. Oumar would be with his herd. Both of them taking care of themselves.

I cut across the yard, the sand peppering my face like sleet. Once inside the house, I pushed the stove against the door to keep it from blowing open, closed the crude corrugated window flaps, wrapped my camera in a pagne and stowed it deep in my pack to give it another layer of protection, discovering a round rock inside, the dehydrated lime for Oumar's limeade. I'd forgotten about it the night Frankie caught on fire. Another time. I covered my nose and mouth with a scarf to filter out the grit. Oumar was right. Thanks to the gris-gris that was now swinging wildly from the doorframe, I had my camera back, and the thief had avoided being frozen in my yard like a statue, a relief for both of us. I'd interpreted the theft as a personal insult, according to my western value system. Oumar showed me how to see from a Tuareg perspective, how to forget myself.

I slid down the wall, the light growing gradually dimmer until it was completely dark, my own hands invisible before my face. I pulled a pagne over my eyes and watched the darkness through the thin fabric. All I could hear was the static of whipping sand. I dozed and dreamt of rain, *its whispered breathing, the sensation falling on my bare skin.* Roy? I said, waking myself up.

Light again, a polished quiet. I moved the stove and pushed the door through the eddies of sand whirled against it. The wind had moved on, but the dust remained suspended as if the air were made of red gauze. Patience lay shiny as a wet rock gnawing on a goat's head beneath the acacia tree. Goat's heads were a delicacy; someone would be mad that he'd stolen it for himself. A dog.

It required three tins of water to wash the sand from my hair before walking to the post office to pick up a letter from home.

#2

April 14, 1989
Dear Lark,

Hope all is well there. Your description of the desert is vivid, tactile, and the cultural details you provide are intriguing. We would love to drink Tuareg tea with Mariama and sweet Oumar one day. Please send our kind regards. Your students sound self-motivated, reminiscent of you growing up. And no one was surprised to hear you got a dog. Patience, very prescient.

Gita wants you to know that she has seen an allopathic doctor. They are running tests thinking it is some sort of blood disease, maybe leukemia. She is obviously making her own decisions on diagnoses and treatments, but we are focusing her diet on ashitaba, artichokes, basil, chicory, brussels sprouts, cauliflower, cabbage, cod and halibut when we can get fresh, mushrooms, olives (in brine), parsley, peppermint, raspberries and thyme.

She doesn't want you to worry; she says she will figure it out. But do keep her in your thoughts, your meditations, your prayers.
We'll let you know as soon as we find out the diagnosis.
Take care of yourself, Lark, and of Oumar.
We all love you~

Leukemia. Cancer of the blood. I would have worried. I walked to Mariama's, looking for arrowheads along the way. All I could see were exposed bones. "My students say you can find arrowheads after a sandstorm," I explained. My voice rang in the thin air as if Gita had blown in on the Harmattan or was always there and suddenly visible like arrowheads. But I didn't see any. Maybe the students already passed this way and found them. Maybe the arrowheads didn't want to be found.

Mariama was bent, sweeping the yard with her hand broom, Izza rocked to sleep on her mother's back from the steady motion. I observed for a while before announcing my presence, not wanting to interrupt. Mariama swept the sand smooth then flicked her wrist a couple of short strokes in one direction followed by one in the opposite direction, creating a pattern resembling bird tracks. Tala told me Mariama once saw a heron on a caravan trek across the desert. She'd described shading her eyes to track it in the vast expanse of sky and memorizing the bird and the precise prints it left in the sand. Nearly half the sand surrounding the compound was perfectly patterned.

"Want to try?" Mariama said without turning around.

She knew I was there. Probably felt my eyes on her.

"Yes." I handed her the dried, crushed henna leaves wrapped in paper. "From Agadez."

"Tanamert, thank you. You come to my house, and we will henna both our hands and our feet." A mix of French, Tamasheq, and gestures.

I responded with the Tuareg's verbal agreement, the first syllable sounding like our negative uh-uh followed by the positive uh-huh. "Uh uh-huh."

She made the guttural clicking sound in her throat, another sound of agreement, and handed me the broom. I bent to the task concentrating mostly on rhythm and direction, two short strokes in one direction, one long in the opposite.

"Bonne," she said. "Continuez."

I was getting in the groove when Mariama touched my shoulder.

"Arrêtez," stop.

I stood up, my lower back spasming, and handed her the broom thinking I made an error.

She held my face with her hands, her indigo stained fingertips edging the scarf up past my hairline to the stubble that remained. "Vous êtes malade, Mademoiselle," sick, Mariama said.

I regarded the Tuareg woman with the deep dark eyes and

ink-black woven hair. The wad of tobacco balanced on her lower lip, baby Izza still sleeping on her back. "Non," I said. "A friend cut it in Agadez." I showed her, again, the deep cracks on my heels as evidence of the drying effect of the environment on my body, but Mariama didn't believe it, wouldn't accept that I'd cut my hair intentionally. I knew that once a baby's hair was shaved to separate it from the spiritual world, the nomads rarely cut their hair. This is after Frankie told me it's bad luck. Before Tala tells me that hair blowing across the sand calls in the djinn, the bad spirits. That even when a single strand falls from a comb when the women are plaiting each other's hair, they rush to pick it up.

Mariama made the clicking sound with her lips in disagreement. "It fell out from fever. You need to rest." She pointed with her chin toward her tent. "Come."

With my scarf on and no mirror, I'd already forgotten my shorn head. "Tanamert, Mariama, but I'm feeling better now." I didn't feel well though; I just wanted to sleep.

As I walked home, I carried the full weight of the sun on my head like the women carried water. I avoided lying down in the house, already hot and suffocating, and unrolled my mat under the acacia next to Patience who was sleeping. With only a couple of deep breaths of the searing air, I felt my limbs melt into the ground.

The vivid garden, then bleak snow, then all we saw disappeared into gritty air. As so many before us inhaling their final figments surrounded by sand, particles of something unnamable, exhaling brown curled petals of chrysanthemums, tree bark from orange trees, dried and scentless, we were senseless. Immeasurable thirst.

I woke up consumed with thirst. Maybe Mariama was right; I was sick with a fever, dehydrating from within. It was almost evening, but I didn't move until dark when I leaned into the gate and walked toward Mariama's encampment. The way was lit with an intoxicating number of stars, a wedge of moon on the edge of the sky. I could hear the sounds of drumming and singing as I neared the camp. When I clapped my arrival, the music stopped, everyone suddenly quiet.

"Ahlan wa sahlan," Mariama said, welcome. Full greetings.

Her eyes said, "I knew you would come."

Her hand lingered on mine as my mothers' used to, as if determining if I had a fever, then she began speaking in rapid Tamasheq.

"You lose your hair, and then your friend catches on fire," Tala translated. "Djinn."

All the women there agreed. I knew that from the Tuaregs' perspective, I put myself at risk from the invisible on a daily basis. My physical explanations seemed ridiculous to them, naive.

"Not believing in the djinn won't protect you from them," Tala said, looking at me in her periphery. "Mariama says doubt may exist for no reason."

Clapping at the door followed by the ritual greetings. "Algheras," always the response, always in peace.

"The marabout is here," Mariama said.

Everyone gathered by the fire for tea. There was a different smell, different from tea, tobacco, goat's meat, millet. "What's cooking?" I whispered to Tala.

"Tree bark."

"To eat?" I asked.

Tala didn't answer.

The conversation seemed to meander randomly maybe because I could only pick up certain words: wind, camels, rain, drought, pastures, president.

"Rain is the true king," I think someone said.

They discussed everything except why the marabout had come.

When he moved away from the fire, Mariama gestured with her chin for me to follow him.

He disappeared into the central tent, Mariama's, and I crouched beside him on the sand floor. I looked toward where his cheek would be, recognizing his wizened brown eyes, the only part of him that wasn't covered—I knew him—the marabout who'd sacrificed the goat and given Izza her Quranic name at the naming ceremony. It felt even more awkward with an acquaintance. I had read little about marabouts beyond that they are Islamic holy men. Nothing about protocol. It seemed he was here to protect me from the djinn. I knew Oumar wandered in the bush alone with the goats. He didn't carry a sword for protection from the djinn as Tala explained the Tuareg men did, but a stick, a shepherd's crook without the crook. Herders spent a lot of time in the wilderness alone. What was the difference? Gris-gris? I wanted to ask the marabout, to hear him explain everything directly, clearly, stripped of oblique Tuareg metaphors. The only sounds the muffled voices around the fire, the low registers of a drum.

Lingering in the extended silence, the marabout closed his eyes and began chanting in Arabic. The words slurred together to my ear like the muezzin's call to prayer. I couldn't make out what he was saying beyond lyrical notes. Then he grew quiet. I listened to his breathing and concentrated on matching my breath with his.

After some time, he opened his eyes and drew a quill, some ink, and a scrap of the blue paper used to wrap sugar from his robe. By the dim light of the lantern and the ambient light filtering in from the opening in the tent, he wrote an ayat, a Quranic verse, on the paper, his movements, methodical, deliberate.

I watched as he poured some water into an empty tea glass, then poured the water over the ink, catching it in another glass, his hands weathered and graceful. He offered the glass of diluted ink to me.

"Drink it." Mariama's voice sounded in my head. I no longer hesitated. The inky water tasted only slightly more bitter than the first round of Tuareg tea.

The marabout produced a remnant of leather, a needle, and thin leather thread, folded the paper into a pouch, reached down to the ground for some grains of sand, added them, and stitched the miniature pouch closed, sealing the contents inside. He strung the bundle on a leather thong, gestured to me to bow my head, and placed it around my neck.

"Bismallah," he said.

I touched the dangling gris-gris. Mokao wore them, the herders; everyone did. "Tanamert," thank you, I said, relieved to be standing.

Before the marabout left, Mariama gave him some money, cheese, and dates. Everyone began singing, drumming. Back to normal.

"Come," Mariama said. "Arabaz."

"Therapeutic massage," Tala translated. "To ward off any malevolent forces."

"Isn't that what this is for?" I touched my gris-gris.

"Yes. But the marabout uses words. Tadeine, the medicine woman, uses trees."

Mariama waved me back into the center of her tent.

"Lie down," Tala said.

I lay on a pallet of blankets Tala or someone had apparently just arranged.

Tadeine poured some grains of millet into her palm. She wore a silver ring on the middle finger of her right hand and multiple bracelets on both wrists.

"Bismallah," she said, circling me three times. She touched my stomach, ignoring my startle reflex and lingered there, listening, as if she understood the language my body spoke. Gita used to massage my back sometimes in exchange for me massaging her feet. "You are only truly independent when you can massage your own feet," she said. Had that meant something else? Tadeine knelt down, added some sand to the slightly cooled liquid from the bark that I had smelled cooking over the fire, and spat in it.

I closed my eyes and tried harder to relax. Tadeine applied the warm, abrasive mixture to my skin, lifting my limbs and making a spiraling pattern with her fingertips on my stomach, tight as a drum from the gentle thrumming, and on my forehead. I could feel the lines engraved there from squinting at the constant glare and from my constant state of uncertainty. I thought of the lizards in Niamey doing push-ups, the bitter, sweet taste of Tuareg tea, the crystalline sound of camel bells. The only noise now, the shifting of Tadeine's bracelets as she touched the ground, the wind. I opened my eyes slightly and glimpsed beyond the tent, a sand sea glittering in the sun. Or maybe my eyes were closed.

Roy and I went to see the village marabout. Anthony. His divine patience might have helped us, but we had none. He carefully penned appropriate sharia on a paper scrap, pouring water over it, drinking the diluted ink. He choked creasing the paper inside the gris-gris, sealing it with needle and thread, his own breath in tiny stitches. He rode away on his donkey.

We were alone then, lost. In the slow sweep of silence, we only remembered each other's breath, feeble whispers dully cleaving the past under a bleached white sky, our lips swollen from disuse, the acrid taste of blood on our numb tongues, so cold lying side by side on the blanket of snow, we turned blue like the Tuaregs in their finest, warriors in the end.

I don't know if the gris-gris worked with the djinn, but they worked with the Tuaregs.

Everyone seemed more relaxed around me, relieved. The nomads, the nomads' children at the school.

"What is the English word for gris-gris?" Tala.

"Talisman," I said. "Amulet."

"It is good you are wearing a talisman."

"Nice sentence."

"Now we will understand you better," Eddoua, the boy with the arrowheads said.

"Your hair won't fall out from illness."

I actually did feel better.

"Your friends won't catch on fire."

"Mr. Frank caught on fire because a flammable gas came in contact with a flame. Science," I explained in English, French, and gestures.

"Yes, the djinn did that."

Frankie knocked on the gate as she entered the yard. Patience jumped up wagging and Frankie gave him something from her pocket.

"Come in," I said.

"Do you mind?" This over her shoulder as she disappeared into the latrine.

She came out, shaking the excess water from her hands.

"How's your burn?"

"Something's seriously wrong."

"Infection? Let me see."

She held out her right hand, healed, the new skin minus whirls of prints, texture.

"Not that. I just came from the shops. It's as if I'm not there. Not even the usual greetings."

Frankie lit a cigarette, blew out the smoke.

"Actually, they're fuckin' avoiding me. The shop owners all acted distracted; no one asks for any product. Ask Oumar if they think I'm a spy."

"They blame your burn accident on the djinn rather than smoking near a flammable gas. You did look other-worldly, surrounded in blue flame like an apparition."

"I'm glad you were entertained, but what do the djinn have to do with business?"

I ignored her ridiculous statement about being entertained by her catching on fire. "Look at it from another perspective. Rather than being glad to see you healed and well, maybe they consider you tainted, toxic. Bad luck."

"That could ruin everything."

"You need a gris-gris for protection from the djinn."

It still felt hot in the rainy season, the advertised lower temperatures nuanced rather than obvious, at least to non-locals, and so far, it lacked rain.

When I asked the students in class when they thought it would rain, one reply: "When Allah wills it."

A different approach. "Tell me about other rainy seasons. What were they like?"

"Sometimes it rains heavily and all at once. One flash flood drowned twenty thousand animals in the Tchirozérine and Tchin-Tabaraden departments alone."

"Sometimes it doesn't rain. We call it welen, sécheresse."

"Drought," I said. "Famine." The French called it la soudure, the soldering, as if lips were fused closed with a bead of hot metal. I couldn't think of a more vivid image of hunger, thirst.

"This is why Mariama's son Ahmed and his friends are not here. They had to leave to find work so their families can buy goats, camels, cattle to replenish their herds, those lost in the drought," Tala said. "The drought, the government break up families."

"There was a nomad whose cattle died in the drought, their tongues swollen from thirst. He severed their heads and brought them to the well and poured water on their tongues," Eddoua said.

"When our animals die, we die."

The image broke my heart. The way he expressed it so matter-of-factly shifted something in my brain.

"I need some goats," I told Tala before class.

The girl was gorgeous. Cool beauty like the moon. Blossoming despite the unrelenting sun. Fifteen? No birth certificates, age, an estimation. Perfect blue-black braids gleaming in the light, supple skin. Her eyes, the golden color of the second round of

Tuareg tea, looked directly at me. Maybe three years younger, felt like thirty.

"Miss," she said, laughing. "You are a teacher, not a herder."

"What if I bought some goats from Mokao and paid Oumar to take care of them along with his family's?"

"Why?"

"Same reasons everyone has them. For meat, trade, the hide." I'd saved enough for a shortwave radio for Oumar, but I owed Mariama.

"For Tabaski?"

"Yes." I'd heard of Tabaski, a Muslim holiday that came after Ramadan but didn't admit to Tala that I didn't know the significance of it.

We began class as always with a range of brief traditional and casual English greetings: Good morning, What's going on? Hey, What's up? How are you doing today? How's everything? How are things? What's happening? How's it going?—and their nuances—Good to see you. Great to see you! Nice to see you. Greetings for different times of day, days of the week, months. Then moved on to discussion. I encouraged them all to add to the conversation. I adapted the usual raising of their hands and snapping their fingers to be called on, with snapping their fingers and freely adding an idea or comment to the conversation.

Discussion Topic: time, with the angle of holidays: "How do you tell time?" I asked.

"The moon is our watch," Eddoua said.

I wrote Time, Moon, Lunar Calendar on the blackboard. "Ramadan is coming up in the ninth month of the lunar calendar. It begins with the sighting of the crescent moon," another student said.

"Yes, the days coincide with the phases of the moon, the lunar calendar."

"Sometimes we can't see the moon if the Harmattan stirs too much sand in the air, so religious leaders from Mecca tell us when they have seen the crescent moon in the sky, and then we begin the fast of Ramadan, everyone together."

"Thirty days fasting, no water, no food, from sunrise to sundown."

I nodded, realizing the gesture meant the opposite of agreement, which still fit my point. "It must be extremely hard to fast in the desert, especially to not drink water." Even thinking of it made my throat parched. I swallowed.

"The most devout don't even swallow their saliva," a particularly attentive girl in the front row said.

"Fasting is one of the pillars of Islam: profession of faith, prayer, alms, fasting, and how do you say, hajj?"

"Pilgrimage to Mecca," the girl in the front row again. "My father has gone there."

"Ramadan is a reminder that a person is not just a physical body that needs food and water but a soul who needs Allah."

I wrote it down on the chalkboard. "That's beautiful, poetic."

"No fighting, no smoking, no sex," Tala added.

Stifled snickering. "L'allah."

"Just prayer."

"Our prayers will be answered if Allah wills it."

"Miss, we do suffer a little from not eating or drinking in the beginning, but we get used to it. Then we break our fast like the Prophet Mohammed, may he rest in peace, did 1,400 years ago, with a sip of water and some dates at sunset. Then iftar, a feast, with family and friends."

I'd broken a fast, eating raisins once when Roy and I were experimenting with deprivation of certain senses to enhance others. We fed them to each other. Such a rich burst of flavor on a cleansed palette. And water. Since living here, I deeply appreciated water. The nuanced taste, the necessity. I'd never been deprived of it, had taken it for granted.

"Ramadan commemorates the time when the angel Gabrielle told the Prophet Muhammad, may he rest in peace, the first verses of the Quran."

I wrote Ramadan on the board. "Because your holidays follow the lunar calendar, you eventually celebrate every holiday in every season, hot, rainy, and cold."

"Yes," Eddoua said. "We talked about this in math. The dates move backward eleven days every year."

I wrote "Solar Calendar" on the board with little rays spiraling out from the "o." "Because the country I'm from uses a solar calendar, our holidays are usually on the same date and always in the same season."

Murmurs of condolence.

Now for my education. "Who can explain the holiday Tabaski?" Every hand went up, fingers snapping for emphasis.

"Most important feast on the Muslim calendar." "End of the pilgrimage to Mecca."

"Feast of Sacrifice."

"Four days long!"

"Celebrates the Prophet Ibrahim's willingness to sacrifice everything for Allah, even his firstborn son."

"Ibrahim, a prophet and ancestor of Muhammed, may he rest in peace."

"But Allah let Ibrahim sacrifice a ram instead."

"I know this story," I said.

Tala spoke last. "Those who can, sacrifice a goat and share a third with those in need, a third as a pardon for any offenses to friends and relatives, and keep a third for the family."

The reason I needed goats. Thank you, Tala. I would give a third to Mariama and her family and Tala.

Oumar came home early that evening. "Tala told me you want to buy some goats from Mokao."

I also wanted to see Mokao. "I would pay you to take care of them for me. Can you? Will you?"

He made the clicking sound from his throat in agreement. "A better purchase than a dog, Miss."

We started walking immediately; still, word reached Mokao's camp before we did. He'd already gathered his herd, separated a half-dozen of what appeared his best goats to sell, not big but fit and unblemished. Mostly white, some with splotches of gray, black, or brown. The locals called them moutons, sheep, rather than chèvres, goats. They looked like goats to me, maybe the name for them interchangeable for uneducated anasaras.

Mokao also kept cows for milk. The Wodaabé didn't eat them for meat. I thought of the image of the severed cows' heads, how the herder watered their swollen tongues even in death.

I could afford three goats but told him I would purchase a couple more in a month or so. I wanted to give him the business, was attracted to him, didn't act on it, but surely he could tell. Until Gita's letter, I always thought people could always tell. On the commune, we were raised to accept biology rather than fight it, but I didn't know the rules here. I thought of the Tuareg man with the hazel eyes at the school meetings who looked away from me every time I looked at him. Maybe I craved a wordless language I could already speak and be understood. Natural language, physical touch, the pleasure of connection. Maybe I hadn't realized what truly being alone felt like. I didn't want to overstep in a culture I barely knew, but I needed to hold someone. Kiss someone. I knew the nomadic women were free, empowered, including sexual relationships like on the commune. Too, anasaras were technically outside of the local cultural standards, but people still judged.

All that didn't matter now, though; the desert had taken that choice from me. I was desirable to no one. I reminded myself that I came to the desert to purify. Embrace the pain of loss and move past it, but I didn't expect to lose my appearance, my sense of self. I adjusted my scarf to cover my butchered hair. Now I was only fit to buy goats, but it would grow back. I glanced at Mokao. He was talking to me.

"Mademoiselle?"

"Miss, ça va?" Oumar.

I turned my attention to him. "What?"

"Mokao says I can get the goats tomorrow on my way to the pasture."

I faced Mokao. "Yes. Thank you." I gave him a little more money than what he asked.

Mokao extended his hand and I grasped it too long but not long enough.

Walking home, I told Oumar I'd seen nothing that resembled pasture, just scrubby vegetation, most with thorns long as your thumb.

"Everything must be earned in the desert, Miss."

It reminded me of when I asked him what to name my dog. "Patience," he'd said. How did a kid so young understand these things? What I needed to know to live here, what anyone needed to know to survive here. A Tuareg education. He not only memorized the Tuareg sayings but understood precisely when to use them. From experience? I hadn't earned anything. I imagined the locals considered me a mad woman, bereft of a husband, family, place, sense, pursued by djinn. Yes, I was teaching their children English, but nothing they couldn't have figured out how to learn on their own. Maybe I was experiencing the slump the trainers alerted us to, once the newness wore off and daily life with no end in sight set in. Second thoughts. Doubt. Homesickness, some called it.

"I'm going to plant the sunflowers," I told Oumar.

"Miss!"

He had seen the seed packets sitting on my fridge and asked about them for months.

"Now?"

"Soon." I needed to see a flower, color, something familiar, and I wanted to give the locals the pleasure of seeing a flower bloom color, offer us all another source of protein, other than goat's meat, that wouldn't spoil, could be easily transported anywhere. I wanted to make a meaningful contribution.

I took the seed packets to school and used them for a lesson on same and different. Same moon, same planet, different landscapes, climates. Same sun, different angles.

The following day, Oumar watered his goats early, returning as the students arrived before school to plant in the early morning of the waning moon. "According to the Farmer's Almanac, flowering plants do best in the phase following the full moon." It proved true most years in the communal gardens.

"The lunar calendar," one of the students said.

"Same moon, different environment."

Some students took turns digging a couple of inches deep into the sand with a wooden spoon, others dropping the seeds in the indentations.

"Nacala," Eddoua said, putting additional seeds in each divot. Another boy taking them out of one and redistributing them in other holes. "Warri. You know this game, Miss?"

"Where do you get the seeds to play it?"

Eddoua laughed. "We play with pebbles and two rows of..." He pointed to the indentations in the sand. "Comment dites hufra?"

"Trou?"

"Holes, pits, indentations?" I offered.

"Oui. Yes."

"A strategy game. Our grandparents taught us and theirs before them, and so on for thousands of years."

"Look." Eddoua quickly began scooping out sand a couple of inches opposite the initial row of holes.

He and Tala dropped an even number of seeds in each pit, then Eddoua and she alternated taking all the seeds from one pit and distributing them in the other pits in such a way as to capture the opponent's seeds.

"Whoever gets the most seeds or stones in the end, wins."

"Usually, two males play but those who watch advise," Tala explained.

It took her about ten minutes to beat him.

"This is why females don't usually play." Tala's laugh, boisterous, infectious.

It only took a half hour to actually plant the seeds, the students alternating digging or planting. Double rows inspired by the game but two feet apart all along the perimeter of the wall. I followed behind watering.

"Miss," Oumar said. "They won't get watered when you're gone."

He was right. I'd wanted to leave the legacy of a perennial that would exist after me, but these varieties were annuals. Someone would have to harvest the seeds and intentionally plant them every year. Maybe me. What would I go back to? I didn't want to live on the commune, Gita was gone. Roy was dead to me. Could I stay? Make a life here? "I know," I said. "Sometimes it doesn't rain a lot where I'm from either. The seeds just need water to get started, to develop their root systems, but they can handle periods of drought."

"Years of it?" one of the quiet students asked.

"No, probably not years."

"Nothing can survive that," Tala said. "That's why we are in school."

I filled the empty seed packets with sand to mark the rows: Hopi Black Dye, Super Snack, Velvet Queen.

That night I thought I'd dream of blooming sunflowers, but I dreamt of drought, of loss, its own kind of drought. The muezzin's call for prayer woke me or maybe the dream. I didn't open my palms, but wrote it down in my journal, then burned it.

Once the dust settles, you only think you're dead, sandblasted body heavy as marble, fragile as glass, broken, immobile, sunken shards involuntarily reposed on shifting ground, no sight, no sound. Bad luck; poisoned well.

Another mirage of the body appearing to others, but not really there. Not real, not there. No mirrors to reflect, no reflections, flesh and blood drained of power. The consistency of powder.

Apply some makeup, some kohl to the eyes, make believe you are alive. Get up, get dressed, smell the perfume, the plumes of smoke that remain of your breath. Imagine a flame out of nothing. Concentrate. Hold on with your mind what remains of your hands, the remnants of your grasp until a discernable pattern emerges, a fevered dream, complicated mosaics like the tiles at Alhambra. You must blink to keep them straight in your head to keep from spinning into vertigo. Where did you go?

I wrapped my pagne around myself, slipped on my sandals, covered my pathetic hair with a scarf, and eased open the gate while Oumar slept. He knew, everyone knew, I still walked out into the landscape by myself. I did it to quiet my mind or maybe it called to me. I considered the gris-gris I wore around my neck and the Swiss Army knife, my miniature sword Oumar called it, tied at my waist a compromise and continued walking alone, though typically during the day, and everyone else felt comforted that I had powerful protection from the djinn.

The night was quiet, the stars less visible from wind the day before lifting the top layer of sand into the sky, thickening it, so even sound muted. I passed the strings of houses, quiet from sleep or prayer and continued into the bush along the route to Mokao's. Too late for drumming and dancing, too early for the drumming of mortar and pestle as the women pounded millet. Maybe I would see our goats; Oumar said they were still there.

I walked beyond the triangle of the acacia landmark, some clumps of stunted prosopis. Kept walking. What I first thought were boulders were the goats sleeping like random stones on the sand. I glimpsed movement in my periphery. Maybe a guard goat stirring from the potential threat of a predator. I looked in that direction, but all seemed still. Then I felt someone standing close behind me. I put my hand on my Swiss Army knife and quickly turned, the element of surprise, to face Mokao. He didn't say anything. No greetings. Neither did he move back, standing extremely close, but not quite touching. Questioning rather than menacing. I dropped my hand from my knife and stayed still, trying to calm my breathing to match the rhythm of his quiet breath on my forehead. We stood there holding each other without touching. Until I moved. An instinctual lifting of my lips to his. When I kissed him, he reacted as if he'd been burned, branded, defiled. I ran, my sandals slapping the sand.

I could hear the goats bleating in the distance, relieved for the curtain of haze as the eastern edge of the sky lightened.

By the time I got home, Oumar thankfully had gone. I dipped some water from the tukunya, filling the basin and stepped inside the latrine, inside the walls. I felt humiliated, rejected, completely misread the situation with Mokao, the cues. I stripped down, stepped out of my cotton bikinis. Blood. That explained a lot. No wonder I was an emotional wreck. Knowing the biological reason though never affected the intensity. Pure despair for no reason, though this time for reasons.

I'd planned to go to the market, but I wasn't yet ready for what this day could bring. Word traveled, especially my business. I didn't think Mokao would be the type to be kissed and tell but I couldn't trust my instincts.

I looked at Patience. "Am I losing it?"

He sat, then scaled the wall leaving me to myself.

I swept out the house, watered the sunflowers, and began sweeping Mariama's pattern of bird tracks in the sand yard.

When I'd finished, mid-afternoon, I could hardly straighten up. My hand on my lower back, I slowly unkinked and eased back into an upright position, the simple physical discomfort a relief from my raging emotions.

I tiptoed along the edge of the yard so as not mess up the surface before Oumar saw it. I took a quick shower and freshened up, then retrieved my sleeping mat from the house, thinking the heat and pressure from the sand would soothe my back like a hot water bottle. Only my butt and upper back touched the ground, so I turned on my stomach, heat searing through the thin fabric like hot breath. Then, the sensation of someone's fingertips drumming that spot, drumming my entire back, my legs like a massage. Rain. I smelled it as it thudded on the sand, took a deep breath, suddenly gloriously happy, turned over, feeling the drops on my face, opened my mouth, tasted them on my tongue. Light rain, but more than a sprinkle. It lasted about five minutes, just enough to replace my bird pattern with its own.

The familiar sound of a truck outside the door. Then voices.

"Better put that out before we go in." Frankie.

I opened the door. "It rained!"

"Yes, Miss! Alhamdulillah!" Tala smiled and stubbed out her cigarette with the heel of her goat hide sandal.

"First time this year I turned on my wipers." Frankie.

"First time I've ever seen a Tuareg woman smoke."

Tala made the clicking sound of agreement in the back of her throat. "Oh!" she said. "This is where the breath comes from for smoke rings." She took Frankie's cigarette and blew a wobbly oval.

Frankie looked pleased.

"You know smoking is bad for your health." Someone had to counterbalance Frankie.

"Physical health," Frankie said. "So are a lot of things. Chewing tobacco, cola nuts, contaminated water."

I expected this from Frankie.

"No food, no power to help oneself," Tala added. "We used to thrive in the desert, but no longer. You see this."

I did not expect it from Tala. "Yes," I said. "Please, come in. I'll make tea," I said, gathering the sugar and tea as I spoke, the brazier, the teapot.

Frankie always took advantage of the latrine before anything else. This time she lit up first. I thought about the stench of the bathroom in the hotel in Agadez. Did the latrine smell bad, and I'd gotten used to it? Was I losing it? It felt like it, but it always felt that way around my period. Overwhelming chaos and catastrophe. "The fuckin' moon," Frankie would say. If I waited a few days for the hormones to moderate, everything balanced out. Patience.

Frankie exited the latrine blowing smoke-rings like the smokestack on a cartoon train.

She made Tala laugh. I wondered if Tala knew Frankie was female. I wondered if it mattered.

"I can't imagine ever thriving in this place." Frankie. "It's difficult enough to survive."

"It is, but the Nigerien government is trying to develop the country, right?" The reason I got my job and her, hers. "Imports, exports, education for all children."

"Uh, uh huh," Tala said.

The ambiguous sounding verbal cue for ultimately "yes." Frankie would figure it out in context.

Tala opened her empty palms and held them out to me.

"Miss. The nomads are being shut out of development. Ignored. President Kountché said the uranium would take care of everyone in the country. The mines are located in the desert, and they have provided nothing for us."

I glanced at Frankie leaning back in her chair, smoking with her eyes closed. "What would change it? Education, like you said in class the other day?"

"Tuareg students like me are limited to a primary education. We learn to read French and know just enough to realize our dire future but not enough to manage it. You know about the males leaving the country to find work so their families can survive?"

"Yes, Mariama's older son is one of them."

"And I can tell you stories of many more. None of us would choose to be exiled from this place. Mariama says that no matter where we go, the Ténéré, the desert, is our home. We may leave the desert, but it never leaves us, and we will always return to it."

"I believe that," I said.

"This is a place of instability and resilience like its people."

That too. The coal in the brazier was barely damp from the scant rain so when I lit some straw, it caught. I filled the teapot from the tukunya and added a handful of tea leaves. "Would you tell me your story, Tala?"

"Miss?"

"What it was like growing up. Your life before coming to school. Your family. Do you have siblings?'

Tala remained silent for a while. Frankie was cleaning her fingernails with the broken tip of my Swiss army knife. Must have left it in the latrine. Maybe I'd over-stepped with Tala, gotten too personal. I excused myself to the latrine to allow some space, to defuse any tension I'd created. When I returned, I talked about sweeping the pattern in my yard just before the rain, stoked the coals under the teapot, and poured the first bitter round.

"You two go ahead," Frankie said. I'll wait for the next round."

Tala covered her mouth with her hand, stifling a laugh. Nobody skipped rounds of tea.

Frankie didn't worry at all about being culturally sensitive. Maybe I tried too hard. Tala and I sipped the boiling tea. It had become such a habitual and necessary part of the day—whenever someone came to visit, whenever someone went to visit someone else—I couldn't imagine not drinking it. For me, the caffeine withdrawal involved not only a pounding headache, but the ache attached to my blood coursing all the way through my body like poison. Maybe the sugar my mothers always warned against. I thought of Gita.

"In the last drought," Tala began. "My family lost their camels, donkeys, and all but two of their goats. After the drought finally ended, it took time for the pastures to recuperate." She hesitated. "The desert took everything for itself. Mariama was my mother's sister. Now she is my mother."

"I'm so sorry. I didn't know." The last major drought ended in 1974, Tala around eight years old. I shivered. The animal bones revealed when the wind blew that we picked up while hunting for arrowheads were probably victims of that drought or another. I hadn't been to a burial, so I didn't know the ritual or burying place of people but did know that the nomads never referred to their dead by name. That Tala was sharing this much was surprising. Maybe she trusted me because Mariama did. Maybe Tala thought I was ready to hear it.

Frankie lit another cigarette and offered it to Tala, who waved it off.

"In the famine, we ate leaves or weeds if we could find them. Everyone depended on the charity of everyone else if anyone had anything, but most of us could only share the drought. It lasted five years."

I felt embarrassed for mentioning the occasional dry period in the Valley when the students and I planted sunflowers and tried to amend. "Our droughts are not as severe because we have resources to prevent and combat them. I've heard people are planting trees along the border of the desert to try to slow desertification, to keep the desert from taking more of the Sahel for itself." No idea how the trees would get enough water to survive.

Tala yawned, covering her mouth so the djinn couldn't enter. I'd been called on that before.

"Many people come from the West with their ideas to try to help, but sometimes they don't understand that our environment, our culture, is not like theirs. My grandmother said, our problems started with the French, in dix-neuf dix-sept, 1917. They created the artificial boundaries that carved the Sahara into separate countries and divided the nomadic tribes of the Azawak into seven different groups, making it more difficult to freely travel in search of food and water for their herds."

"Your grandmother is right, but if you hadn't been the nomads on the receiving end, would you have done the same?" Frankie.

I glared at Frankie. Our own government military forced the Native Americans from their land for its own purposes, drawing its own artificial boundaries for a culture it knew little about. It felt like history repeating itself. Did Frankie not see this?

Tala straightened up in the chair, lifted her chin. "Maybe. But we are nomads. Before the last drought, our amanukal, chief, owned herds of thousands of camels, cows, sheep, and goats that grazed in pastures extending into Algeria and Libya. Since then, most of us camp near the desert villages that have water pumps like those dug by U.S. AID in Tchin-Tabaraden. Sometimes anasaras get it right."

"Good to hear." I added more water and sugar to the teapot. Reading. I would concentrate on teaching reading English. The nomads could easily learn to speak English but reading English along with French would open the world to them, at least the region. If they had access to books. I needed to figure that out. I wondered what Frankie was thinking. If she were questioning her short-term philosophy. If she thought peddling cigarettes to the nomads was getting it right.

Patience scrambled over the wall then went straight for the bone under the acacia. I took advantage of the teaching moment, Tala doing the teaching. "I know having a dog for a pet is a Western, anasara, notion. Oumar says not to play with a dog because it will lick your mouth."

"That's a Kel Tamasheq saying referring to the unclean, but keeping a dog as a pet doesn't bother me. I find it amusing."

I hadn't heard this term. "What's Kel Tamasheq?"

"Most people call the nomads Tuaregs, an Arabic term that some interpret as meaning abandoned by God, but my mother said those people don't understand the desert or its people, that Allah gave us the desert. Allah gave us our animals, and Allah sometimes gives us droughts. She said it's a complex relationship that only we understand."

Tala paused. "But I've never understood it."

Frankie smiled at this.

"We call ourselves Kel Tamasheq, those who speak Tamasheq, but we aren't concerned that others call us Tuaregs. We're used to it, just as you get used to being called anasara by everyone but other anasaras."

Tala was right. At first, I considered it an insult to be generalized together with all people from the West as if we were all the same, but that generality was all they knew about me. Nothing personal. I actually preferred anasara to Miss but I'd gotten used to that here, too.

I served the second round of tea, raising my arm up over my head to pour it, the steaming stream of liquid gold funneling perfectly into each shot glass, as Oumar taught me for dramatic effect, although he said it cooled the tea.

Frankie shot me the overdoing-it look.

I knew we weren't supposed to talk politics but "Do you mind if I ask you a little about politics?"

Tala shrugged. "Tea unties tongues."

"I read that President Kountché ousted your first president in a coup because of how he mismanaged earlier droughts, but then he did no better. Now Ali Saibou is President. What do you think of him? Are things improving?"

"Don't you need to add some water and sugar to the teapot?" Frankie.

She didn't know anything about making tea, but she was right; I added.

"I hope that President Saibou addresses our nomadic issues, but we have always suffered from the government. It uses our landscape against us."

Frankie lit another cigarette. "Besides government corruption and ineptitude, there is the isolation of living in such a desolate place, surrounded only by sand controlled by political and economic boundaries."

"Do you think the government is corrupt?" I put it out there.

"Miss."

Too direct. Maybe dangerous. Niger's government, military. I looked at Frankie as if I meant the question for her.

She studied her cigarette for a good minute and finally

responded. "Niamey is a long way from Tchin-Tabaraden. Things pass through many channels, many hands. But regardless of the country, power corrupts. From what I know about the situation, more and more male Tuaregs have been going north to Algeria to work or to Libya to the training camps run by Ghaddafi. He's a strong proponent of the rights of the Arab and Bedouin, Tuaregs, the native people of the Sahara. The Popular Front for the Liberation of Niger, the FPLN, has its headquarters in Libya." Frankie took a drag. "Ghaddafi has promised the Tuaregs a revolution, hasn't he? For a Kel-Tamasheq state."

I'd never heard Frankie say anything serious.

"Yes," Tala said.

I poured and served the final round of tea, the one described as sweet like death.

Tala finished hers first, thanked me, and excused herself. Something at school.

I turned to Frankie. "That sounded like intel."

"Rothmans studies their markets. Foolish not to. Everyone knows the nomads are struggling. Living off the land can't last, especially in this sand, this environment. The Tuaregs all know it; it's fracturing them."

"You mean because the families are having to split up?"

"That, and the generations see the solution differently.

Tala, for example. You've said yourself how open she is, how much more direct than Tuaregs in general."

"Because I'm friends with Mariama. Plus, she's fluent with multiple languages."

"Maybe, but she is also the younger generation. She thinks differently, expresses herself differently from her parents and grandparents."

"That's how generations tend to work."

Frankie handed me her empty shot glass and shook another cigarette from her pack. "Do you mind?" she said as she lit up. Her signature grin followed by a deep drag. "Another lesson for the teacher."

She waited until I wrapped the chipped cone of sugar in its blue paper and took it inside, rinsed out the shot glasses, returned from the latrine, and finally sat back down.

"After the drought in 1974, the Tuaregs here in the Sahel essentially split into three different groups: the traditional and impoverished nomads, who would never complain, essentially prisoners of their own misery, the elite nomads who moved to the cities to try to find a viable way to survive by adapting to the environment, and the ishumar, the unemployed and disenfranchised who have been exiled and are biding their time to regain the honor and autonomy of the Kel-Tamasheq, the Tuaregs."

"What are you, a spy?"

Frankie's face lit up. "What do you think?"

"I think you know a lot about the Tuareg situation that has nothing to do with the Rothman packaging they prefer."

"Hard packs," she said. "For traveling."

Oumar appeared as I was finishing the evening watering of the sunflowers, where the sunflowers would be. I stared at each indention for any hint of green. Not yet.

He formally went through the greetings. Unusual for him, for us, then followed me from indention to indention as I methodically poured water from my cup. Usual. "You want to water?"

He made the negative sound with his lips. I know he thought I wasted water by pouring it onto the sand where it disappeared instantly.

"Why don't you wait for the rain like the grass does?"

Because I'm not that patient. Because I need to see a flower. Besides I thought some clever insect might discover the seeds underground and eat them before they germinated. "I thought I'd help Allah by getting them started, then let him take over with the coming rain."

Oumar leaned against the wall surrounding the porch, crossed his arms, and watched me.

"What's wrong?"

He shrugged.

"Mariama okay? The goats?"

"Mariama says, an eye that sees what it likes, keeps glancing."

I paused mid-pour. "What?"

"Mokao said you were looking at the goats in the middle of the night."

"I couldn't sleep." I lifted the gris-gris from my neck. "And I have this for protection against the djinn." I resumed watering.

"You weren't there to look at the goats."

I didn't want to discuss this with a kid or with anyone. "Is that what Mokao said?"

Oumar's smile lit up.

"He said he was pleased you'd come."

I couldn't believe he would tell Oumar about it. "He didn't seem pleased to me." I was glad I had to focus on what I was watering.

"You don't kiss someone on the lips."

As in certain people or anyone? "Is that some sort of offense?"

"Miss. It's." He wrinkled his face. "We never do it."

"Tuaregs don't kiss?"

"Not on the mouth!"

"But you kiss other places?" It just came out. He was probably glad I was concentrating on watering, too.

"Miss."

I glanced over at him. He covered his mouth with his hand.

"Please tell Mokao I apologize. I didn't mean anything by it. I didn't know."

"He knows."

"It won't happen again."

"Miss? Mokao likes Frank."

Of course he does. Everyone did. "I'll introduce them." They could work out the logistics.

"Miss?"

Finished watering, I put the cup back on the tukunya. Oumar was still studying me. "What."

"I thought you were going to meet the man who is looking for you."

"What man?" The Tuareg man at school with the hazel eyes?"

"An anasara."

"The anthropologist you thought was my father?"

"No, not him."

"Anthony?"

"Who?"

Maybe Joel had come for a visit from wherever he'd been posted.

"How old of a man?"

Oumar shrugged.

"What did he look like?"

"Dressed like a Tuareg, but his hair, pale. His eyes light."

I remembered the Tuareg I'd glimpsed driving out of town with Frankie with hair the bleached sand color of Roy's.

"Did you tell him where I lived?"

"Mariama said not to tell him anything."

"When did you see him?"

"Which time?"

"He's been here more than once?"

"He rides with Frankie sometimes."

Was that the Tuareg I saw get in the driver's side of the Scout after Frankie burned her hands? "Is he here now?"

"I haven't seen him today."

Anyone who wanted to see me would have shown up at school or stopped by my house. Everyone in town knew where the anasara worked and lived. Unless he didn't want me to know he was looking for me. That ruled out the anthropologist, Anthony, and Joel. Nick? But he would have driven his own taxi from Agadez. Had Roy traveled across the world to stalk me?

The thought of Roy brought up mixed feelings as it always did, especially when the moon was involved. I still loved him, would always, but I would never admit it to him, never get back with him. I could not go through losing him again. He knew that; I'd made it ever so clear. So why was he here? He knew I'd reject him. Did he I think I'd wear down? Thoughts ran through my mind as I lay on my mat, Oumar already asleep or pretending to be. My last thought: pissed that Roy would show up here after what I went through to get away from him. I already had to deal with him in my dreams, but even they had moved on from the sublimity of when we were together to the desolation at the end of the relationship.

Where did you go? Beside yourself, apart from the glare of time. Instinctually surviving such massacre of your making, the body carved by its own history, spontaneous souvenir.

It is clear now; the other you is dead, voice silenced, breath still. Cleaved so completely, perhaps you never were. What were you thinking? Arise and wander away from this place before it takes you, too. Don't listen to the wind's fingers of sound, signing in noiseless voice, useless phrases, pointless points. Move forward in any direction, at night when mirages are invisible to keep from sleeping when they are not.

It's best not to see, hear, feel the acidic aftertaste. Suck on aromaless, innocuous stones while you move the very stones that stoned you, pebbles, sand, glass ground between your teeth. There is no danger, no emotion, nothing but make believe.

Roy, finally gone, I dreamed me.

Frankie made the product drops on her route the week ahead of Ramadan. Most people in Tchin-Tabaraden besides children didn't travel, eat, or drink anything, let alone smoke during the day once the new crescent moon was spotted. I'd still not seen anyone smoking at all except Tala, but the shop owners kept buying more cigarettes.

"I imagine you're planning on fasting for Ramadan," Frankie said.

"Hadn't thought about it." I'd thought a lot about it and decided it was exactly what I needed to do. Divine intervention for my weakness of body and soul. Atonement for my misstep with Mokao.

"You're not a Muslim."

"I don't think Allah or anyone else around here cares about that."

Mariama had invited me to break the fast at her encampment during the month of Ramadan, and I thanked her but told her I would be doing my own version. Next year when I was whole again, I would participate with her family.

"What about you?"

"Me fast? Are you crazy? Why put yourself in such a vulnerable position? This landscape alone can fuckin' kill a person."

We carried on with class as usual, the students sharp as ever, couldn't tell they hadn't eaten for hours and wouldn't eat or drink for hours longer. I felt a little woozy the first couple of days but followed the pattern of eating and drinking at sunset, then again before I slept, after the first prayer at 4 a.m. when the muezzin called on the loudspeaker. I mimicked how I'd seen others pray and recited the words with the gestures, Allah 'akbar, God is great. Some words I knew the meaning of but others I repeated like lyrics, when you sing the words without understanding the meaning, some referring to passages I'd found in the Quran. Other sounds carried at that time of night, drumming, voices. I lay down and listened, dozing until before dawn when I drank water and ate protein, usually goat's meat or cheese Mariama continued to send with Oumar to break the fast. My own stash of powdered milk that was hard as a rock only when desperate.

During the day, I swallowed my saliva if I had any, and sometimes I watered my sunflowers before dark. After abstaining from drinking water, the biggest challenge, not drinking tea to get through the day. Oumar checked in before breaking the fast at Mariama's. I prayed the common prayers to Allah pre-dawn, noon, 4 p.m., 7-ish, and 9-ish and added in my own requests for forgiveness, for patience, for gratitude. I wrote a poem and sent it up to Gita:

Thirst is the mute language of desire, simple on the surface, complex in its depths. Everyone plumbs it eventually. First imbibing the prescient pleasure, plums fresh from the imagined tree to the parched mouth, one sweet violet moment on the tongue. Forgive that it doesn't last past the full-bodied erupting taste, past the quiet violence of consumption. Take, eat, as often as you can. But when you can't, learn the art of conservation, conversation. Discuss plums, politics, the poetry of water. Move toward each other. Wander together the barren landscape, Search. It will take every ounce you have lost in the process, but there is more beyond the surface.

Allah didn't answer my prayer for rain. I imagined he had notes about that tied in every fold of his garment—if he was a male, wore garments, and wrote prayers down—but even so I regained a sense of calm, of being, a reason for being here. I attributed much of that to fasting and praying. Emptying out. Cleansing. Opening my palms instead of making fists. I knew this but had forgotten it.

I'd quit dreaming of Roy and wondered about Frankie. Pointless to question her about driving Roy to Tchin-Tabaraden when she dropped off product. What difference did it make? In this place, you would give anyone a ride who needed one if you had the means. But Frankie herself? Two sides to her at least. Besides the male/female dynamic, the easy going, joking, charming persona with the engaging smile and glinting eyes as if she were talking to you personally, intimately, there was the articulate Tuareg intelligence she contributed in other circumstances. While it would be uncomfortable and complex to see Roy because I knew him so well, I was resolute in how I would handle it. Pure rejection, whatever it took. But Frankie was like no one I'd met before, and now I wasn't sure I knew her at all. It wasn't mistrust as much as the feeling that I was still wading in the shallow end.

By Tabaski, two months after Ramadan, I had fallen into a natural rhythm, slowing down, calming down. Maybe it was the desert environment exerting its dominance that I'd finally accepted or maybe it was Allah exerting his or her will, or maybe I was beginning to adjust.

The marabout faced east and with a quick movement sliced the goat's jugular vein before it even blinked. Sacrifice. Once the blood drained out, Mokao skinned the goat by gouging a hole in a back leg and blowing the animal up like a balloon. He hung it from its hind legs in a tree, as a crowd of children gathered to watch the ritual, then he removed the head, the local delicacy. It lay in the sand, one eye looking up at me. This should have been disturbing, but maybe because the process was respectful, because every part of the goat was used for survival, it was not. Mokao skinned the hide to transport and keep water cool, moved on to the organs.

I held out my hand for the knife and sliced some of the rich organ meat for the children, who ran off shrieking with delight.

Mokao moved on to the rest of the meat, wasting nothing.

I saved the prized head for Mariama and divided a third of the rest of the meat between Mariama, Oumar, Tala, whom I considered family, a third to Mokao and the Tuareg man with the hazel eyes and his family as a pardon of any offenses, and a third to the wandering madman, the neighbor children, and the students at school. I thought about taking some to Frankie, Nick, even Roy. Forgiveness, peace, and love, but would the meat keep? Food poisoning would be a disaster. Nick would think I was trying to kill him.

I opted to divide the meat locally, delivered it, and stayed at each place through every ritual of Tuareg tea. I felt forgiven, absolved, restored. Buzzed. Giving everyone the benefit of the doubt, including Roy, including myself.

It'd rained only the once for five minutes during the rainy season, but the nomads, both Tuaregs and Wodaabé, were prepping to go to In Gall where the Tuaregs celebrated the Cure de Salée, the salt cure, and the Wodaabé celebrated the Worso, the Geerewol. The annual reunion of nomads and, because of the curative power of saltwater and the typically rich pastureland, a reward for the herds.

"You and Frankie must go," Oumar said.

I fingered pommade through my short strands and scalp to add moisture. It'd already grown several inches since Frankie's barber had shorn it.

"So much of attractiveness is in your own head," Frankie said.

Sounded like something Gita would say. I could keep my head covered. Besides, was I really so shallow that I wouldn't go some-where because of my hair? I couldn't not go for that reason.

"I could drive us to the Cure de Salée; we could go and then leave whenever we want, when you need to. Mariama would love it."

The route from Abalak to In-Gall would take longer, but it was paved, worth it. Oumar, Mariama, the women I'd met braiding hair, Mokao. "All the nomads who aren't in school will be there. How can I go if my students can't?"

"I'll take product and we'll need some camping gear, but I think I could make room for a student."

After a rousing discussion on the Cure de Salée in class, I told Tala that Frankie planned to drive there.

"Miss! You're going too, yes?"

"I don't feel right going if the students can't."

"Miss, those with the opportunity to go will go. The students would think it's foolish not to."

"Frankie says there will be room to take one more person in the Scout."

"I would love to ride with you!"

Mariama had the tailor embroider a tekatkat, a white blouse stitched with the local designs in red thread for both Tala and me, and I bought some indigo cloth for Tala and Mariama. She offered to lend me some Tuareg jewelry to wear, and I took a few simple bracelets but left most of it for Tala. We got together to henna fresh patterns on the sides of our hands and feet.

Mariama handed me desert pants, robe, a tagelmust in sugar wrapper blue, and a pagne the same color with a black embroidered top. "Give this to Frank." Tell him, he can wear either one."

CHAPTER TEN
RAINY SEASON, EN ROUTE TO IN GALL 1989

A few days later, Tala, Frankie, and I left from my house, both wearing our best pagnes, tops, and new goat hide sandals. Frankie wore her khakis and Rothmans shirt.

"Way to get in the spirit of things."

"All that cloth makes me claustrophobic. Besides, it's a fire hazard if you smoke and talk with your hands like I do."

"What about the pagne and blouse?"

"I don't want to suddenly dress like a woman. It'll fuckin' confuse people."

Tala laughed. "Mr. Frank, everyone knows you're a woman."

Frankie took her eyes off the road to look directly at me.

"You told her?"

"No," Tala and I both responded.

"Then how did you know?"

Tala shrugged. "We just know."

I didn't just know but I kept that to myself. Tala changed the subject and talked about the recent run on purses and accessories at the Friday market in Tchin-Tabaraden this time of year.

"The men buy up anything that's bright, that will move, catch light, or draw attention in some way."

"Shiny objects." Frankie.

Tala considered. It wasn't a word we'd discussed in class. It only took seconds for her to figure it out.

"Shiny, yes. Zippers, locks, watchbands, and always traditional Tuareg silver—they clean it all with Omo, you know, the laundry soap, and a lemon if they're lucky enough to find one, until everything shines, then mix the silver with leatherwork, shells, and feathers. The males accentuate their feminine beauty with makeup and extravagant accessories trying to get the attention of the females."

"Cross-dressing. You'll fit right in, Frankie. Sort of."

"You know what this fête is about, yes?" Tala gestured with her fingers as I did in class to elicit multiple responses.

"A reunion of nomads in the area." I looked at Frankie.

"A celebration of the rainy season, such as it is."

"Access to salt and pasture for the animals."

"And?"

"A courtship ritual for the Wodaabé."

"The place to marry the person you want. Teegal. The opposite of an arranged marriage. Koobgal."

"Do you know Mokao?" Tala to Frankie.

"Never met in person, but I know him as the Wodaabé truck driver who gave Lark a ride to Tchin-Tabaraden. The herder Lark got her goats from, her dog from. What am I forgetting? Oh yeah, the one she kissed."

"I never told you about that."

"I just know. Everyone does."

"Mokao is dancing at the Geerewol," Tala said. "He's favored to win the beauty contest."

CHAPTER ELEVEN
RAINY SEASON, CURE DE SALÉE, GEEREWOL, WORSO, IN GALL 1989

Frankie parked outside the encampment itself, and we walked in on foot. The hundreds of camels ornamented with colorful Tuareg saddles, tasseled silver bridles, and thousands of herders decked out in shimmering indigo cloth, copious silver rings, earrings, bracelets, gold necklaces, elaborate hairstyles and headdresses, the Wodaabé and their herds of Zebu cattle exactly how Tala described it on the drive there. I stood still and saw for myself the colorful display of life under a sky of bleached slate. If it rained, they would celebrate that.

Besides the nomads driving their herds along the fringes of the encampment, Tala explained that the women were unpacking their household finery and putting it on display. I counted fifty ceremonial carved calabashes of different sizes and patterns that one Wodaabé woman arranged on tables. Tala said the white substance I thought was paint, used to emphasize the designs, was curdled milk. She pointed out the men constructing temporary shelters out of branches with grass carpets that would serve for the Geerewol dance events.

Drumming and ululating erupted, the crowd growing raucous. Tala grabbed my hand, pulling me along. "Camel dances," she shouted in my ear. I glanced back to see Frankie keeping pace. She moved in little stutter steps, sashaying sideways, following us through the sea of people like a nymph or maybe a djinn.

A long line of riders took turns performing for the audience. A pure white camel decked out with multi-colored leather fringed headgear with a string of small bells that hung from its neck and a tasseled colorful blanket across its back stepped forward. The camel looked regal with its Tuareg saddle and ornate gear and held its head accordingly. The rider, dressed in traditional indigo robes and tagelmust, only his eyes visible, trotted the camel to the center of the spectators, side-stepped in one direction and then in the opposite direction. He spun, with one of the camel's back legs planted, making a 360-degree circle, and repeated it in the other direction planting the other hind leg. "Zéro!" people were shouting. Then the rider tapped his camel and it bent down on its front knees crawling and jingling the bells until it was a couple of feet in front of a Tuareg woman. She looked stunning with the indigo scarf draped over her woven hair, a Tuareg gold necklace shining in the filtered light through the clouds. The camel bowed its head and stood up again as the crowd cheered and the women ululated.

"Those two will marry."

"So, his performance singling her out is like a marriage proposal. His skills are impressive."

"Especially for an anasara."

"What? From where?"

"Agadez."

I laughed out loud even imagining it could be Nick.

Agadez was a big place, must be someone else. "Do you know his name?"

Tala shrugged. "Camel races!"

The camels ran full out, hooves kicking up dust, the cloth of the mounted nomads billowing out behind them toward a finish line I couldn't see, the crowd going wild. Women wearing tekatkat, the white blouses embellished with red thread patterns like Mariama had given Tala and me, sat majestically on tasseled red and turquoise leather cushions and blankets, rolled to display their colorful diamond or striped patterns.

I estimated hundreds of nomads, twice the number of animals. We walked past the area where people could buy camels, cattle, goats, or sheep for transportation, milk, or meat. An impressive nomadic market.

As everyone else, Tala and I were dressed up for the occasion. Tala paired her blouse with a black pagne embroidered with white thread and draped the indigo cloth around her head, the ends hanging past her shoulders. I wore my blouse with a pale blue pagne embroidered in black along one edge and a blue and black scarf that I thought looked good. Frankie wore her traditional navy polo with the Rothmans embroidered in white script and a clean pair of khakis. If Mariama hadn't gifted me the blouse, I wouldn't have worn it. It felt uncomfortable dressing in something so meaningful to the nomads and their special occasion. Though rude to disregard another's gift, I knew that Mariama would take no offense to Frankie rejecting both outfits she'd given to her. She'd probably laugh about it. Somehow, people understood Frankie or were drawn to her regardless.

The complex henna patterns stained on the sides of my hands and feet felt more natural to me. Maybe because some people dyed their hair with henna at the commune. Mariama had woven a gris-gris into my mini braids, and I wore some of her bangles on my wrists. Tala and I were holding hands as nomads do, milling through the Ifulan, the Fulani, Wodaabé camps, following a group of young women and girls. They wore dozens of colored glass and plastic beads and cowrie shell bracelets on their arms, some with thick bronze anklets, and multiple silver hoop earrings lining the perimeters of their ears. The scarification patterns on their faces, little fans on each corner of their lips, a series of tiny rectangles under their eyes, and cross-hatch markings on the forehead and chin, were darkened with kohl, and bundles of leather gris-gris mixed with the necklaces swung from their necks.

In contrast with the Tuareg, the fabric the Wodaabé women wore was black with striped and hieroglyphic patterns in red, white, and yellow thread in their juxtaposing scarves, blouses, and pagnes. They looked at the displays of other women's possessions as they walked, and when they saw something they especially liked, they clapped, sang, and danced.

I glanced up at one point and mentioned to Frankie that I felt, and then saw, a Tuareg man staring at me. I wasn't close enough to see his eyes to determine if I could recognize them, but the way he was standing looked familiar.

"With these kinds of celebrations, the usual decorum is a lot more relaxed," Frankie said.

As if she knew about decorum. Maybe she did and intentionally ignored it. Sometimes we caught a glimpse of a man primping his hair and makeup in a tiny hand mirror for the Geerewol, the Wodaabé beauty contest. I'd brought my camera but felt torn between it being more insulting to take their pictures or not to take their pictures. I decided just to take everything in for the moment, maybe I'd get it out for the dance. The contestants' clothing and makeup even more elaborate. Besides braiding shells, coins, beads, and gris-gris into their hair, they painted their faces red or ochre, depending on the dance, often with black, red, or white stripes down their noses and other decorative markings to accentuate their features. Their eyes were ringed with kohl and their lips blackened to provide contrast for the whites of the eyes and teeth, which along with their height, they considered especially beautiful. Maybe next year they'd be using sunflower shell dye. The conical straw hats or turbans with ostrich or horsehair feathers made them appear even taller.

Oumar stood with Frankie and me watching the yaake dance. The goal was to show charm and charisma through facial expressions.

The men's faces painted ochre accented with black and red designs. Lined up, moving slowly forward together, bending their knees and then rising on tiptoe, nodding and wagging their heads and again rolling and crossing their wide-open eyes to emphasize the whites. Alternatively making exaggerated smiles and puckering their lips making sounds that reminded me, at least, of kissing, then speeding up their movements and sounds to ratchet up the spectators even further. One man quivered his eyes directly at Frankie.

"Mesmerizing," she said. "I can't look away."

None of us could. Slow-motion ecstatic dancing.

Afterward, Oumar led us through the throng of people zigzagging through a maze of tents for several kilometers.

"How can you find your way?" Frankie.

"Tracks in the sand," Oumar said, gesturing with his chin to the trampled sand, then laughed. "It's organized by tribes and families."

When we reached Mariama's camp, we greeted her and the extended family, Mariama introducing everyone.

"Is your husband here?" I asked.

She put her hand on her heart. "No."

"He, her son, Ahmed, and thousands of others will be returning with the mass reintegration from Libya and Algiers," Tala explained. "This is what we are celebrating. Come eat!"

"I thought Mariama's husband had taken their herd to find grass."

"They have no herd now, just the goats Oumar is watching," Tala said.

The goats were here, too, grazing with all the other livestock from the region.

"And thousands of nomads exiled? I'd imagined dozens."

Tala ignored this and passed the bowl of milk. "Drink."

We passed the communal bowls of meat, millet, and milk, using our own wooden spoons to eat, drink. I took some to be polite but didn't have an appetite.

Frankie ate enthusiastically and dribbled some milk on her shirt.

Mariama said something, and Tala translated. "You have plenty of other clothes."

Frankie said, "Tell her I'm not worthy of such beautiful desert clothes. I'm saving them for Oumar and Izza."

I was still thinking about the exiles. "When are they coming?"

"Who?" Mariama said.

"Your husband, Ahmed, the exiles?"

"Soon," Mariama.

"We call them ishumar, the unemployed, those who had to leave our country to find work," Tala explained. "President Saibou is inviting them back to work through our history of difficulties. He says he wants to reunite everyone."

"That's wonderful news!" No wonder they were celebrating. I reached out my hands for the bowl of milk and drank.

After eating, the older people stayed in or went back to their tents, while the young gathered more centrally, and the music really started. Drums and strings. They sang about love and warriors, their history. The drumming emanated from my gut and reverberated through my entire body. The lyrics were always in Tamasheq, and I could only understand a word here and there—ténéré, desert, ehan, tent, iloudjan, camel, akh, milk, tindé, drum, adhou, wind, tafoud, thirst, tafouk, sun, aman, water, achai, tea, l'horba exile, assouf, longing—but I easily recognized the syncopated rhythms as the gait of camels. The mortar drummer picked up the beat and another pounded on a hollowed-out calabash floating in a shallow tub of water. They called it an asakalabo. The music had a bluesy sound. Anzads, the single stringed guitars, and a couple of western guitars, women's, sometimes men's, voices. I could make out some themes: honor, the desert, longing, water, power/Kaocen.[1] The western guitarists were the ishumar, the unemployed, who had had enough. I picked up from some ragged strings of conversation that all the exiles were waiting to see if what President Saibou said was true about the Tuaregs gaining their due and their respect. Mariama said that she hoped it was true that they would be welcomed and reunited. Someone else said they would make it so.

Oumar grabbed my hand and Frankie's sleeve. "It's almost time for the Geerewol! We can't miss Mokao!"

We ran to catch up with Tala, but she disappeared into the crowd.

The spectators stood in a semicircle facing the dancers with the men on one side and the women on the other.

"Anasaras can stand on either side," Oumar said.

Because we didn't fit, but we were welcome. Frankie naturally embraced this. I tried not to overthink and just be present at the famous beauty and endurance contest.

Oumar explained that the men's faces were painted red so that their natural beauty could be more clearly judged, and each wore a woman's pagne pulled tight across the hips and tied at the knees with a leather thong, restricting them to tiny steps to accentuate their long, lithe limbs and silhouettes. "Miss. They will love if you take their pictures."

I removed the pagne draped over my shoulder, took the lens cap off my camera, adjusted for lighting and captured these images: A leg adorned with an iron anklet with rings that clanked in rhythm with the dance. Close-ups with colorful beads, glinting silver jewelry, and leather bundles of gris-gris. Strings of white beads across a torso leading to multiple narrow decorated belts wound around the waist, again emphasizing their forms. A sinewy arm bound with leather bands and goat hide with the white fur still intact. Faces framed with long strands of shells, beads, and dyed leather. A white feather that stood up from a stark white headband.

"Ostrich plume," Oumar said.

I took another full frame from ostrich plume to ceremonial staff.

"The dancers don't eat much but drink a strong mixture of pounded bark and grass mixed with fermented milk to increase their endurance, their skill, their beauty."

Their features seemed genderless, both genders, the face paint captivating, the accessories definitely drawing attention. A magical, ephemeral beauty.

There were maybe fifty dancers, at first chanting then swaying and turning their heads left and right, big smiles and wide eyes showing the whites. After some time, they danced faster, stomping the ground with their feet, controlling the emotions of the crowd. This trance-like state continued for at least an hour, all of us hypnotized by the dancers and the flickering bonfire. Frankie wasn't even smoking. I kept shooting pictures. Some of them looked directly into the camera and posed.

"Watch. Mokao will win," Oumar said.

"Which one is Mokao?" Frankie whispered in my ear.

"Not sure." I loaded another roll of film.

Finally, an old woman dressed in black came out from the crowd, walking up to the dancers, studying each one intently. Some other old women joined her, also scrutinizing the dancers, who themselves remained focused and emotionless, even when the women callously dismissed someone they didn't like or bowed and let out a shriek when they saw someone they did.

"That's Mokao," Oumar said pointing with his chin to the man the old women were admiring.

When the women were through, there were only a dozen men they hadn't eliminated. Then three stunning young women came out, acting totally uninterested but watching the dancers' every move in their peripheral vision. After a few minutes, the young women sank to their knees, their left hands shielding the left side of their expressionless faces for another twenty minutes or so. The crowd hollered and ululated in contrast, until finally each young woman chose the winner by getting so close as to touch him, but not quite touching him. The women all chose the same man.

As Oumar predicted, Mokao won, the most attractive, seductive, and captivating among them. I captured the image and put away my camera, leaving some shots to take of Mariama and her family if she wanted.

"I feel like he's looking right at me," Frankie said.

"He is. Want me to introduce you?"

"Not now. I need a cigarette. She fumbled for her matches, her hand trembling slightly as she lit up. "Let's walk."

We wended through the crowd, through the drumming, the people, animals, tents, beyond the commotion. Paused by the lake, where some white birds—egrets?—preened in the water and people sat along the banks watching the long-limbed graceful birds that Oumar said the Wodaabé dancers tried to emulate. I stopped to take a photo before continuing into the bush. The sky silver, the crowd sounds so muffled we could hear the wind blowing through the blades of grass, then someone walking in small, hurried steps toward us. We both turned toward the sound.

"Foo-foh, hello," Frankie greeted Mokao with her limited Fulfulde vocabulary.

He smiled, his black stained lips revealing unnaturally white teeth. His makeup had run some; there were two trails where beads of sweat had run the length of his face from his temples. He advanced so that he was standing extremely close to Frankie, not quite touching. No introductions necessary, I started walking back toward camp. Slowly.

"Teegal," I heard him say.

Then "Sey jaango."

That either meant "See you tomorrow" or "Goodbye."

Frankie caught up with me within minutes.

"What'd you say?"

"I greeted him."

"No, when he asked you to marry him."

"What?"

"Teegal. Remember? He wants to marry you."

"I know what he meant, but I don't think a marriage is necessary."

"You'd make a striking couple."

We walked on in silence. Frankie may have been thinking of Mokao, but I was thinking of thousands of displaced Tuaregs coming to Tchin-Tabaraden. Thinking that if it involved children, I could start a new class. Thinking I could help deliver the necessary supplies so many people would need. "Have you heard the term 'ishumar' before?"

Frankie lit another cigarette exhaling the smoke in a sigh. "The unemployed Tuaregs who left for Libya and Algeria to find work and are finally returning home."

"Right, but when we were talking about it, Mariama's expression, response seemed subdued rather than excited."

We walked past some children that were kicking a ball they'd fashioned from rags.

"For years, the government has not wanted the Tuareg exiles back," Frankie said, her voice lowered. She took another drag, sighed again, and continued. "In what seems a good faith effort to establish a relationship between them and the Nigerien government, President Saibou along with Abdoulmoumine Mohamed, a Kel Tamasheq leader, met with the ishumar community, and he invited them to return home to Niger."

I quieted my voice, too. "That's what I mean. This sounds like the most positive thing I've heard regarding the nomads since I arrived. After all the years of hostility between the Kel-Tamasheq and the Nigerien government, President Saibou has promised that all will be pardoned."

Frankie looked behind us, and seeing no one, continued. "From my view, the government has been hostile to the Tuaregs, the nomads, since Niger's independence in 1960, denying them assistance during droughts resulting in loss of their pastural livelihood. When entrepreneurial nomads have tried to start businesses in town, they shut them down. The nomads are treated not only as if they don't exist but as if they don't deserve to exist."

"The nomads have valid trust issues, but the ishumar did meet privately and decided to accept Saibou's offer. They've chosen the path of peace and reconciliation."

"That's one way to look at it."

We walked on in silence. I wondered why Mariama never told me her husband was one of the ishumar but led me to believe he was searching for grass and water for their animals. Maybe she thought it none of my business. Maybe he didn't want her to. I wondered if he still thought I was a spy.

Passing the lake, Frankie said she thought she saw Mokao. "I'll find my way back."

"Sure, have fun. See you later." I walked toward camp. It was too dark to see well, which heightened sounds. Drumming, the chiming of bells, animals lowing, an occasional high human note, someone singing, a disembodied voice.

"No, Miss."

The voice seemed to originate from the landscape itself, but then two figures materialized, one moving toward me, the sound of bells. A woman, I could make out now, a queen.

"Salaam alyakum. You shouldn't be here."

It was Tala. "Alyakum a salaam."

"We were looking for you."

She looked stunning, gris-gris and strands of small bells woven into her hair. I reached out to grasp her palm and startled at the sword in her hand.

"The djinn, Miss. They are waiting for the single women."

I glanced toward the other figure watching us.

"To steal those to be married, for themselves," she explained.

A wad of tobacco balanced on her lip as she spoke.

"Are you getting married, Tala?" Her companion stood in the shadows.

"Koobgal," she said. "Arranged before my birth. I won't be coming back to Tchin-Tabaraden."

"What about your education?" I said, but I meant that I'd miss her.

"Don't worry about me, Miss."

"No, of course I won't. I know you can take care of yourself. Wait, a photo." I focused the Roelli.

Tala arranged her hair and looked straight into the camera, her regal pose.

Then I took another shot with the used Polaroid my mothers had sent. No one even knew I had it yet. My mothers said the film was really expensive; they only sent photo paper for a dozen exposures.

"Watch," I said, holding the corner of the photo paper and fanning it in the air, as Tala's likeness gradually appeared. With less lighting, it was a little under-exposed but very clearly her.

"L'allah," Tala said, waving her fiancé over. "Polaroid! Like a mirage opposite. I love!"

Her fiancé was completely swathed in desert garb. Difficult to even guess his age. At least not an old man. He looked directly into the camera, eyes the gray-brown color of acacia bark. Again, I captured a shot with the Roelli for myself and one with the Polaroid for Tala.

"Alhamdulillah," the man said as the couple's image developed before their eyes.

"Here," I said, handing the camera to Tala. "A wedding gift. But there're only ten pictures left unless you can find more photo paper."

"Don't worry, Miss."

I watched the couple disappear into the dusk and continued on. The sky overcast, only a few stars visible away from the firelight.

I felt someone following me and turned to face the person. "Lark," he said.

I recognized the voice, the stance. Djinn. Roy's ghost, but I didn't acknowledge its existence. I remained indifferent, in control. The desert had taught me that much. I kept moving forward. When I reached our camp, I unrolled my mat and lay down inside the tent and heard my voice outside myself.

Mechanical motion, so like the real thing. No rush, no time but the present direction. Keep moving toward water, toward rain. This is your body; do it in remembrance. Follow the dogs, stoned themselves, to the well. No water yet, no reflection. Even if there were, there wouldn't be. Matter doesn't always.

Moving is everything. Only stop to get a drink. Be smart: Walk at dark, find shade after noon, take a camel, a scorpion's horse. Even if you could care, you wouldn't. Moving is the only thing. All else is past, waste. Concentrate on the surface, beyond which is oblivion, infinity. Stay focused on the patterns in the sand, Harmattanic art, tracks from someone else still moving. You are not alone. Nomads are sweeping patterns in the sand with bundles of sticks, a language everyone eventually learns, a recognizable repetition of symbols.

Try to see the big picture, the abstract pleasure under your feet, toughened now against the heat, a hide you can live with, deep fissures designed on leather skin. Beyond pain, unrecognizable but practical. Wash the dust off with spit; you have arrived.

When I got up the next morning, there was a scorpion on my mat where the small of my back had been.

CHAPTER TWELVE
COLD SEASON, TCHIN-TABARADEN 1989

A knock on the gate. The cold season wasn't as hot as usual, but the wind pelted sand at my face on a more regular basis. Frankie must have forgotten something. "I was joking the other day, Frankie. You don't have to wait for me to invite you in," I said as I opened the corrugated gate.

"Lark."

Roy. Again. This time in broad daylight. The sun shone on us like a spotlight. His hazel eyes. His voice, a single note that reverberated deep in my gut. Dressed in light blue Tuareg garb, his blonde hair visible along the edges of his turban. My body wanted to pull him to me, kiss where his hair grazed his temple, work my way to his mouth, but I looked through him as I'd trained myself to do. My eyes blank. I read initial shock in his eyes before he blinked and recovered. Judging my appearance as if that had anything to do with anything ever again. Still, a cut, barely perceptible on the surface but deep. I didn't flinch but wedged my foot against the bottom of the gate. "What are you doing here?"

"I wanted to see you. Knew you went to Africa, did some research and found you went to one of the most desolate regions in one of the poorest countries on earth."

I heard "what the hell" in the pause.

"Wanted to see if you're all right. Got concerned when I saw you at the Cure de Salée. You acted like you didn't know me, couldn't see me."

"I'm fine."

"You're. You look a little anemic or something. Maybe it's that outfit."

I happened to be wearing one of my better pagnes, the green plant leaf pattern not yet faded from the sun and my celery colored tee.

"Wild sandals."

I glanced down. He was wearing his old Chucks, sand now embedded between the rubber toe and the off-white canvas. He wore them when we met every night at my secluded place in the field of grass, under the field of stars. I liked sleeping outside, making love on the land, brought him into it. I'd wake up in the night seeing those shoes, a strange object glowing on the natural landscape. Seeing them now made me want to lay my pagne on the sand, introduce him to the desert stars, entire galaxies, the magnified moon.

"What's that around your neck?"

"I said I'm fine, Roy." I glared at his eyebrows to avoid his eyes and raised my voice. "Now get the hell out of here, leave me alone, and go back to your own life." I know I said that about peace, love, and benefit of the doubt after Ramadan, but you can't give a former love an opening unless you want to open yourself back up. It's your only chance for control, for survival. I'd learned that much.

"Lark. I've come all this way. Can we just talk?"

"We said everything in the States. There's nothing left."

Frankie knocked as if Roy wasn't standing there beside her, and I wasn't looking right at her.

"I heard yelling. Everything okay? Roy said you were old friends, wanted to surprise you."

"Your intelligence isn't quite accurate, but he did surprise me, and he's just leaving, apparently with you." Awkward silence.

"Everyone's still at the Cure de Salée, so there's no reason to be here, to stay. A wasted trip all around, I guess."

Frankie headed for the latrine taking in the sunflower seedlings. "I like what you're doing with the landscaping." Over her shoulder.

Roy. "You're not even going to invite me in?"

He unwrapped his turban. It draped around his neck, exposing his face, his skin still smooth, his supple lips protected from the sun. His hair longer than mine, silky. He craned his neck, took in the yard: the rows of fragile sunflower plants, the spindly acacia tree with my laundry draped over it to dry, the faded string chairs, the brazier with a cold enamel teapot, the porch, the outside of the house. Patience had gone to the Cure de Salée for all I knew. Some guard dog. "No, I'm not."

Frankie appeared and lit a cigarette. I couldn't take another six minutes or however long it took to smoke one. I gestured toward the semi open gate. "Bye," I said to Frankie. "Nice gris-gris."

"Got it at the autogare."

The sunflowers were now taller than Oumar due to my constant watering and a little goat manure. Some with green flower heads.

"Magic," Oumar said.

"You know about magic?" I was thinking "Jack and the Beanstalk."

"Yes."

I tried to make it fit. "Like the gris-gris the marabout makes?"

Oumar made the negative sound with his lips. "Magic from sorcerers."

"But not as potent as this." I held up my gris-gris.

"Both are powerful."

"How do you know which type you have?"

"If you get a gris-gris from a marabout, you know it is authentic. Like yours."

"Frankie got a gris-gris from an autogare. What about that?"

"Only locals trying to make money from tourists who don't know any better would sell them there."

So maybe Frankie wasn't a spy or maybe she was and played ignorant. "Do you think Frankie is a tourist or a spy?"

Oumar side-stepped. "Marabouts are holy men. Their words are from the Quran. They don't do their business in large public and defiled places like the autogare or the marché."

"What if the man in the autogare bought the gris-gris, for example, for safe travels, from an authentic marabout and then sold them in the autogare as a convenience to non-locals?"

"It doesn't work like that."

"So, the amulet Frankie bought is worthless?"

"Not worthless. It just wouldn't have come from a marabout, but it could have been sorcery."

"Is there a gris-gris against sorcery?"

"Yes, Miss."

I cupped the unripened head of a sunflower. "This is science," I said. "It's powerful, too."

"When are they going to look like the pictures?"

"Some of them may bloom soon; others another month, another moon."

"And they'll look like the pictures?"

"Yes, and you can take the seeds with you when you're herding and eat them when you're hungry."

"Do they taste like dates?"

"No. Not sweet. More like the first round of tea, but salty rather than bitter."

He looked doubtful.

CHAPTER THIRTEEN
COLD SEASON SANDSTORM, EN ROUTE
NEAR TCHIN-TABARADEN 1989

"The gris-gris worked," Frankie said. "The vendors are back to normal, better than normal after their time at the Salt Cure."

The placebo effect? The power of positive thinking? I wasn't here to figure out Frankie and what she knew or didn't know. Whatever. "I feel like going for a drive."

"Let's go." Frankie lit a cigarette, "Where to?"

I knew she'd be up for it. "The bush. Beyond where I go walking." I finished watering the sunflowers, emptying the tukunya. I'd get up in the middle of the night and refill it.

"Not off the laterite road, even for a few minutes."

Oddly, sometimes Frankie sounded very hands on hips.

"That's all it takes to get disoriented."

"Okay, the laterite road then," I conceded. "I'll drive, and you can tell me if I veer off."

I ignored Frankie's previous statement about not being a good passenger. Her Scout was an automatic and there was no traffic. Probably the reason she agreed to let me drive. White with rust damage, the Scout actually looked like a tank at close range. The driver's side window open, the cab still smelled like smoke, petrol, and tobacco. I put it into gear and drove out of town, children running alongside to race us. I let them win.

Frankie pointed to a couple of wooden stakes pounded into the sand. "That's the road. See it?"

Barely. "Yes." The stakes marked the different texture, more like a snow cone than sand. I could see it if I concentrated hard, but if a tourist were tired, it would be so easy to miss it, to forget momentarily and get lost.

"You might pick up the speed a little, your pace is putting me to sleep."

I accelerated. Flat, no traffic, easy. Frankie smoked and took in the scenery. She was right. It felt good to be the driver in control rather than the passenger at the mercy of the driver. She rolled down the passenger window, a good cross breeze through the cab. I navigated the road for a good thirty minutes of silence. Neither of us brought up Roy. She had gathered my position on that situation: I didn't want to talk about it. For my part, I appreciated the silences of conversations, no longer feeling the necessity to fill them. Driving faster, I let any thoughts about the past blow out the open window and back behind us. Then the wind suddenly picked up with some velocity; dried plant life darted in front of us. Felt like the onset of the previous sandstorm.

Frankie the first to speak. "Maybe you're finally going to get your wish for some rain."

"I don't think it's rain," I said. "We should turn around. Might be a sandstorm."

"I'll drive," Frankie said.

I immediately pulled to a stop in the middle of the road. We switched places. Frankie revved the engine and did a donut to turn the Scout around. Such a show-off.

As she drove, the sand lifted around us. I rolled up the passenger window. Even with the steel protection of the Scout, Frankie's shirt whipped in the wind rushing through her window. Her binding might have protected her tenderest skin, but even my face and arms stung from exposure, sand peppering us like sleet.

"Pull your shirt over your nose and mouth as a filter," I said, pulling my shirt over my nose and mouth.

Frankie ignored me, drove faster, trying to make it to the village before the storm, saying the truck might get swept up in a flash flood.

"Those are silica clouds," I said. She didn't seem familiar with sandstorms. When it grew darker, she turned the headlights on full beam. It made it more difficult to see, the constant dizzying movement of the particles of sand. Reminded me of the Aralen dream I'd had when the nurses mistook dysentery for malaria, and I'd overdosed. Frankie switched headlights to dim as you would to see better in fog or heavy rain, but it made no difference.

"I can't see the road. We're going to have to stop."

She pulled off what may have been the sand road onto what she imagined the sand shoulder for safety, as if there were a difference and anyone else would be driving in this.

"I've never driven in a sandstorm."

The wind was blowing so hard, she couldn't get her cigarette lit. "It'll be okay," I said. "Seriously, Frankie, pull your shirt over youth mouth and nose as a filter. It's not good to breathe in sand." I got as comfortable as I could, slunk down into the seat, and closed my eyes. Every time I started to doze, Frankie would say something.

"In this situation, it's best to stay in place, so you don't get more lost."

We had already determined this, but Frankie continued to fill the staticky silence. She seemed afraid. This surprised me about her. I knew the storm would pass and we would figure our way back with reason and a clear head. "I don't think we're lost," I said. "You stopped when you couldn't see the road, and we're only thirty minutes out."

I listened to the static like white noise.

"Getting lost can happen so quickly; you don't realize."

"We might as well get some rest until it blows over, then we can reevaluate." I sort of turned over for emphasis.

"Someone's coming."

"What?" I sat upright in the seat, shaded my eyes like a visor, and squinted through the windshield. "Someone else is driving in this? Where?"

"Maybe it's a djinn."

I almost laughed. "Not likely, besides we're wearing our gris-gris for protection against them unless yours is a fake."

"It's a Tuareg. Eleven o'clock. See?"

I could barely make out the blur of a figure crouched over moving against the wind. As it got closer, I saw the tail of his turban trailing like a kite behind him.

"Maybe someone saw us and is coming to lead us back to Tchin-Tabaraden," Frankie said.

"No. It's a djinn. Roy."

"Why would he be walking in a sandstorm?"

"He's having trouble letting go."

"What is it with you two?"

So, she knew. "It's over between us, but you keep giving him a ride to Tchin-Tabaraden."

Roy grabbed the door handle, and Frankie let him in.

"You're fuckin' crazy," Frankie said.

I said nothing and neither did Roy. He was, though.

"I'm driving. You'll have to sit in the middle."

Roy crawled over and now sat between Frankie and me. Bizarre and unnerving. I slid over as far to the passenger door as possible, but I couldn't get away from his familiar scent, cracked the window and dozed with my head against the glass.

It became light again sometime the next day, not the stark brightness I'd grown used to. The wind had moved on, the dust remained suspended as if gravity didn't exist, but at least we could see, sort of. Roy's knee was touching my thigh. I pretended not to notice.

Frankie looked around to gain her bearings, but the entire

landscape had shifted; the few recognizable landmarks I thought I'd remember, no longer existed.

I heard grit in the hinges as Frankie pushed open the door through the eddies of sand that had whirled against it. The outside of the truck was shiny like Patience had been after the last storm. The Harmattan even sandblasted the rust off. I pointed this out, but Frankie couldn't hear it because she couldn't see the road. She thought it blew away. I thought it still there but buried. Roy, to his credit, kept his mouth shut.

"Fuck," Frankie said. She drank some water and passed the canteen to Roy, who drank and passed it to me. I made no eye contact with him, didn't acknowledge his presence in any way, only the presence of water.

"That wind must have been blowing 50 miles an hour. I didn't think I was going to make it," Roy said.

Frankie lit a cigarette, blowing the smoke out her window. The only reason we'd let him in the vehicle, or maybe I was reading into Frankie's actions.

The sun stayed hidden in the dusty atmosphere, not that we could trust it for help. Although the road meandered some, I knew Tchin-Tabaraden was mostly west and thought if we continued straight ahead, we'd run into it. Our other option was to stay there and see if someone showed up. Like Mokao. The rest of the water in the jerry can of water in the back would last a couple of days if we rationed it.

We stayed in the shade of the car through the afternoon, drinking water.

"Do you carry a teapot?" I asked.

"No, I told you that the last time. I also don't carry tea or sugar. I only drink the stuff to be polite. Besides, we don't want to use up any water making tea."

"You're wearing a gris-gris now; I thought you might carry a teapot. Right back," I said, and hiked off a short distance to pee.

When I returned, Frankie was fiddling with the compass she said Rothmans issued to its drivers, while Roy studied the map.

"I understand true north and magnetic north but have no idea about the exact angles of our location."

"The wind was blowing from the east if that makes any difference," Roy said. "The sand dunes moving like waves."

I didn't react to his observations, but I'd love to have seen the desert moving like waves. All Frankie and I saw was a chaos of individual sand particles, moving, vibrating, colliding, bouncing off each other. "Tchin-Tabaraden has to be mostly west and south of us," I said. "Why don't we drive straight due west for fifteen kilometers. If we don't see Tchin-Tabaraden, we can drive south."

Frankie worried about this, said she couldn't figure a precise direction and didn't think we should risk driving without it, but by nightfall she was out of cigarettes. We drove west for several kilometers but did not see the village. Frankie veered south, then backtracked east. By then our water was gone. We stopped. Waited.

It grew dark. The sand in the air dissipated, the stars visible, but now our heads were fuzzy. We hadn't eaten for a couple of days. Our throats dry, our mouths parched. Cotton mouth, Roy used to call it.

Frankie studied the west, squinting. "Look, someone else's smoke in the distance. A fire. Fuckin' Tuareg tea. Unless it's a mirage. Are they visible in the dark?"

"Doubt it." Roy.

"Let's find out." Me.

We climbed back into the Scout and drove toward it.

We arrived at the campfire in one of the Tuareg encampments outside of Tchin-Tabaraden. I did not know the people, but they knew us, welcomed us. They apologized that there was no water for Tuareg tea, only the fire. They gave us food and gave Frankie a couple of cigarettes, since she asked, and invited us to stay the night. They said the sandstorm clogged the pumps. No water now, but eventually.

After loosely conversing with the family through a blend of French, Tamasheq, and charades, we lay on borrowed mats, our eyes watering from the blowing sand. Frankie seemed to immediately fall asleep. My tongue felt thick, my throat scratchy from particles of sand. Everyone else must have felt the same. I closed my eyes and tried to relax, but the sound of Roy's breathing made my heart race. I tried to match my breath with Frankie's, tried to meditate, to imagine a river within a grain of sand. My head pounded. Dehydration. And now Frankie lying on her back smoking a cigarette, miniature toxic clouds hovering over me.

CHAPTER FOURTEEN
COLD SEASON, TCHIN-TABARADEN 1989

In the morning we drove on to Tchin-Tabaraden. I directed Frankie to stop at Mariama's encampment on the outskirts first. She would know where to find water, probably had an emergency stash. No one there.

Frankie. "Let's go to your house. You've got water in the tukunya. We can ration it to drink. No showers."

"My tukunya is empty," I said. "Used the rest of it to water the sunflowers." The sunflowers! Did they survive? The wall would have protected them from a direct hit by the wind, but they would have suffered from the flying sand and lack of water. I was afraid to see the damage. Patience, I didn't worry about. He would take care of himself. It was bred into dogs here.

"What about the pump in your yard?" Roy kept talking to me as if I were listening to him.

"We'll have to wait until tonight to see. There's never any water in your pump during the day, right?" Frankie.

"Right. If the pumps work tonight, I'll fill the tukunya." We would drink and I would water whatever plants remained.

Driving down the sandy roads of the center of the village, I saw through an open gate a group of women sitting in a circle in a sand yard. "Stop." We would take advantage of the local custom, when you visited people, they would give you something to drink, to eat, and lodging if you needed a place to stay, just as the Tuaregs did the previous night, though we hoped someone here had water. I also knew that men did not typically show up to a group of women. Glimpsing Mariama among them, I thought she might come out to see us.

"I was afraid you got lost in the sandstorm!" she called to us and gestured us in.

We recited the ritual greetings; no one seemed to be disturbed by Frankie's or Roy's presence, probably because we were anasaras.

At the ritual response about the night passing in peace, in health, Frankie whispered, "in hell."

Roy nodded.

"Algheras," I said. We passed the night in peace.

The women continued bantering about the sandstorm, the Cure de Salée, the lack of rain, new babies, everything but the lack of water and the intensity of thirst. Their stoicism reminded me of Ramadan, but this time we weren't postponing drinking water until after sunset, we didn't know when we would drink water again. The locals seemed to trust Allah on this. We were not as confident.

Eventually, a woman brought out a small decorative calabash, a dried gourd cut in half and hollowed out with chalky white designs that looked like suns engraved on the outside and handed it to the woman sitting to her left. The Wodaabé carved them and passed them down through their families. The women in the yard I recognized as Tuareg, Wodaabé, and Arab, sipped from it then politely passed it one by one. When it came to me, I hesitated only briefly when seeing the whitish liquid with sticks floating in it, thinking certain dysentery, tuberculosis, or worse if I drank it, just before drinking a couple of swallows. Thirst. I would have drunk anything liquid. Anything. And I doubted that I was thirstier than anyone else. I could not tell if Frankie swallowed. Roy looked directly at me as he drank, though I watched him in the periphery. He was making a statement. "I would die for you." Too late.

Given the circumstances, Frankie and Roy would stay at my place. They had to have water before anything else. We all did. Awkward and annoying, but I would remain aloof, detached as planned. As if I couldn't see him, as if he didn't exist. I hoped it hurt him as much.

I opened the gate to a sand ocean fixed in time. Great waves lapped high up on the inner row of sunflowers, burying the entire bottom half of the stalks. Heads bowed, leaves beaten, shriveled, wilted. Only half the shorter, five-foot plants had flower heads, the rest bent and broken from the wind. I left the sand in place for support and possible insultation for holding any moisture in. Everything needed water.

Tipping the heavy clay tukunya on its edge, I rolled it across the sand floor, hefted it on top of the mini fridge, and poured about a cup from the bottom that included thick sediment. I moistened my mouth with a couple of sips that tasted earthy, gritty, and offered some to the others. Disgusting but wet. Frankie declined, but Roy drank because I did or maybe because he was as thirsty. The sediment soothed my dry lips like a mud mask. I blotted it like lipstick and covered the cup with a book against evaporation, rationing what little remained, in case.

I hadn't drawn water since before the sandstorm, and neither had the women who typically lined up at the pump in my yard to fill their water buckets in the pre-dawn hours. I pulled up the pump handle stiff with grit. Nothing. The copious blowing sand clogged the gears of the water pumps. Otherwise, water trickled from it in the middle of the night, I supposed because the other pumps were watering herds until then, lowering the water pressure. An anemic stream typically began at 3 a.m., slight but steady for a couple of hours. If only I were drinking the water, I could make the cup last a couple of days, but water, food, and tea were always shared with visitors. That meant at least Frankie and Roy, but maybe my students would drop by, Mariama, Tala, Oumar.

If Frankie and Roy hadn't have stayed at my place, I would have spent the day a kilometer or so away from my house to avoid offering nothing to thirsty guests. Still, I tried to stick to the routine. After writing my lesson plans, I sucked on a date pit and read Blake and Auden beneath the acacia, while Frankie and Roy played spades. We were all trying to distract ourselves from the dust in the air that exacerbated the dryness in our throats. "Thousands have lived without love," Auden wrote. "Not one without water." The reason I was reading Auden, one of the thousands. I'd thought the human body could only survive three or four days without water, but clearly that wasn't the case, or at day four the locals would be panicking. I was uncomfortable, thirstier than I'd ever been but had no doubt water would come because the nomads said it would.

By night, even Frankie drank some sludge from the bottom of my tukunya. I fell asleep until the women came with their empty buckets, pulled up the handle of the pump in my yard and bent their heads to listen, but there was no sound, no water again that night.

When we woke the next morning, we drank the remaining muck from the cup. Now we were entirely out of water. Surely there would be some that night, though none of the locals said so. No one acknowledged thirst, so I didn't either. My head was pounding, my eyes dry, burning.

I waited until afternoon before we visited the wife of one of the shop owners who lived nearby.

"Why the fuck are we waiting?" Frankie.

Because I didn't want us to appear weak. To take water from the locals who had abstained until they could no longer stand it. I didn't respond.

There must have been thirty women or so there with the same

idea of quenching their thirst, including Mariama, who smiled at me. Everyone greeted one another as usual, admiring braids, joking, and finally sitting in a large circle continuing the banter that I tried to contribute to though I didn't like opening my mouth to the dry air.

My students didn't mention the lack of water in class either; everything carried on as usual. How did they know they weren't going to die of thirst? Were there stages they knew that we hadn't yet reached? An internal thermometer they could rely on? Did they simply accept death? I didn't want to show my ignorance, my weakness. Oumar would have explained it without my asking had he been there, but he had to take care of his goats, our family goats. What I understood: There was no water, so you dealt with it, adapted. Complaining didn't help; it showed weakness, used energy. There would be water for those who were patient.

Day three Frankie became subdued, unanimated, quiet, serious, but only in the confines of my yard. If she stepped out in the public domain, she was the old Frankie, Frank as it were. Responding to greetings with her usual swagger, though I recognized her forced smile. She didn't stay out long or go out often. It took too much. She rationed her cigarettes as if crucial to her survival. She smoked, but less, with less relish, only to give herself some control over six fucking minutes of her life.

Roy tried to stay out of my way. He may have been pissed coming all this way only to be shut out, but he wasn't as pissed as I was. He didn't speak directly to me but had a constant concerned look on his face. For me, for all of us. He might have first thought I was playing at running away from him to stoke the chase, but he could see now for himself that was not the case. Oumar, Mariama, Tala, and some of my students stopped by to check on me, Frankie, to check out Roy. I was embarrassed I had no water to offer. They expected this, but I wanted to show them different, show them some strength, some patience, that I could pare down when necessary. Adjust. What I had already learned from them about how to live. Roy could see this. I didn't have to explain it to him. He knew he had lost the person I was.

I was calm, like when your vitals slow to survival mode. Like a possum. I conserved energy, stayed out of the sun. I knew there would be water, had developed the patience to wait for it.

On the fourth day, a water truck arrived from Tahoua. It parked in the center of the village and people came from all directions to fill their buckets. I don't think we could have gone another day. We anasaras couldn't have gone another day. Frankie, Roy, and I knew it but never mentioned it. Just drank, deeply, but not too deeply, our bodies revived, alive. Survived.

That night, Patience showed up, and the pump in my yard once again pulled water from deep below the sand. The women returned in the middle of the night, noisier than usual, their buckets clanging like percussive windchimes, the women themselves laughing rather than quiet. I raised up on my elbows and greeted them.

The next day, Frankie and Roy left for wherever they came from. Roy, convinced that I didn't need him, moved on, freed to go back to the States and pursue his happiness and leave me to pursue mine.

I wrote my mothers and described my students, detailing Tala and Eddoua planting the sunflower seeds, the game they played, strategically placing seeds in the shallow holes of sand, the stalks now five feet tall in double rows that followed the perimeter of the yard. The green in the yard made it so much cooler, the shade, the chlorophyll, the oxygen they breathed out. "By the time you read this, some of the sunflowers will be blooming. Oumar is so anxious to see them. He asks if they will bloom every morning."

I described Mariama's therapeutic massage and getting the

gris-gris from a marabout against the djinn, left out mentioning Roy—if they knew he was here, they weren't mentioning it either—described the sandstorms and the rain, left out the lack of water for four days, talked about my goats and Ramadan and Tabaski, left out Mokao and the kiss. I described the Cure de Salée and Mokao winning the beauty contest, thanked them for the Polaroid but didn't tell them I'd given it to Tala as a wedding gift. I inquired after everyone's health, the dogs, the garden, requested news. "Besides raising sunflowers for protein, I want to create a library of books for the students or whoever can read them. I'm going to call it Gita's Library. I'm focusing on teaching reading English, a skill that could affect their future," I wrote. "Please send books: science, physics, agriculture, design, nutrition, and poetry." I scratched out poetry because I would leave my collection. "Hopefully there is some sort of flat rate, or some way to get them to Niger without too much expense and trouble." I included some loose Tuareg tea and directions on how to brew it, on a brazier, including how to pour it from a great height into shot glasses, inside the aerogramme, a greyer shade of blue, folded and sealed it. Beside the bland pre-printed stamp, I drew one of a stylized sun, heat waves spiraling, radiating from an inked disc and beside it a flower moon with dewdrops of water on the petals.

In class, for our discussion topic, I wrote "water" on the board, thinking it would elicit some vivid personal experiences of the ordeal we'd just been through, but the students didn't see it as a dramatic ordeal but what it was like living in the desert.

"Miss. Aman, water, is life." End of discussion.

I pushed a little. "My perception is that nomads seem to drink less water than what seems normal, necessary, what the desert environment demands."

"Miss, we drink what is necessary. That is why we are here."

That evening, I told Oumar to tell Mokao I was in a position to buy two more goats.

Maybe I could give Oumar the money and he and Mokao could work out the deal without me getting involved, avoiding the lingering awkwardness since the kiss. But I didn't want to avoid Mokao. Nothing to be embarrassed about, I reminded myself, a simple misunderstanding. "Find out when it's convenient for him, and I will be there."

Oumar's eyes shone, his lips quivering as if stifling a grin.

"I'm just going to buy goats."

"Yes, Miss. I am happy about the goats."

The sunflowers that survived, bloomed in December before the holiday break. Oumar noticed the tightly coiled colors on multiple sunflower plants and somehow knew one would bloom the next day, but Mariama saw it first. I came home from the school, opened the gate. She stood the same height as the plant, looking at the single yellow flower face to face. "Salaam alyakum." She was talking to the flower, but her smile flashed at me. She turned so baby Izza could see. Izza reached her hand to grasp the bright yellow just as Mariama took a step back. They both laughed at the color, the size, the softness of the petals.

"Where are the thorns?"

"No thorns, just seeds you can eat." Maybe they would develop thorns if they survived long enough. I explained the seeds, source of protein, etc., but Mariama wasn't ready to hear it. Flowers were enough. More than enough. I nearly wept myself to see them. I wouldn't mention the dye until the heads were dried, the seeds shelled.

She leaned close to the flower and breathed in.

I hadn't detected a scent.

"Adhou," she said.

They smelled like the wind.

She pointed to the dead stalks with her chin.

I nodded my head meaning "no," as in dead.

Mariama bent and lifted some strands of dried fiber and wove them together.

She would weave a mat—what I slept on, though the Tuaregs slept in low portable wooden beds—for protection from the sun. I should have thought of it myself, using all the plant. "Yes," I said. Take them." They pulled easily from the sand. Mariama left happy. She carried the stalks in her arms like a baby, not enough to carry on her head. Iza bound on her back.

The next week, the Velvet Queens started blooming. The yard, a mosaic of colors resembling a kaleidoscope. The Queens featured multiple flowers on each stem. I cut one that looked like an orange yellow sunset and wove the stem through Mariama's braid.

"Save it," I said. I wanted to harvest the seeds.

"Yes, forever."

After Mariama, people paraded through my yard on a daily basis to see the gold, crimson, and blood orange flowers for themselves until it seemed everyone in the village and beyond had come. More than the first day I arrived when all the Tuareg men asked me to be their friend. The Tuaregs in the bush, the people in town, my students, the director and his family, the Tuareg with the hazel eyes and his wife, Oumar, Tala, even Mokao. He laughed, did a little dance when he saw the flowers. Many people I'd never seen before from further out in the bush.

The Black Hopis in the back row bloomed last. The yellow heads with the blue-black seeds the same color as the dye in the Tuaregs' finest cloth, Mariama's favorite. When the head dried, I would invite her, Tala, and the women to come to my house and we would pound the shells with a mortar and pestle and make black dye for cloth. Make a powder to accentuate the eyes. The Wodaabé men too would be interested before the Geerewol beauty contest the next rainy season.

Some of the seeds I'd harvest, rather than process, to plant in

Mariama's compound. If others were interested, I'd plant some at the school, the post office, outside the dispensary. Maybe get a cottage industry going producing seeds for the locals' consumption, possibly expand to the entire regional nomadic market. Maybe the Tuaregs could get salt at the Cure de Salée and sell seeds to the other nomads gathered from across Niger. If it was the right kind of salt. And if they liked the seeds. The Tuaregs' food didn't taste salty, but they recognized the curative aspects of salt for their herds, and their ancestors hauled it on caravans and traded in it. Tradition. I knew salt helped human cells somehow maintain a balance of hydration but also that too many sunflower seeds make you thirstier. What was the balance? I'd ask my mothers.

The students looked forward to the upcoming Noël holiday break. They didn't celebrate the holiday itself but learned the French customs. I added some common traditions from the States.

"Same," someone said.

They found the discussion about the holiday entertaining but looked forward to spending time with their families.

I dreaded it. Different. All the volunteers were required to gather for a meeting in the nearest city of size to talk about issues and problems, to socialize, support, reconnect. I preferred to stay where I was, working through my own issues and problems: languages, customs, sandstorms, thirst, djinn, Roy, raising sunflowers in sand. I'd done all right and felt more comfortable here with the locals, life at a slower pace than the idea of spending a weekend with a large group of loud, excited Americans drinking tepid beer, which I'd never developed a taste for, instead of Tuareg tea, which I had. The nearest large city to Tchin-Taba-raden was Agadez. I could get a ride at least to Tahoua with Frankie when she dropped off product. The bush taxis stopped at Tahoua for petrol and to cram in more passengers. They always had room for one more. I dreaded that ride, too.

Because of the lack of rain, Tala told me after class, Oumar had taken the goats to find pasture. She didn't know where he went or how long he'd be gone. I'd leave some food out for Patience and water the sunflowers before leaving for the weekend. I knew I shouldn't keep watering them. Oumar had said as much. Especially as they were established, my excuse, but I was afraid to let go. Afraid the one thing I'd contributed wouldn't survive. The desert might take them for itself. Allah might think the water better used elsewhere.

CHAPTER FIFTEEN
COLD SEASON, EN ROUTE TO
AGADEZ 1989

After stopping by the latrine to preempt any need to stop along the route to Agadez, I climbed into Frankie's Scout with my guerba of water and my pack. "Thanks for the ride."

Frankie glanced over with her infectious smile. "I'm going to Agadez anyway, but you'll need to find a ride back unless you're staying for a month."

I got situated, tucking the guerba between us and stowing my pack in the back so I could extend my legs. "A month in Agadez? What, do you have a boyfriend? Girlfriend? Both?"

This elicited a boisterous laugh. Maybe it was some kind of de-briefing. Frankie never said she wasn't a spy.

She drummed the steering wheel. "Come and find out." She pulled out a cigarette and lit up.

Such a flirt. "Wouldn't want to ruin our platonic friendship. And my transportation."

"Truth hurts."

"There's a mandatory volunteer meeting; otherwise, I wouldn't be going to Agadez at all."

"Rothmans is putting me up in the Hôtel de L'Aïr during the

Paris-Dakar off-road race. If you need a break from the college crowd, you're welcome to stay."

"Thanks, I might." We passed through Kao without stopping. I watched it disappear into the distance from the side mirror.

Frankie took another drag and checked her look in the rearview. "The Dakar is huge; Agadez is going to be packed. You know about the race, right?"

I took a swig from the guerba. "Yeah." I didn't hand it to her, just paused with it in my hand midair. She would say if she wanted a drink.

She shook her head. "The route insanely is going through the Ténéré desert next month. Can you imagine 400,000 square kilometers of desert with no road, 160,000 square miles? They use a compass, map, and intuition. Fuckin' crazy."

She flicked the butt out the window.

"I wish you'd quit doing that."

She winked. "Thanks for reminding me. Anyway, Agadez is one of the stops, and it's mandatory that I do some preliminary groundwork."

I let that sit awhile. Preliminary groundwork. "So, you not only peddle cigarettes, but you also work for the Dakar?"

"You know me better than that; I'm strictly on-road. They wouldn't like my routes. Rothmans sponsors vehicles in the Dakar. They're painted just like the cigarette packages."

She pulled the pack from her pocket to illustrate. "A lot of people attend these events, a lot of smokers putting their health at risk. I'm there for them."

"Clearly twisted. If you don't need me to drive, I'm going to doze a little."

"Good idea," Frankie said. "Rest up."

I closed my eyes. Relaxed into the syncopated rhythm like a camel's gait.

The water pump is still broken, nomads restless and cheerful as usual. They are used to the edge, adept at hiding their faces from wind, rationing saliva to get them through during

Ramadan. The devout don't swallow, preferring suffering as sustenance.

Follow their tracks in a trance, intricately weaving blues and blacks. Dance for a drink of water. Don't despair if there is none. Crying is wasteful, impossible, pointless, weak.

I woke when we hit the paved road at Tahoua. The first time I'd dreamt in French. A different rhythm.

While the gas pumped, Frankie sat back down in the driver's seat. "Thing is," she said as if we hadn't quit talking hours ago. "I heard your ex took a job as a mechanic in Niamey."

"I thought he was leaving. Why would he stay?"

"The Dakar; at least that's what he said in passing as we drove to Tahoua."

"You didn't take him to Niamey?"

"No, and I didn't take him to Agadez either. That's the Dakar's first stop in Niger, then Tahoua, and Niamey. But the racers won't arrive for another month." She hung up the nozzle. "Want anything?"

I always kept eating and drinking to a minimum when riding with Frankie. She didn't consider stops beyond petrol necessary. "No thanks."

I stayed in my seat, reviewing. I tried to look at the situation practically: Roy loved the Dakar. He also knew mechanics.

This could have nothing to do with me. He was already here, an opportunity to see the Dakar in person.

He could easily get a job as a mechanic and subsist until the race.

Maybe he didn't have immediate prospects back in the States.

Maybe he needed to get away like I did.

Maybe I hadn't convinced him that I'd moved on.

I couldn't control what he did, only what I did.

Niamey was at best eleven hours from Tchin-Tabaraden. Agadez, far enough at seven and a half. The odds that we'd run into each other were slim.

If he persisted in stalking me, I'd persist in rejecting him.

Frankie returned with a Fanta and started the car. "Everything okay?"

I handed her some bills for gas money. She waved them off. "Look," I said. "I'm a volunteer, but I'm still more financially stable than 95% of the population."

"Save it."

I settled back into my seat. She knew all about me. Maybe if I didn't talk, Frankie would start talking. About herself.

Even after a good 15 minutes of silence, she didn't. The sun coming in from both the windshield and the passenger window acted as a sedative, making me squint through the waves of heat at the disappearing pools of water on the asphalt, then pass out completely.

CHAPTER SIXTEEN
COLD SEASON, AGADEZ 1989

I roused at the checkpoint for Agadez when the Scout slowed momentarily as Frankie flashed her credentials and tossed the guard a carton of cigarettes.

"Why are you always so tired?" she said.

"A natural preventive for motion sickness."

"I used to get that before I started driving. Where to?"

"The Agriboun hotel."

"Budget."

"What else?"

We drove to the west side of Agadez, a few blocks from the mosque.

"Thanks for the ride, Frankie."

"You know where I'll be."

I didn't check in to the hotel but greeted the Tuareg man at the desk who guessed I'd come for the meeting. He led me to a sandy courtyard and a boisterous group of anasaras drinking Flags, dancing to the same mixed tape from training.

I drank, danced, learned the anemic guy had gone home—health issues. No one knew anything about Joel.

"It's as if he disappeared," someone said. "But I thought the same of you, and here you are." He raised his glass. "Salut!"

I raised mine.

Stacia was living with the Egyptian doctor, Roz had her front tooth knocked out in a bush taxi accident, and their parrot could perfectly imitate the Big Ben chimes at the top of the hour on the BBC.

"Let's dance," Roz said with a slight lisp, pulling me center courtyard. "Can your feet handle it?"

"Sure. They're numb now, callused. Hey, sorry to hear about your accident."

"I'm fine. Losing a tooth is pretty minor in the big picture."

Everything here was on a scale. I wondered if that also meant she wasn't getting it fixed. "I've been meaning to ask. Do you know anything about the dispensary in Tchin-Tabaraden? I think it may have been built when the school was, several years ago. It's shut down, but there are bottles of medicine labeled in German inside."

The music switched from *Coming in from the Cold* to *Bette Davis Eyes*.

"I'd guess someone came in and built it, ran it for a short time, and lost funding."

We weren't really dancing. Barely swaying as we spoke into each other's ears. "When nomads need medical attention, they have to travel a long distance by camel or donkey, even on foot, to the nearest place with some sort of facility. Sometimes they come see me and my copy of *Where There Is No Doctor*."

She took a swig of beer.

"I've heard they are not always admitted to facilities. One nurse told me there are no accommodations for the nomads because they're mostly uneducated, that the medical staff isn't able to communicate with them because they don't speak nomadic languages, that they have their own methods."

Now, I drank. "That's ridiculous. Most of them speak some French and they can communicate through gestures, context. My guess is the medical personnel are not trying to understand them."

"Exactly."

It wasn't just the nomadic languages others didn't want to understand, and it wasn't only medical staff and government officials. Niger in general seemed to reject the nomadic culture, their lifestyle. Nomadic vs. sedentary, rural vs. urban, non-formally educated vs. formally educated. "Buy you another beer?"

"Sure." Roz sat down at the table with the others.

I ordered a gin and tonic and a beer, offering her either. She took the gin. "What about some sort of mobile health vehicle that could go to the nomads in remote locations on a regular basis?"

"I'll look into it."

I glanced around the table. Mostly acquaintances. Fisheries, nutritionists, another teacher. "Does anyone know if Nick's coming?"

"Hope he brings his wife."

"Nick's married? I've never seen him with anyone."

Stacia passed around an order of brochettes.

"He married a Tuareg woman at the Cure de Salée. That's not too far from Tchin-Tabaraden. I figured you were there."

"I saw an anasara perform in the camel dancing event. That was Nick?!" Nick who struggled speaking anything but English, Nick? "Talk about adjusting to the culture."

He and his wife arrived then in full Tuareg regalia as if they'd come directly from the Cure de Salée. We all gave them a standing O.

They both seemed happy. I greeted her in Tamasheq, her Tuareg gold jewelry glinting on her neck, her ears. I wondered how he afforded her dowry. I grasped his hand Tuareg style.

"Bold move. Wow."

"Thanks," he said. "This is Raïcha."

"Toutes nos félicitations," congratulations, Stacia said.

"She doesn't speak French." Nick.

I looked at Nick. "You speak Tamasheq?" If so, why was I still struggling?

"Learning. But we don't speak it to each other. Yet. I don't want to sound like a two-year-old talking to my wife."

"How do you communicate?" A fisheries guy.

"Gestures, context. Like we all did when we first got here."

"The taxi business must be going well." That'd be the only way he could afford the dowry. It varied but at least an ox for the wedding meal, household goods: millet, sugar, tea, a bed, jewelry and clothing gifts for Raïcha, something for her mother. A camel wouldn't be out of the question. He definitely wasn't the type to ask for money from anyone.

"Even better when I can retire from teaching."

I asked Raïcha what she wanted to drink.

"Flag," she said. "Tanamert."

Two? I gestured to Nick who nodded, describing meeting the parents, meeting the marabout, meeting the dowry, the ceremony.

"The wedding was seven days long," he said.

I'm sure I wasn't the only one trying to figure out how he pulled it off. He must have a lot of help figuring out the cultural nuances from a generous kid like Oumar or a bright enterprising student like Tala, or a mother figure like Mariama. Maybe a father figure.

"My business partner explained the logistics and I did my best."

Or a business partner. "I saw you at the Cure de Salée. Impressive." I described in detail his performance to the riveted audience. "But how did you learn to ride a camel, let alone teach it to dance?"

"Worked my ass off. How else do you think?"

"A gris-gris?" I didn't know he had it in him. I'd never even heard him string two sentences together in English.

"I do need another assistant. All the drivers have one, for helping with minor repairs, finding parts, handling the paperwork at the checkpoints. The kid who was helping me moved on. If you know of a young kid who isn't tied up with school whose family needs the money, let me know. I'll make it worthwhile."

"I might know someone," I said. "Talk to you about it later." A Bob Marley song came on and I asked Raïcha to dance.

The next song, Nick cut in and I sat back down at the table watching them watch each other. I wondered if they felt like Roy and I had. Their body language open, inviting. The moon. Someone had said the rooms with fans were booked. I decided to get a taxi to Frankie's place. I excused myself and waved to Nick and Raïcha.

"Wait!" Nick shouted over the music. "We'll give you a ride."

I felt like a child in the backseat, the adult married couple up front.

Nick looked in the rearview. "Tell me about my potential new assistant."

"His name's Oumar. Bright, ten to twelve years old. His father and older brother are in Libya working. He has a small herd of goats, but someone else could watch them, add them to their herd. His mother is my best friend. I'll ask her what she thinks. At least Oumar would still be in the country, and she has a baby girl to take care of."

"Tell her I'd give her some cash up front and a shortwave radio."

I asked Raïcha if she knew Mariama from Tchin-Tabaraden. That's when I realized I didn't know Mariama's last name or anyone else's. But Raïcha knew a Mariama whose husband and son Ahmed were in Libya, with a son Oumar and a baby daughter Izza. She made the clicking sound in her throat.

"She knows him?" Nick.

"His mother," I said. "Her husband, an older brother and knows about his baby sister."

"Raïcha is going to have a baby."

"Congratulations, again!"

I couldn't believe I was talking to the same person I'd met the previous hot season.

"I'm not the same person," he said.

"None of us are."

"Where to?"

"Hôtel de l'Aïr."

"I know it. Kaocen's palace." He drummed the steering wheel. "Kaocen ag Mohammed, leader of the Tuareg insurrection in the Aïr Mountains in 1916." He looked in the rearview. "I'm not only a taxi driver; I'm a tour guide."

Frankie had left the door unlocked and bathroom light on, but she was already sleeping, the hum of the air conditioner accompanying her rhythmic breathing. I moved quietly, maneuvering my pack to avoid knocking into furniture. I entered the bathroom— it smelled like smoke—took a good look at myself in the mirror, ran my hand through my hair. It didn't look like my old hair, someone else's, reddish gold but healthy. The face stared back, tanned but not dry, green eyes less stark against a darker shade of pale, eyebrows no longer surprised. I leaned in, my lips touching the mirror, closed my eyes and lingered there, feeling the weight, the pressure, my own breath warming the surface, then pulled away. "You're losing it," I whispered.

I washed my face, my lips with soap, stripped off my clothes, and stepped into the cold shower. I stood directly under the nozzle and let it rain down on my head like a downpour until I could barely breathe through the water.

I toweled off so I wasn't dripping, but I wanted to feel cool. Easing in beside Frankie, I pulled the sheet up, edging back just until I could feel her body heat, and closed my eyes.

"How was it?" she said.

"Do you think you could hold me without... Just hold me." Suggestive. Needy. The usual effects of the moon.

"Fuckin' maybe," she said, put one arm under my shoulder, the other around my waist and pulled me in.

The desert persists drawing its sandpaper tongue across your wrists. Think of rivers to wallow in, swallow the entire Nile. If you drink, you will return. Drink, walk on water, drink a shot of tea whenever it is offered, bitter or sweet, take, drink, taking care to step over the brittle bones of others arrived before you. Listen to what they don't say, might have said, can't say, like the echo of a single match striking, creating ripples of sound waves, superfluous light you could drown in. Clap and announce your presence. Ahlan wa sahlan.

A knock on the door. "Excusez moi, Mademoiselle. Your car is here for you."

Must be Nick. I unwound from Frankie. She bit my arm, her face lit up, amused. "Thank you," I said toward the door. "I'll be right down."

We arrived in time for beignets and Nescafé, the director already speaking. He gestured for us to sit, eat. He talked about the importance of keeping up on our vaccinations, treating our water, taking our vitamins, physical health related issues, then moved on to mental health. Someone had been evacuated for psychological issues. The rumor was the blonde. "It's important to talk with someone, get support if you're struggling with anything."

Someone told him I'd been sleeping on a mat on the ground.

"We'll deliver a metal frame and mattress to you, Lark."

"No. Thanks. Really."

The director left after the Q&A had subsided and lunch had been served: rice with a red sauce and goat's meat and a lettuce and tomato salad with vinaigrette. I closed my eyes to focus on the taste of fresh vegetables.

We didn't start drinking beer until afternoon.

I started the discussion as if in class but more direct. "Do you feel like we're doing any good here?"

"Not sure," the fisheries guy said. "How do you know? Any positive effects will take time. People need food, a livelihood. In my case, smoking fish preserves it. People can eat it and sell it at the market."

He opened his pack and pulled out a bundle of newspaper. "Try it." He unwrapped it and passed it around. "If you're hungry, it tastes pretty good."

"Kind of looks like blackened fish."

"Smells fishy."

I wasn't that hungry.

"Fishing requires water though." The other teacher.

"And a taste for fish." I ordered another round.

"Anytime you can add vitamins and minerals to the diet, it's a positive." The nutritionist. "I feel like we're doing some good providing information on the maternal diet affecting the fetus, looking for opportunities for a variety of food."

"It's a developing country though. Knowing what to eat versus access." I sounded negative even to myself. The moon.

"Yes, but that's the point of the fisheries project, right?"

"And clean drinking water. We're encouraging breast-feeding rather than feeding babies formula from the west that's for sale in the markets. Mixing it with contaminated water causes diarrhea, dehydration."

"That requires water, too though, and access to food for the mothers," I said. "In the Sahel, the nomads can get water, grains, protein, and dairy when there isn't a drought, but the aftereffects of a single drought can last for years."

The fisheries guy spoke up again. "I know about the forestry tree planting project to slow desertification, but again, it will take years to take effect, but it's better than doing nothing."

"Is it?" I was starting to sound like Frankie or Lao Tzu. "The nomadic way of life is at stake. Sometimes I think it might be better for the nomads and the Nigerien government to work things out for themselves." I took a drink of tepid beer. "But then remember how that worked out for the Native Americans and our own government? Are we on the right side, here?"

"We all have doubts and questions," Roz said. "But when it comes to the individual level, do you think you are making a positive contribution to the community in Tchin-Tabaraden, Lark?"

"I'm focusing on teaching the nomads to read English. Coupled with being able to read French, they can choose to educate themselves and accept, reject, or modify western ideas if they can gain access to such reading material. I'm working on that. Hope to start a library."

"Good idea." The other teacher.

"And I planted sunflowers, drought hearty, the seeds as a protein food source."

"Great idea." A nutritionist.

"Oil too, good for the skin, good to cook with." The other nutritionist.

"But they're annuals. Someone will have to intentionally plant them every year." I got to my point. "Did you know the exiled nomads are being relocated to Tchin-Tabaraden?"

"Yes, I've heard this at the hospital." Roz. "The government is encouraging them to come back from living and working in Libya and Algeria."

"It's good the nomads will be coming home, sounds promising, right?" I looked at the faces around the table to gauge reaction. "Their history with the government has never been positive, but hopefully that's about to change."

Stacia raised her beer. "To the first step of reconciliation." We toasted.

I shared a taxi ride to Tahoua with Roz and Stacia. Spent the night. Heard their parrot chime like Big Ben at the top of the hour on the BBC and ask me, "What do you think you're doing?" every time I moved. At night, it mimicked someone coughing. I couldn't sleep inside. Oumar called houses the tombs of the living.

After an omelet with herbs and chilled diced mangoes on the side and rich Egyptian coffee brewed by the doctor, I spent several hours people-watching at the autogare before managing a ride to Tchin-Tabaraden and my own sleeping mat.

CHAPTER SEVENTEEN
COLD SEASON, TCHIN-TABARADEN
1989-1990

I walked out of my gate and in again thinking I'd entered the wrong yard. Not a trace of a single sunflower. Only miniature hoofprints spackled across the sand. I felt shock mostly. Disbelief. One of those disturbing dreams when the lush landscape dissolves into dust, an arid mirage of water just as you take a drink. Had I actually grown sunflowers, or had I dreamt the packets arrived in the mail, the students and Oumar coming to the house to plant them? The watering, the sprouts, the stalks, the gold and crimson blooms. No evidence.

Inside the house, I found the letter from my mothers describing how the Hopis made dye from the shells, the protein content of the seeds (28oz = 6 grams of protein), the Lepidoptera moths that might pollinate them, directions on how to pollinate the flowers myself. It was good to read the words, the letter in my hand. Good to have something to hold onto.

Judging from the footprints, famished goats ate the green stalks, the soft petals, the crunchy seeds. Someone let them in to graze. I would not ask Oumar what to do or who it was, practicing for when he was gone, and I couldn't ask. I would figure out what happened. Maybe someone would tell me without my asking.

When Patience showed up, I fed and watered him. Asked him about the sunflowers just to see if he had any reaction. He sat.

When Oumar came in, we greeted each other warmly as usual, maybe warmer than usual.

"Miss. Did you see? Your flowers are gone."

Calm. Patient. "Yes, I noticed that. It looks like goats ate them." I gestured to the pocked ground. "I wonder how they got in."

"Someone let them in, Miss."

"Is there a gris-gris for that?"

He made the clicking sound with his lips. "No."

We unrolled our sleeping mats and lay down.

"You saw your people in Agadez?"

My people? "Sort of, yes. I guess."

The sound of drumming in the distance. "Oumar?"

"What, Miss."

He probably thought I would ask his advice about the sunflower situation. "Would you want to be an assistant to a taxi driver in Agadez?"

He looked directly into my eyes, delighted.

"Yes! And before the Dakar!"

"You'd have to find someone to herd your goats, but you'd get paid for your work there of course. You'd have to live in the city, away from Tchin-Tabaraden, away from your mother's tent."

"I'm not a child."

He wasn't, but he was. "I know someone who needs an assistant. I'll talk to your mother about it."

"The anasara who married Raïcha? She knows."

Oumar and I walked together to Mariama's before the sun rose. He couldn't wait any longer, talked non-stop the whole way about the Dakar and the excitement of the city, while I felt conflicted. I wanted him to take the opportunity, but I didn't want him to go.

"You okay, Miss?"

"No. I mean yes," I said.

"I will make you some tea when we get there."

I listened to the rhythm of his feet on the sand, studied his profile, breathed in his scent, grabbed his hand, memorizing everything about him I was going to miss.

He held on to my hand.

"What about the djinn at night when I am sleeping alone?"

"You have your gris-gris and your guard dog, Patience. And your tiny sword. These will keep you safe. Besides, my mother only thought it was the djinn tormenting you; now she realizes it's not."

"What does she say it is then?"

"You."

"What?" I stopped walking, our clasped hands reeling him backward. "What does she mean?"

"She says Allah created countries full of water for people to live in and deserts for people to find their souls."

"That's what I'm trying to do." I started walking again. Forward motion to emphasize my point.

"She knows. Be patient, Miss. Everything comes to you from your mother."

Did he mean Mariama? She felt like a mother to me, my desert mother, and she treated me like her own. "Yes, but I will miss you."

"That's good, Miss."

"You are my brother."

"Yes, Miss. You should marry Ahmed and stay here."

I squeezed his hand, trying to check my emotions as we entered Mariama's compound. Maybe she would forbid Oumar to go until he was older, until I was gone.

"Salaam alaykum," she said, opening the woven stick gate. The ritual greetings gave me time to collect myself. Everyone and their family members fine, in health, in peace.

"And how was your trip to Agadez?"

"Good. Kind of like a reunion—not like the Cure de Salée—but interesting, in some ways surprising. I found out the anasara camel dancer at the Cure de Salée was Nick, the English teacher I know in Agadez!"

Mariama laughed. "Love."

"I met his wife, your friend Raïcha. They do seem in love. Happy." I was talking too fast.

"Yes," Mariama said. She was talking even faster in the opposite direction.

Oumar translated. "She says I can help Raïcha's husband with his taxi business."

She did know about it.

"And I should go to Agadez before the refugees return. She wants you to go with me, get me settled with Nick."

I understood the economics but didn't understand the timing. "Before they return? Won't you want to see Ahmed and your father first?"

"They will see each other," Mariama said.

Did she mean before the refugees arrived? After they were settled? "When are the refugees coming?"

"Soon."

No hesitation. She didn't mention the sunflowers either.

The students knew the sunflowers were gone but didn't seem to know how it happened.

"Someone thought he needed them more than you," one student offered.

"What will you do, Miss?" Eddoua.

"I will get more seeds and replant. Try again."

"And don't leave them this time. It's a good plan."

Oumar had suggested the same, that no one would water the plants when I was gone. I understood that now, but once they saw the value of them as a food, fiber, and a source or beauty, if the powdered eyeliner idea worked out, someone would tend them. I wouldn't leave before that happened.

They also knew that Tala had married and lived elsewhere. "A man from her home village."

"Do any of you know him?"

No one.

"Koobgal, Miss. Arranged marriage," the girl in the front row said.

"What do you think about that?"

"It's a good match for the families." A male student.

"But will Tala be happy with a husband chosen by someone else?"

"If Tala isn't happy, she will cast him out of the tent."

Everyone laughed.

That sounded like Tala. "Yes, but is that true for anyone?"

"Yes." Another female student. "The older women, relatives of the bride, construct the tent before the wedding. First, a small nuptial tent." She came up and drew a small tent on the blackboard. "That first night the man treats the woman like his mother."

Another outburst of laughter. They enjoyed educating me.

"The women strike the tent down and rebuild successively bigger every day." She erased the tent and drew a larger one. "The second night the man treats the woman like his sister."

More laughter.

"But always the djinn will try to steal the single women. The women burn incense to mask their own scents and cover their heads to protect them from the jealous djinn."

Someone else erased the tent and drew another larger, then erased and drew an even bigger one with some simple figures inside, their heads covered, with wispy lines indicating the fragrance of incense wafting upward.

I remembered Nick saying the wedding lasted a week, but I'd missed the details. "So is the actual wedding ceremony on the last day in the final tent?"

"Yes, Miss. On the seventh day, after a short ceremony the couple move into their own tent that belongs to the wife."

"Matrilineal." The girl in the front row.

Oumar told me that Mokao was taking the fonctionnaire who had first shown me the school and my house to Agadez to see the Dakar racers come through on their first stop after driving through the Ténéré desert.

"We can get a ride with Mokao and him after the market on Friday."

"Are you sure you want to go?"

"Miss. It's the Dakar. People from all over the world will be there. Cars, trucks, motorcycles! A lot of them! A big fête!"

His enthusiasm about it made it sound appealing. "It does sound exciting."

"Miss, we must go."

"It's an opportunity to see the Dakar. We'll take it. But what about afterward? I mean actually living there. Will you like that? It's a city. Your life will be different from life here where you sleep in the sand. Under the stars."

"Miss. The desert holds Agadez in the palm of its hand."

CHAPTER EIGHTEEN

COLD SEASON, EN ROUTE TO
AGADEZ 1990

"The Dakar brings in drivers and spectators from all over the world!" the fonctionnaire effused.

He took off his fake glasses holding them up to the light, looking for a pesky smudge as if they had lenses.

"You know the story, Oumar? Monsieur Thierry Sabine, after getting lost on his motorcycle in 1977 in the Ténéré desert near Libya, was inspired to design the Dakar course to challenge both the drivers and their machines through the most brutal landscape on the planet. Our desert."

"Didn't he almost die?" I knew he did but thought Oumar should, too.

"Monsieur Sabine was wearing a gris-gris given to him by my brother, Ahmed," Oumar said. "He said the desert let him live, and the desert reminded him of that."

The fonctionnaire pulled a kola nut out of his pocket, offered it to Mokao and Oumar who declined, then to me, laughed, and bit off a piece.

"After he was rescued, he vowed to share with the world the power and beauty of the desert," he said, gesturing with both arms the sweep of the landscape we were driving through. "Over 600 cars, motorcycles, and trucks are registered for the three week/13,000 kilometer route from Versailles—that's outside of Paris—south through France to the Mediterranean coast, connecting by sea from Sete, to Algeria, then Niger, Mali, Mauritania, and finally Senegal to the capital city of Dakar! Anyone with a vehicle can get in it."

"You have to be 18," I added.

The fonctionnaire made the clucking sound in his throat in agreement. I felt it important to clarify this when Oumar was about to get into business with Nick and gain access to a car.

"Pardon, mademoiselle. Anyone 18 who wants to race in the desert. This year, the first leg in Niger is from N'Guigmi to Agadez, 780 kilometers."

Mokao was quiet, eyes on the road. He may not have understood the fonctionnaire's French or understood and chose silence. Maybe he disliked the Dakar. I kept at it. "Didn't Sabine die at the race a few years ago?"

"Yes, but he wasn't racing. He was riding in a helicopter searching for vehicles stuck in the sand to rescue them. Heavy winds, blowing sand. The helicopter crashed at night into a sand dune 27 kilometers high near Timbuktu."

"The desert always wins," Oumar said.

Oumar's excitement brought to mind Roy watching his first Dakar on the television in the common room at ten years old. Gita and I were working in the garden and heard the loud sounds of the motors and crowd and came inside to see Roy sitting by himself, enthralled. That may have been what inspired his love of machines, mechanics. But what struck me was hearing that Mark Thatcher, Prime Minister Margaret Thatcher's son, had gotten lost in his Peugeot 504 on the desert leg in Algeria, and a massive search including spotter planes and helicopters from four different countries along with the Algerian military was tasked with finding him. Him and forty other racers lost in a sandstorm. When it cut to the rescued Thatcher, he said he'd done absolutely no preparation for the race. Roy had turned to me and said he couldn't imagine thinking like that, surrendering so much control to chance.

I felt responsible for Oumar since Mariama entrusted me to get him situated with Nick. Did she trust Nick because she trusted me? Was Nick trustworthy? I worried about that, and that Oumar might be influenced by the city, by a lifestyle he didn't understand, but he reminded me he was more thoughtful than that. He was right. I relaxed then and dozed, the truck warm and bumping along, the engine, their voices white noise.

You are welcome, invited. Translate the dead goat as love, a sacrificial offering of the eyes, the brain. You would have refused once. No longer. Now you understand how every bit is used, would voluntarily do it again. Nothing is waste, even the headless empty body filled with water that others might drink.

A shift had occurred. I dreamt, and thought only in French, translating any Hausa and Tamasheq phrases into French rather than English.

Nick met us at the autogare. He introduced himself, recited the Tuareg greetings to Oumar, then turned to me. "Agadez is swarming with both racers and spectators, probably a million dollars' worth to the businesses here."

A microcosm of the world blown into the ancient Tuareg city. I'd thought Mokao would want to see Frankie, but not in this traffic, this crowd. And I wouldn't see Roy.

Nick showed off his taxi. "A 1976 Peugeot 504."

"Where'd you find it?" His transformation still surprised me from helpless monolingual anasara to French-speaking businessman.

"A French couple drove it across the desert and were headed back to France. I'd seen it parked outside the hotel, walked into the bar, and easily found the car's owners."

He walked around the car and opened the back.

"It's called a family car because of the cargo room. The couple said they bought it used and gave me a good deal."

So, it had at least made one trip across the desert. Was it safe? I could only evaluate the appearance, didn't see any major rust spots or dents, though there were some minor scratches in the blue paint job. No glass in the side windows but the windshield's intact. "The tires are worn."

"Oumar can scout for better ones for it, can't you?"

"If you have the money for them, this is no problem," Oumar said.

"Right. The gas gauge and odometer don't work, but you can keep track of that."

Nick handed Oumar a pad of paper and a pencil. I'd never seen Oumar write. Did he know his numbers? The interior, a dustier blue than the exterior, included some cracks in the seats. Still, it appeared top of the line compared with the other cars I'd seen in Niamey, Tahoua, and this Agadez autogare.

"A 4-door with a V4. You ready?" Nick.

Oumar sat on the console and the fonctionnaire took the passenger seat. I thought we were going to take it for a drive, but Nick shook my hand and Mokao's Tuareg style. He handed me the shortwave radio for Mariama, got in the driver's seat, and started the engine. I ran around to the passenger window and handed Oumar some money. "In case," I said. I didn't know how responsible Nick would be with a child. This way if Oumar got hungry, he could take care of himself. I lingered in the window. "You're wearing your gris-gris?"

"Miss."

Nick put the car in gear and pulled away. "Come see us in Tchin-Tabaraden!" I said, following them as they gained speed. "You can listen to the shortwave!" I shouted to Oumar.

He leaned out the window and waved as they drove toward Agadez.

I turned on the shortwave radio. Dead.

"Batteries," Mokao said, pointing with his chin to a nearby vendor.

I inserted eight C batteries in the sandy compartment and tuned the radio to a French station reporting about the Dakar.

"Two fatalities in the Ténéré. A Dutch engineer thrown from his truck when it hit a sand dune at about 180km and somersaulted several times," the announcer reported.

"The Dakar is cursed," Mokao said.

I agreed that it ripped up the landscape for western entertainment. Risk and danger the draw. Air pollution, noise pollution. It also helped the local economy exponentially. I turned off the radio.

True to driver behavior, Mokao lingered at the autogare. We shared a brochette, and I drank a cool Fanta with him. He preferred orange, so I got the grape; they both tasted sweeter than the last round of Tuareg tea. If I still had my deck of cards we might have played, but there was a lot of action in the autogare, a lot of tourists coming in and some locals wanting to leave. We stayed even after the autogare closed. I thought we might spend the night there, but a couple of Tuaregs showed up four fingers from sunset, at least according to my arm held extended straight out, the width of my fingers that fit between the horizon and the sun. A tip from the commune mothers so we children would know how much time before we had to be home by dark. Mokao laughed. Nomads used the shadows in the landscape.

The two men greeted Mokao, said they wanted to go to Tchin-Tabaraden. They may have said the ishumar had arrived, or they may have said they were coming. Thousands of them.

CHAPTER NINETEEN
COLD SEASON, TCHIN-TABARADEN 1990

I gave Mariama the shortwave and a wad of bills from Nick.

She patted her heart, touched my face. "Tanamert."

She didn't ask about Oumar. Probably knew he'd be fine, or she wouldn't have let him go. Maybe because she trusted me. Or maybe because she trusted Raïcha and consequently Nick, her husband.

"My husband and Ahmed have returned home."

I scanned the yard, her tents.

"Not here. At the refugee camp." She gestured northeast with her chin.

"Alhamdullilah! Have you seen them?"

"Not yet."

"Will they be coming here? Staying here?"

"Not yet."

"When can I meet Ahmed?"

"Soon."

My students were elated their fathers, brothers, cousins had returned. They spent as much time at the camp they said, as on the school grounds. I often saw clusters of them walking hand in hand down the sand road toward the encampment. I knew Mariama was waiting for the right time for me to meet Ahmed, but I wanted to at least see the camp.

"Eddoua," I called. He was walking with a group of students. Are you going to the camp?" I didn't wait for his response. "Can I go with you? I won't stay long."

They stopped and waited for me.

"Yes. Come see, Miss."

We'd just started walking when Eddoua knelt down.

"Look," he said.

A marble. Roy's marble.

"What do you think this was used for?"

"A child's toy," I said.

"Not from here."

"No," we have them in the West."

"Then it belongs to you."

He put the marble in my hand where it remained inert.

We continued walking beyond Tchin-Tabaraden to the far side of the dunes, talking as we went, looking for arrowheads, the wind adding resistance. As we crested a dune, Eddoua stopped and pointed with his chin. Thousands of people drowning in a vast sea of sand; the few tent sails rippling in the wind could not possibly shelter the masses of people bobbing around them. I'd interpreted the rumored thousands to be a couple thousand, but there must have been 20,000 ishumar, exiles who had finally returned and were camped with little protection from the environment. We pushed our way across the sand, the wind stippling our faces with grit and dust, my skirt clinging to my legs.

"Anasara," rippled on the wind as we neared the encampment. I hadn't seen so many Tuaregs gathered together since the Cure de Salée, the fête where the nomads reunited in their finest to dance, feast, and celebrate the rains while their camels grazed, drank from the salty pools of water, and grew strong. Ahmed was here, Mariama's husband, my students' siblings, fathers, friends. This reunion in Tchin-Tabaraden was subdued—without the shimmering indigo and embroidered cloth, without the copious silver rings, earrings, and bracelets glinting in the sun. No ornamented colorful Tuareg saddles, no tasseled silver bridles, no camels, no sound of braying donkeys. No one dancing. The encampment stark, spare. The ishumars' faces haggard, aged, their desert garb, drab, worn from the blowing sands. I saw no wares except some battered mortars, an occasional shortwave radio, enamel bowls collecting sand, some braziers and enamel pots for tea. Shared necessities. The Tuareg women's hair woven into simple designs without embellishment. Fewer plugs of tobacco balanced on their lips. No singing, no sound of camel bells. The opposite of the Cure de Salée. I thought I heard a guitar in the distance and turned toward the sound, noticing a man in proximity making tea.

"Salaam alyakum."

He made the ritual response, standing and dusting off his hands to greet us. The students asked after people they knew.

"Do you have enough food and water?" I asked. "Where are the tents?"

He pointed with his chin at a gendarme.

"Bonjour," I greeted the official. "I heard the exiles were coming home but had no idea there would be so many! Where are the tents, the provisions?"

The military man looked exhausted himself.

"The aid hasn't arrived yet," he said. "Tents, blankets, more food are coming."

"When?"

"Soon," he said.

I glanced over the crowd; many of the youth could have been students. "I live in Tchin-Tabaraden, teach at the school. What can I do to help?"

"Go home," he said dismissively. "We have things under control. It's dangerous for you here."

I returned to the Tuareg man making tea. Some of the students had gone to find their loved ones, their friends. Eddoua lingered, crouched beside the others, explaining to me that Algeria had driven out all the ishumar, Tuareg exiles, and relocated them in the camp of In-Guezzam near the Nigerien border. Nigerien officials had said the Tuaregs were Malian, and Malian officials had said they were Nigerien.

"Nobody claimed us," the man making tea said. "Nobody wanted us."

He offered each of us a shot glass of tea. A little boy watched, half hiding behind the man's leg, reminding me of Oumar as a child only last year. When he saw me looking at him, he ran away, disappearing into the crowd. I didn't want to accept the tea because clearly supplies were limited, but it would be rude to refuse it, to acknowledge how dire things were.

"Tanamert," thank you, I said. It was the last round. I would bring some tea, milk, and millet when I returned. "Welcome home. Some of you at least are in your home country."

The man slurped his tea and collected my glass, Eddoua's, and those of the others who were crouching around the meager fire to guard it from the wind. "Niger finally accepted those of us you see here."

I made the sound in the back of my throat of agreement. Were there more? The population of Tchin-Tabaraden had already multiplied exponentially.

"The United Nations will help them reintegrate into Niger and the other Kel-Tamasheq into Mali," Eddoua said.

"Bien sûr, of course they will." I thanked the man for the tea and said I would be back. I opened my palm and offered the marble to him. "Give this to the boy. It's a glass ball, Marbre, marble. Made from melted sand."

"Miss." The gendarme, military police, hissed.

As I turned to leave, I saw Mariama. When our eyes met, she seemed startled, almost cold.

"What are you doing here?"

She said it, as if I were a stranger to her, an anasara. It was likely an act for the gendarme's benefit, but convincing, disconcerting. I didn't know if she was protecting them from me or me from the gendarmes, but I played my part and left the camp.

I struggled to maintain a slow pace, resisting the wind now urging me forward until Mariama caught up to me. Even then, we walked in silence.

"The refugees look rough," I finally said. "But they'll recuperate with some rest and food, the younger ones will have proper lodging and food at school."

Mariama made the clicking sound with her lips in disagreement. "None of them or their children are allowed to go to school, to work, or travel. They're forbidden to do anything but wait."

"Maybe until the government sorts things out, until the supplies arrive, and everyone is able to travel to their own homeland. Otherwise, that makes no sense."

We arrived at Mariama's encampment, where she busied herself with her hand broom.

She said something about hearing at the Cure de Salée that tents marked from the French Embassy were being sold in the markets of Niamey and Agadez.

"The tents meant for the refugees? That's illegal. They can't do that," I said.

"That's exactly what they do."

She didn't look at me but continued sweeping the pattern of bird tracks in the sand.

I knew the Tuaregs were still waiting for the grain that had been promised to them during the drought in 1985. It still hadn't materialized since I'd arrived in Tchin-Tabaraden four years later. I'd seen for myself the occasional sack of millet, sorghum, or powdered milk marked from the U.S. and France, always for a price. "But this time," I said. "President Saibou invited the Tuaregs, the Kel Tamasheq back. He wants to reunite everyone."

"Yes," Mariama said. "Maybe that's true."

By the next staff meeting, weeks after the refugees' arrival, it seemed nothing at the camp had changed. I brought up moving the youth I'd seen in the camp to the school.

"The dorms would be too crowded." The director.

"Not as crowded as at the camp. They could get regular meals and go to school while the government works out the logistics."

"We have no extra food."

"Let's get more food."

"Miss. Even if we request it, it comes from the government. More food and supplies are already coming for the refugees."

"They've been waiting for supplies for nearly two months now."

"It takes time, Miss. Patience."

I looked around at the other teachers, all silent. Patient.

After the meeting, I went to the market. With the cold season ending, blankets no longer a priority, I bought tea, sugar, rice, millet, tomato sauce, piment, and Omo. No wind but a sepia haze as I walked back toward the camp. I couldn't see it through the veil. It didn't exist until I was physically there.

I left the supplies with the tea man. He would give some milk and food to the little boy, the children, to those who needed it most. Not even close to enough but better than doing nothing.

I didn't worry about Oumar and Tala, but I missed them. They knew what I didn't understand, what I should know. Maybe what I shouldn't.

At school, the students seemed in a state of suspension. Class as usual but limited discussion about the refugees, about why they were refugees. They didn't say much about the situation, though I pushed. Less that I tried to provoke, more that I couldn't understand the value of patience sometimes. Of waiting. For what? "How can they stay like this? They can't move." Such questions hung in the classroom as if rhetorical.

It seemed the same elsewhere. Mariama remained aloof. And where the hell was Frankie? She'd missed a month on her product delivery schedule. The vendors when I asked if they'd heard anything, unconcerned.

Tchin-Tabaraden seemed a different place than when I'd arrived. A different environment. Or maybe a different me.

CHAPTER TWENTY
HOT SEASON, TCHIN-TABARADEN, 1990

I saw Frankie arrive from my vantage point in the market. A couple of Tuaregs got out of her Scout and disappeared into the crowd. After she made her usual deliveries, she caught up to me. I bought some Tuareg cheese to take to the little boy at the camp and continued walking. I tried not to act like I missed her. "You saw the refugee camp?"

"Hard to miss. So many nomads, as if they are the writhing landscape."

"Some 20,000 arrived when I was in Agadez. According to the gendarmes, the government is helping them reintegrate, and I want to believe that, but they've been here for months in squalid conditions. The government is isolating and restricting them, holding them indefinitely." She would know this had she been here. "I know things move slowly here; time is slow; education is slow; change is slow. But. I can't help thinking that our own government military forced the Native Americans from their land for its own purposes. What if President Saibou's invitation to the Tuaregs to return home and work things out is another broken treaty?"

Frankie, after a long pause. "I think you may be right."

"Where have you been?" Too harsh, needy. "Thought maybe you and your Scout joined the Dakar."

"Maybe in another lifetime and if I were a different person."

Things lightened. "You'll always be the same person, Frankie Frank."

"You love me, don't you."

It wasn't a question. She winked.

"Doesn't everyone?"

"I followed the race," she said. "Selling to the Dakar crowd at Tahoua, then Niamey, then into Mali. Threw my schedule off though. I didn't charge my vendors here for product because I missed a drop or so."

Or so. "Where is the product going? I never see anyone smoking, besides Tala." I imagined her blowing a wobbly smoke ring. "I miss her and Oumar."

Frankie hesitated, then patted her pocket that contained a single cigarette. "We'll see Tala and Oumar again." She held it unlit on her lip. "Speaking of. Saw Roy working on vehicles at the stop in Agadez. Seems he's earned a reputation and some money."

She was trying to read my reaction. "He's a mechanic and seeing the Dakar live, a dream."

"We had a beer with Vatanen, the Finish driver who won the leg to Agadez and went on to win the race." She lit her cigarette. "Nick, too."

She took a deep drag, then put the cigarette out on the sole of her wingtip and back in the pack in her front pocket.

"Trying to fuckin' quit."

"Whatever happened to you, I like it."

Her face lit up. Pure mirth.

"Nick talked Roy into working as a mechanic in Agadez. He said he'd have all the business he can handle, but I think Nick wants him for his personal mechanic."

She watched me in her periphery.

My jaw may have clenched. I thought I'd taken care of this, but I could avoid Roy for the rest of my life if necessary. "I don't care what he does as long as it doesn't involve me. Agadez is half a day's drive away. I'll never see him."

"I wouldn't count on that. He's determined. Obsessed. You two must have had quite the relationship."

"Had."

We arrived beside the blacksmith. Greeted him. "I've never seen so many bracelets and rings for sale in one place, even in the city."

"The refugees are selling their jewelry for food and tea," he said.

Frankie and I looked at each other, pooled our money, and bought as much as we could.

"I'll give the money and jewelry to Mariama to take to the camp. She'll distribute it or buy whatever is necessary. They won't accept it otherwise. I think they'll only accept food, milk, and tea from me because they always provide for travelers themselves."

"Like you."

"And you."

"Have you met Ahmed, Mariama's son?" Frankie said, toying with another cigarette.

"How do you know Ahmed?"

"Raïcha's cousin. You know, Nick's wife."

"Ahmed has lived in Libya for the last couple of years at least."

"I didn't mean I'd met him. Just know of him."

Right. "I have some fura at home. After we eat, let's take some supplies to camp. Maybe we'll see him."

We walked back to the Scout, greeting people as we went. I hesitated at my gate, letting Frankie walk in first.

"Where are the fuckin' sunflowers?"

"Goats ate them. Also while I was in Agadez."

"Whose?"

"Doesn't matter."

"You're right."

While Frankie disappeared into the latrine, I mixed the millet and sour milk in a hollowed-out calabash.

"Here." I handed Frankie a wooden spoon. "Fura tastes kind of like yogurt."

She touched the tip of her tongue to a tiny amount. "Too sour."

I handed her the cone of sugar with a shot glass. "Add some sugar."

She gave it back without even attempting.

"How do you manage without me?" I struck the cone and handed her some bits of sugar. "I'm going to buy a goat from Mokao and donate the meat to the camp."

"Why not butcher one of your own goats?"

"Those are for Mariama."

"Does she know that?"

"I've never said anything directly, but she knows."

"I'll see Mokao tonight and mention it to him."

"So, you're staying there then?"

"Fuckin' maybe."

While I arranged the millet, rice, tea, sugar, and cheese in my pack, Frankie went out to the Scout and brought back the clothes Mariama had given her, the ones Frankie said she was saving for Oumar and Izza.

"I thought it might be better to dress in local garb to go to the camp rather than my Rothmans uniform. The gendarmes might think I'm peddling cigarettes outside my jurisdiction. Don't want to get arrested."

She came out of the house dressed as a Tuareg man. Her tagelmust wound perfectly. "Who taught you how to do that?"

"Down time during the Dakar in Agadez. I've been practicing."

We walked to the camp, to the same place I saw the same man making tea. The sun dipped below the horizon, the sunset colorless.

The man greeted us, knew Frankie before I introduced her. "Rothmans," the man said.

I handed him the supplies, spotted the little boy. "Takomért?"

His eyes wanted the cheese, but he didn't know me, stayed frozen in place.

The man called the boy's name. "Ibrahim, come."

He advanced shyly followed by a half dozen other children who left the marble in the sand to share some cheese.

The man turned back to us. "Follow me."

We followed him further into the interior of the camp. He gestured for us to sit around the fire. As my eyes adjusted to the dim light, I could see a group of men already assembled, some of them with musical instruments. We all greeted each other, and someone started making tea.

They played the music I'd heard Mariama sing about Kaocen, songs I'd heard at the Cure de Salée about honor, the desert, longing, water, power. The sounds of traditional instruments blended with western guitars, and always drums. No one danced, though. The people here only played, sang, or listened, and drank tea. After the second round, a man somewhere to my right spoke.

"You're Lark. My mother has told me about you."

"Ahmed?" The man beside me switched places and Ahmed crouched down next to me. He wore his turban like a scarf that hung loosely from his neck, played a western guitar. Both chords and fingering. His skin was smooth, the same clear tea color as his eyes, as Tala's eyes.

He drew his palm across mine. I wanted to tell him I'd missed him, but that sounded too bizarre even though true. I'd missed him through Mariama. "Your mother and brother, Oumar, and Tala have been so kind to me."

"Kindness is a mark of faith," he said.

One of Mariama's sayings.

"And I know you from her, Oumar, Tala, Eddoua, and your friends," he said.

He'd switched to French, but I wasn't sure what he meant by my friends. He'd just named most of them, or did he mean my anasara friends? He wouldn't have access to Roz and Stacia in

Tahoua. Frankie? She said she hadn't met him. I looked at her. She stared at the fire.

Another man started playing some notes and everyone joined, the music rising as if from the flame.

Someone tapped me on the shoulder.

"Miss."

A gendarme. The same one who'd confronted me before.

"Why are you still here? You need to go. Now. It's very late."

I didn't want to cause trouble for the nomads. I stood up, brushing the wrinkles, the sand from my pagne. "Yes, of course, thank you for your concern. The music makes me lose track of time."

The gendarme seemed appeased, moved off.

I left after the third round of tea. Frankie, my escort, the gendarme looking on from somewhere; I could feel his gaze. Any danger I felt, due to him.

We walked back in the twilight of shimmering stars. I waited for Frankie to confess, the waxing moon shining directly on her face. She looked pleasant, unperturbed, said nothing as usual. Maybe she was used to lying.

"Why did you tell me you didn't know Ahmed?" I finally said just outside my gate.

"What difference does it make?"

"The difference between a lie and the truth."

"The truth is I'm your friend and, like you, a friend of the nomads."

Patience was home, so I wasn't entirely alone. The relationship with my dog, also technically based on a lie. He obviously could not understand French. I had trained him that when in doubt, to sit. Not useful in this culture, in any culture, even for a dog. Patience. Every time I said Oumar's suggested name for him, I thought of the quality. I had become more patient with the pace of life in the desert, with what I could do without, with Roy's persistence, but since the refugees arrived, such patience seemed wasted, counterintuitive, or maybe I was still impatient after all. For others.

The exiles' detainment, Frankie's words kept me awake, questions running through my head. How well could I really know the nomads in a year's time, or ever? How well could she? I still struggled with Tamasheq, the nuances of their culture, their sayings. But I had no doubt about my friendship with Mariama, Oumar, Tala, even Frankie, conflicted as it was.

I got up early and walked to Mokao's before class. Frankie was there drinking tea and furiously smoking. She'd said she was quitting. I wondered if they'd had a fight and she was taking it out on the cigarette. Or maybe I'd interrupted something else. Maybe whatever it was she was lying about. The tip glowed like the center of the sun. Sparks shot out like rays. I could feel the collateral heat.

I ignored it and greeted them both.

"I told him about the goat," Frankie said pleasantly. "That you wanted the meat to go to the exiles."

"Oui," Mokao said, always genially. He showed me the goat he had in mind, good sized.

I paid him, said I had to go. School day. Another topic on same and different: water and salt—priming them for sunflower seeds—and home remedies and dispensary medicines. I glanced into the distance to check for the goats, squinting against the light. "What's that?" I shaded my eyes with *Where There Is No Doctor*. Something glaring in the sand. A metal feeder?

Mokao spotted it immediately. "Mota!"

Voiture, car. What was it doing out there? Out of gas? Stranded? At least they were close to civilization, to help.

We piled into the Scout, Frankie at the wheel.

As we got closer, we could see the car rolled on its side.

Someone might be hurt. Closer, a blue car. I clutched the dashboard straining to see. "That looks like Nick's taxi!"

No movement around the vehicle as we pulled beside it. A still life, smelling of petrol and hot rubber. I crawled over Mokao and ran to the car. "Oumar!" I called. "Nick?"

I looked inside the car. "Personne," I called. No one. A can of mosquito repellent, an emergency kit, tools scattered across the seats and floor. Two jerry cans in the back knocked over. A pack of Rothman Racers lay on the driver's side floor, a few loose cigarettes lay like pick up sticks. No glass in the windows besides the front and back windshield, and they were intact, only some dents, some scratches, some shards of red and clear plastic outside the car. Maybe Nick and Oumar had hiked to town. Maybe Oumar was at my house waiting. Then I remembered no seatbelts.

"Voici!" Mokao said waving Frankie and me over.

Oumar lay face down in the sand, completely still.

"Fuck." Frankie.

Mokao said something I didn't comprehend. I bent down to Oumar's ear, touching his shoulder, warm, from life or the sun? "Oumar? We're here. You've been in an accident. Can you hear me? Talk to me." I tried all the languages I knew in rapid succession. No response. Only Frankie walking around calling Nick's name. Oumar's body lay inert, unconscious, but no obvious breaks or bleeding besides some abrasions. Mokao and I gently rolled him over. His face looked like a sleeping child's. I bent down, my cheek close to his nose. No breathing. I pressed my fingers against his carotid, nothing. "Frankie, the book, CPR!"

I cleared his airway. "Bismillah," I said as I positioned his head and gave him mouth to mouth breathing—three breaths, then two compressions as Frankie read.

"They aren't going to understand what you're doing," she added.

I heard Mariama's voice in my head. "When the music changes, then the rhythm must."

Mokao disappeared.

"Three, two, three, two," I repeated in my head like a mantra. Oumar's heart started beating on its own after a few compressions. "He's got a pulse!"

"Okay," Frankie said. "This says he's getting 17% oxygen, 4% carbon dioxide from your exhales, and that's enough."

I kept breathing for him. Ten minutes, twenty? I'd forgotten how to measure time by a watch.

"We didn't find anyone else," Frankie said. "Mokao thinks he was by himself, stole the car." She touched my shoulder. "Let me give you a break."

"I'm not tired yet," I said, focusing on keeping a steady rhythm of breath. I would breathe for Oumar for the rest of his life if necessary.

"He probably hit his head. Might be in shock," Frankie read, flipping through the book while pacing back and forth, trying to be helpful.

"Neither Nick or Raïcha would have allowed him to drive by himself."

Frankie kept talking, maybe out of nervousness, out of the helplessness of not being in control. She lit another cigarette and then another.

"How did he even know how to fuckin' drive?"

I composed my own interpretations, my thoughts the rhythm of breathing. Oumar needed the car more than Nick. He wanted to see his brother.

"Lark," Frankie said. "It's been nearly an hour. I've smoked a half pack of cigarettes."

"I love you, Oumar. Come back to me," I whispered in his ear, then looked up at Frankie. I was not letting go. "Is there water in the Scout?"

Frankie brought the guerba.

I should have thought of it before. "Water is life," Eddoua said in my head. I poured some on Oumar's lips. "Come on Oumar."

The deep rumble of Mokao's truck broke the stillness. I didn't look up but heard Mokao's and Mariama's voices and those of two other men, Oumar's father, and probably Ahmed.

I felt them looking down at what I was doing. Mariama, Ahmed, Oumar's father, and Mokao.

"Anasara," Oumar's father said.

I kept going despite what they might think of my putting my lips on Oumar's, not pausing, not breaking the rhythm of breath, and I would keep going until somebody stopped me.

I smelled pungent herbs. I hoped Mariama had a gris-gris for this.

"A marabout is coming," she said, touching my shoulder.

I sat up and she bent down in my place.

"Oumar." Mariama cupped his face in her hands.

His eyes fluttered open.

I got up then and stepped away.

My female students gathered around my desk.

"For you, Miss."

One handed me some earrings. "Red, I said."

"Like your hair," another said.

The earrings tapered into a triangular shape engraved with two lines just below the lobe. "They're beautiful. Where did you get them?"

"Oumar's car. We walked out to the place of the accident and gathered the bits of broken plastic."

What was left of the taillights. I put them on. "Tanamert, thank you."

"Allah saved Oumar's life," Eddoua said.

"Yes," I said. "Alhamdulillah. I didn't even know Oumar could drive."

"Apparently, he couldn't." The girl in the front row.

"I heard he swerved to miss a bush cat and caught the back end of his car with an acacia."

"I heard he fell asleep."

"It wasn't the djinn. He wore a gris-gris against them."

"You met Ahmed?" Eddoua again, to me.

"Yes, twice now. It surprised me he plays a western guitar."

"He got the guitar from an American," someone else said. Frankie?

"But he'd learned to play it from listening to bootleg cassettes in Libya."

Frankie. "He's very good."

"He will play for my wedding," Eddoua said.

"Are you getting married, too?"

"When Allah wills it."

Making the simple click of agreement from my throat had become second nature.

Eddoua continued. "Mariama first thought you and Ahmed would get married, why Allah put you on her path."

"She thought the djinn were trying to steal you. Then she realized you love someone else."

"Love is stronger than the djinn," someone else said.

Who? Frankie? Mokao? Surely she knew they were together. The Tuareg man with the hazel eyes? "Who does she think I love?" We hadn't discussed who/whom.

Eddoua shrugged. "She says love has nineteen switches that beat the one in love."

Roy. Change of subject. "I was also surprised at how casually Ahmed wore his tagelmust."

Eddoua laughed. "Rock and roll. The style of the ishumar."

"The unemployed."

He clicked in agreement.

"Can we talk about them in discussion today?"

"No, Miss."

Instead, we began with typical ways to say goodbye. Thoughts of Oumar and Tala reminded me, though I hadn't actually said goodbye to either. I wouldn't. I kept things light, temporary: Bye. Bye-bye. See you later. Talk to you later/soon. Take it easy. I'm off. Have a good evening/weekend. Take care.

We discussed the recent birthday of the Prophet Muhammad.

"Founder of Islam."

"According to the French calendar, the Prophet Muhammad, may he rest in peace, was born on 22 April, in Mecca, Saudi Arabia." The girl in the front row.

"The prophet says, four things support the world: the learning of the wise, the justice of the great, the prayers of the good, and the valor of the brave." Eddoua, of course.

Then we talked about the salt cure, the Cure de Salée. If I wanted sunflowers to survive beyond food for animals, I needed to give them a good reason. I wrote one of their phrases, Water is life, on the board.

"The salt cure is good for our animals," a female voice said, as I was trying to draw the inside of the human body, should have practiced. "Yes," I said, erasing and re-drawing an outline of a human like at a crime scene. "And today we're talking about the scientific reasons water and salt are good for people, too. First, water." I turned around and wrote: Human body=60% water

Biological Functions of Water:

Provides structural firmness of cells—I drew a cell.

Makes blood, lymph, gastric secretions, urine—more arrows and bubbles.

Forms blood plasma (transports oxygen, etc. to muscle and tissue carrying away carbon dioxide and lactic acid=cramps)—We traded our experiences with cramps.

Lubricates joints: I demonstrated bending my elbows and knees. A girl mimed grinding millet with a mortar and pestle. "Exactly."

Controls our body temperature through sweat—The thermometer confused them.

Finally, Eddoua. "Yes, Miss," repeating the phrase I began with. "Water is life."

"Right, and besides water, we also need minerals. Sodium, salt, is one of those." I wrote, Sodium (Salt):

Maintains water balance

Activates thirst response

Prevents cramps "L'allah," someone said.

Enables nerve impulse transmission—This concept difficult to explain.

Maintains normal blood pressure

"My plan with the sunflower seeds is to cure them in sodium, salt, then when you eat them while traveling, you will get protein and sodium, both necessary to good health." I thought about how I had eaten entire bags of sunflower seeds before, too much sodium, and then having to drink a copious amount of water to rebalance the elements. But I knew I didn't have to explain this. They conserved their food, water, their energy every day.

"Yes," Eddoua said. "Plant them again, Miss."

We moved on to home remedies and medicine with a focus on how things work. I handed *Where There is No Doctor* to the girl in the front row.

"Where do I begin?"

"Look at the front of the book at the table of contents or look at the back at the index that lists all the subjects you can read about. When you see something that interests you turn to that page and read that." They took turns reading "Family Planning—Having the Number of Children You Want," "Home Cures and Popular Beliefs," "Health and Sicknesses of Children," "Health and Sicknesses of Older People," "How to Control Bleeding from a Wound," "Bullet, Knife, and Other Serious Wounds."

"This is different from what we usually do," someone said.

"Options," I said. "Different perspectives."

Eddoua flipped to First Aid, then read the first page of "What to Do When Breathing Stops." "This is what you did to Oumar."

"Yes."

I caught Mariama just as she was leaving her encampment.

She looked strikingly beautiful as when I first met her, though less adorned.

"Lark" she said, touching her heart.

I greeted her. "I'm so happy for you to have your family back together."

She touched her heart again. "I'm planning a méchoui. We will roast a goat at my house in honor of the ishumar and Oumar who have come back to us. You must come."

"Yes, of course. So the refugees can leave the camp?"

"Some of them will be there, Ahmed and Abdullah, and Oumar is coming with Nick."

We did not talk about Oumar stealing Nick's taxi so he could see his brother, nor that he almost died. We all understood this. I did find out that Oumar learned how to drive from Mokao and that Roy, Nick, and Mokao righted the taxi with some chains and Mokao's truck. Frankie reported that the taxi was still drivable, though a crumpled side fender, the scratches and dents the length of the car on the driver's side, the broken taillight, that Nick could open the driver's door, but it was stiff as if bent and no longer true. All things Roy could easily fix.

Mariama touched my chin, turning my face. "Nice earrings."

I started to take them off to give them to her since she admired them as was the custom, but she made the negative sound with her lips.

"Yours," she said.

Entering Mariama's encampment the evening of the méchoui, I saw what I'd smelled at my house in the village, a goat splayed on crossed sticks stuck into the sand, roasting over the fire. I scanned the crowd for Oumar:

Mariama playing the anzad, single string guitar, while others drummed. Izza now toddling, spinning, dancing to the rhythms.

The other matriarchs who also lived there singing about the

Tuareg warriors, the epic poems that traveled through their history.

Frankie, dressed as a Rothmans associate, an unlit cigarette stuck on her lip, dancing with Mokao.

Abdullah, Mariama's husband, once thought I was a spy. What did he think of Frankie? Still cool toward me, aloof. He'd spoken directly to me only once when I'd first arrived. "You clearly are not French." We hadn't spoken since he'd returned.

Alhassane, the first ishumar I'd met at the refugee camp. The man who made tea for visitors, who consoled the children, distributed supplies.

Ahmed, guitar slung on his shoulder in place of the traditional tâkoba, sword. Tagelmust draped below his chin, scarf style.

A dozen of Ahmed's friends or cousins. Turbans also askew, informal. They moved through the crowd together.

El Hajj, the Hajji from the restaurant who served me scorpion the first time I ordered a meal.

Tadeine, the medicine woman. The woman who presided over Izza's naming ceremony, the first person to plait my hair, the woman who gave me the therapeutic massage with the powerful properties of tree bark.

The marabout who made my gris-gris: the first to get my camera back and the next two for health and protection against the djinn.

Several clusters of Tuaregs I didn't know.

A lone Tuareg. Probably Roy.

Tala, cool and beautiful as ever, hair perfectly braided and her husband, Sidi, deep in conversation with someone I didn't recognize. I'd find them later.

Nick, but I couldn't see Raïcha.

Oumar! Half a foot taller it seemed, thinner in the face and jaw. Still wearing the goat's hide sandals exposing the splayed big toe on his right foot. He gave me a little wave, and I ran to him. Same huge smile.

We greeted. "You're tall as a sunflower."

"But I don't require as much water."

"It's so good to see you, Oumar."

"The eye weeps yet withholds tears."

Another of Mariama's sayings. I glanced over at her. "How's Raïcha?"

"Healthy, but she can't travel 30 days before giving birth. Besides we rode camels, the white taxis, left the blue taxi in Agadez."

We wouldn't talk about the accident. "How is business? Do you miss the rural life, or are you a city boy now?"

"Business is good, alhamdulillah, but I still get out in the bush. Nick and Raïcha live outside of Agadez in the Aïr Mountains. He just stays in town the nights before he teaches at the school."

"Do you miss me as much as I miss you?"

"Always." The smile.

Oumar's father started carving the goat and the crowd shifted toward him.

"How is... Patience?" Oumar asked, a little hesitantly.

"Fine. He asks me when you're coming home every day, Quand Oumar rentre-t-il à la maison?"

"Miss, no."

"I'm sure he'll stop by to see you or to try to steal the goat's head." I laughed but Oumar appeared serious.

"Miss, that anasara, Roy is here."

"Yes. I thought I recognized him earlier; thanks for letting me know. Don't worry. He's not a danger to me."

"Why is he still here?"

"It's complicated. Come on, let's get some food. Looks like your brother is getting ready to play some music."

Oumar's father filled a bowl with meat and handed it to me for both of us. Then he added some of the brain gesturing with his chin from it to me. A delicacy, a gift.

"Tanamert, thank you."

He responded with the click from his throat.

It tasted like escargot.

When the music started up again, we moved by the fire. The songs, familiar. I could sing most of the lyrics from memory, even the words I couldn't translate in my head.

The musicians played for a while before Oumar's father began making tea. The blend of the sounds of the traditional instruments with the western guitar changed the music, transformed it.

The crowd had thinned by the first round of tea, when talking took the place of singing.

"The government is not welcoming us back. The military has corralled us like wild animals," Alhassane, the ishumar who made tea and disseminated the supplies at the camp. He said the same the first day we met in the cold season, months before. Ahmed poured tea from two teapots, handing a glass to everyone there and bringing more tea leaves to his father, who added it to the pots of water, blowing on the embers in the braziers.

"All the promises of reconciliation and aid have never materialized," another man continued. "They're like mirages."

I could only pick out certain words in Tamasheq: promises, reconciliation, mirage. I constructed into sentences what I heard blended with context, and my own imagination, perspective.

I knew the Tuareg refugees were forbidden to do anything but wait. Mariama had explained this much to me, and I had seen it for myself.

His words sounded like how the first round of bitter tea tasted.

Alhassane saw me looking at him and adjusted his tagelmust. Maybe out of respect or maybe because it wasn't my business. He murmured into the crowd, but I could no longer make out discernable words. I was not asked to leave, but everyone spoke Tamasheq, which I understood only some of. I kept glancing at Frankie, who must have been completely lost, we the only obvious anasaras there. She seemed focused but must have been distracted, thinking about, I wouldn't even hazard a guess. When I looked at Mariama, she didn't look at me. No smile but concentration. She would expect me by now to figure things out for myself. I kept trying.

Someone else spoke up. "When some of our young ishumar asked about the promised international aid, they were interrogated and arrested."

I heard young, promised aid, interrogated, and arrested. "What?" I said aloud, a reflex rather than intentional.

Oumar touched my hand. "Miss."

He was right. It wasn't my place to say anything. It only felt like it. My place, my landscape. The desert demanded it. The desert created Tuaregs and recreated me. I had forgotten my language, my culture, fruits, and vegetables. Everything replaced with sand. Mariama, Oumar, Tala, my students, they were the reason I'd survived this place. I loved them, but I could see now that wasn't enough, not even close. I could see the injustice of the Tuaregs' situation that mirrored my own country's discrimination against its indigenous people. Maybe I was trying to make up for that, too.

"We have to do something about this," Ahmed said.

He plucked at the strings of his guitar and Oumar got up to pour the second round of tea.

I heard another voice say, "It's time to stand up for ourselves."

Or maybe it was a line from Bob Marley playing in my brain. Get up, stand up.

"Tomorrow," Ahmed said.

Again, everyone talking at once, including Nick, crouched between Tala's husband and Ahmed.

Ahmed continued. His voice calm but rising above the other sounds. "A few of us will occupy the military police post to protest the arrest of those of us who've been unjustly jailed and demand attention to the conditions of the camp."

I heard tomorrow, occupy, military police, arrest, unjustly jailed, demand attention, conditions, camp.

A mixed reaction from the others.

"You have weapons?" Tala's husband asked.

Weapons. This stirred people up.

I caught Tala's eye on the opposite side of the fire.

"No, it's a peaceful protest," Ahmed said. "We'll be unarmed."

I heard peaceful, protest, unarmed. Alhamdulillah, but I kept my thoughts to myself as Oumar reminded me in every language. I wanted to whisper to him that such a balance of strong passive resistance mirrored Martin Luther King, but that would take time to explain, another time.

Ahmed stood up and spoke with Mariama, then moved around the circle talking to different clusters of people. Oumar hit the cone of sugar smartly with the shot glass and, as always, a handful of young children materialized to collect the smaller bits of sugar. When Izza toddled over, he handed her a piece. I had known Izza her whole life, longer than her father, who now stoked the coals, adding the larger splinters of sugar and water to the teapots. But only in the sense of chronological time.

I told Oumar the peaceful protest reminded me of the equal amount of sugar and bitter leaves in the second round of tea we were drinking.

He smiled. "Yes, Miss."

More discussion ensued, mostly people talking with those hunkered beside them.

All speaking Tamasheq. I could hear some dissention, feel some tension, but they all seemed to agree that action was necessary.

I glanced over at Frankie conversing with Mokao. Two of my favorite people, happy together.

Oumar got up and poured the final round of tea from a standing position hitting each cup perfectly, spilling not a drop. Frankie's and my eyes locked for a second before she resumed her conversation with Mokao. I never understood the Tuareg saying describing the last round of tea as sweet like death. I guess death could be considered sweet in extreme cases, but I agreed with Dylan Thomas: Do not go gentle into that good night.

We drank our tea and talked among ourselves or, in my case, listened. No one was talking directly to me, but they allowed my presence. I tried to be present as much as I could while knowing only a smattering of their language, trying to string words together to make meaning. There seemed to be a consensus that if the peaceful plan didn't work, they would try something else.

Another man suddenly stepped into the circle of Tuaregs crouched around the fire, each immediately feeling for his tâkoba, sword, except for Ahmed, who carried only a guitar. I first thought a gendarme had been listening and they were busted, but the man lowered his tagelmust and I recognized Roy at the same moment Frankie did.

"Roy," Frankie, Nick, and I all said at once. I kept "What the hell are you going here?" to myself.

"He works for me," Nick said as if reading my mind. "Best mechanic in Agadez."

A few people had heard of him.

"Excusez, Roy said. Sorry. "I came to... hear the music." He knelt down on his knees, the closest he could get to an extended squatting position.

I heard Frankie mumble, "Fuckin' idiot."

"I know him," Mariama said.

What? How? My inner voice.

"He is not concerned with our business." Mariama.

That much was true. She knew him that well. Everyone relaxed then and Oumar handed him a shot glass of tea.

Roy held it with the folds of his boubou. "I initially came for the Dakar then stayed in Agadez working as a mechanic."

Why was he still talking?

"But I'm returning home, very soon now," he said to whomever was still paying attention to him. Me. Nobody else cared.

"A good mechanic is always welcome," someone said.

Oumar made the clicking sound with his lips and whispered

in my ear, "He is not here for the music. He is here for you. No matter what Ahmed or my mother says, I don't trust him."

"What does Mariama say?"

Oumar made a double clicking sound with his lips, that he disagreed, that it wasn't worth repeating.

I saw Ahmed walk over to talk to Roy, so I went the same direction to eavesdrop before finding Tala. Ahmed was holding his guitar in one hand and Roy's arm in the other as they walked.

"I heard you made a name for yourself at the Dakar. Nick says you are skilled."

"Thanks. It's my passion, like playing the guitar seems to be yours."

"Yes," Ahmed said. "Where are you staying?"

"Camping near here. Your guitar music carried; I had to see, to listen."

"You will stay with my family tonight," Ahmed said. "Our guest."

The Tuaregs were generous. I left the vicinity of Ahmed and Roy and caught up to Tala, now talking to Frankie.

"Tala!"

"Miss!"

"You look stunning as always. How is married life? Your village? Do you have anything to read?"

"I am happy, at least for now. Not many books there."

"You should write one." Frankie.

"I could title it, *Teaching my English Teacher* or *How to Find Happiness in Your Koobgal Marriage*."

I couldn't imagine an arranged marriage but maybe I lacked imagination. We caught up on the fate of the sunflowers and that she and her husband had come to see their friends and relatives living in the refugee camp. Frankie told her she had quit smoking and revealed that she was thinking of growing a desert variety of organic tobacco, possibly creating a cottage industry for the Tuareg women, but at the very least the tobacco would contain no additives, chemicals. The women would enjoy a healthier chew.

Frankie. Frank. People were starting to disperse. "If anyone needs a place to stay tonight, I'd love it," I offered.

"Roy does." Frankie.

"Funny," I said, trying not to imagine Roy and I spending the night alone. "Believe it or not, Ahmed invited him to stay at Mariama's."

"I believe it," Frankie said. "They took us in, didn't they? But I can't believe Mariama stood up for Roy tonight when he showed up out of nowhere when they were planning the protest."

"Trying to keep things calm. She's right that he isn't concerned with their business. He wouldn't understand anything discussed in Tamasheq, but he is fluent in the language of vehicles, and everyone in this country appreciates that."

"He's still a fuckin' idiot."

Tala and Frankie both offered to walk me home, but my house was in the opposite direction. "I can find my way," I said. But I was bummed. Didn't want the night to end. Didn't want to be alone.

When I got home, even Patience was out. Still wide awake, I lit the kerosene lamp so I could see to sweep out the house and burn some energy. Shook out the mats and hung them over the porch railing. A beautiful night for sleeping outside as was every night except during the Harmattan. It took all of five minutes to clean house. Hot in there anyway.

I put the wire lamp handle around my wrist and started sweeping the yard in a sunflower pattern, a sort of moving meditation. The sunflower design, a kind of modified monochromatic pointillist style. Seurat but not. Blooming heads big as dinner plates, dashes of seeds, the petals, three short strokes wide, tapering to two, to one. The stems and leaves, longer strokes. Six flowers per row. I was on the fourth row when I heard a vehicle outside followed by Frankie coming in the gate, arms full of beer, wine and, "Is that whiskey?"

"Girls night in," she said.

"What about Mokao?"

"He's a good Muslim, doesn't believe in this stuff."

"Alhamdulillah."

"What would you like?"

"Let's go in order. Beer, wine, whisky, and just a little. I'm not used to it."

We clinked bottles. She took off the jacket she'd worn on the drive over. A pack of Rothmans and a Bic slid out beneath her chair.

"To the desert," I said, pouring a little on the stem of a sand sunflower. "And to its people."

"Don't waste even cheap beer on sand. What is that? A fuckin' sunflower? Looks like I got here in the nick. Are you losing it?"

"Not yet." I didn't bother talking about meditating, sweeping, or Seurat with Frankie. "It's good the Tuaregs are staging a non-violent protest tomorrow."

"Yeah. Ahmed is organizing it. His father isn't joining him, though I think Mariama supports the idea. A few other ishumars all around Ahmed's age."

"I admire Ahmed, but I'm glad Oumar's not going. Even though it's peaceful."

Frankie shrugged. "Well, he has a job so he's not actually an ishumar."

"True, and Nick's taxi business is doing really well. I know it's helping out Mariama."

"Glass of wine?"

I made the affirmative sound from the back of my throat. "Please." I went in the house and retrieved my two enamel cups.

"Here's to the greater good and good wine."

We clunked enamel cups.

I took another drink. And another. "Do you love Mokao?"

"How could I not?"

We raised our cups again. "I'm happy for you. Love is such a sublime feeling. Everyone should feel that. And then there's sex."

"Except no kissing in my case, but I'm not complaining. Not kissing is very sensual."

"Yeah, but eventually, I'd miss it," I said. "I miss it so much."

"Time for a shot of whisky."

"I'll get the tea glasses."

"You mean shot glasses."

Frankie muttered something about loving the nomadic culture, except for the fuckin' tea as I entered the house.

I set the glasses in the sand. "It's an acquired taste, acquired from politely drinking it whenever it's offered." She shook her head, which could have meant agreement or disagreement. "If you drink as much tea as I have, I think it actually replaces your blood. At least that's how it feels when you don't drink it."

Frankie poured the amber liquid like the Tuaregs poured tea, from an impressive height and not spilling a drop.

"I remember how strange I thought it was to drink tea out of shot glasses; now it seems strange to drink liquor from them."

"To strangeness," Frankie said.

"To leaving a legacy of kissing on the lips," I said.

"An anasara can dream."

We raised our shot glasses and drank. It burned all the way down.

Frankie poured another. "Tell me about Roy."

I studied the sand sunflowers, angled my ear toward some distant music, then looked at Frankie, who was staring at me through a veil of smoke. "Pay attention because I'm only going to say it once and it's going to be brief." The second shot didn't burn at all. "Ready?"

"Maybe I need another shot first," Frankie said.

"We definitely do."

She poured and we drank.

"Once upon a time, for several years, Roy and I were deeply

in love." I held my glass out for a refill. "It was perfect on every level, sensual, spiritual, sexual. Perfect. Until one day, it wasn't. Roy and my best friend Gita got together—reasonable on a commune that practices the dissolution of one-on-one relationships. But I couldn't be reasonable. I couldn't breathe. So, I pretended he was dead, and I ran. Here. To this landscape. To these people. To you." I raised my glass, swallowed the shot, then held up my hand for emphasis. "Now, here he is, changed his mind, regained his mind? Whatever." This is where Frankie was supposed to ask me if I still loved him, but she didn't. "Of course, I still love him; that I can't control, but I will not, cannot, refuse to lose him again. That much, I've learned, and he hasn't. The end."

"Like I said, he's a fuckin' idiot. And Gita?"

"After I arrived here, she wrote that she loved me, not Roy. I never knew that. How could I not know that she was in love with me?"

"Sometimes it's like that."

"Then she died."

"Sucks, but at least you knew the truth," Frankie said.

Not that I expected condolences or even empathy from Frankie. Maybe I did.

She handed me another shot instead.

"I don't know the truth." I traced Gita's name in the sand with my free hand. "Is the only difference between love for a lover and for a good friend, sex?"

"Love is a fuckin' lab experiment—all those chemicals, human elements, variables. You make a hypothesis, but it's not always correct."

"A true romantic."

"I love Mokao. And the others I've loved before him, I regret none."

"Maybe the commune has it right. Human beings aren't meant to spend their lives with one person, monogamous like 90% of birds."

"Maybe it's your name." Frankie got up. "Or that you're just in love with the idea of love." She disappeared into the latrine.

I grabbed the pack of Rothmans from under her chair, lit one of her cigarettes and poured another splash of whisky.

Frankie lifted her head slightly as she exited the latrine, catching the whiff of smoke. She gave me the side-eye as she sat down and lit one of her own.

"To love," I said.

She raised her eyebrows.

"Who doesn't love falling in love?"

She raised her shoulders, eyebrows, and her glass. "Gets trickier after that."

"Exactly what I'm talking about." I took a shallow drag. "I mean you could enjoy a series of falling in love with people your whole life."

"To falling in love," she said, her glass still aloft.

"But after the magic of the fall, you never get to the depths, the complexity of two human beings sharing a life together."

Frankie tilted her glass to me. "Take the corner out of that, will you?"

"It takes effort, right? Intention. Like learning how to live with yourself."

Frankie blew a trademark smoke ring. "Not bad logic, especially at this time of night, but this is exactly what you didn't do with Roy, which kind of negates your argument."

She was right as far as reasoning. I turned my empty shot glass back and forth in the sand, made a cup holder, and changed the subject. "I've been thinking of staying on after my contract ends next year. By then I'll be more fluent in the languages. I already love this place, and I can't imagine leaving Oumar, Mariama, Tala, you."

Frankie didn't miss a beat. "You could take Oumar's advice and marry Ahmed. Mariama would love it."

"Koobgal. I can't even imagine agreeing to arranged marriage."

"Right, because what could fuckin' go wrong with a marriage based on hormones and pheromones?"

I raised my glass.

Frankie was gone by the time I woke up, but Patience was there thumping her tail. "Shh," I whispered. She sat. It was late, excruciatingly bright, but at least it was quiet without Frankie, probably out peddling her idea of organic tobacco to the vendors, or maybe she was with Mokao. Good for her. She'd left her Rothmans uniform and wore her boubou, the desert clothes Mariama had given her. My plan, to stay home nursing my headache and do some laundry. I should have been drinking water between alcoholic beverages, a forgotten tip from my mothers. My brain felt like a dry sponge.

I didn't think anything of it when Nick stopped by looking for Oumar. "Not here. Did you try Mariama's? His mother will know where he is." I filled the enamel wash tub and sprinkled in a handful of Omo, looking away while stirring the blue powder in dizzying circles with my pencil until it dissolved. T-shirts easy, I scrubbed, rinsed, wrung, and hung them on the acacia, the thorns anchoring them like clothespins. Pagnes more difficult, so much material in a small tub, the tedious rinsing to get all the soap out, then wringing them out. I plodded through, my head floating too close the sun. The throbbing reminding me of those blinking lights that keep planes from hitting vertical obstacles.

Only a short time later, apropos of nothing I could determine, everything changed. An armored car stopped outside my wall, and some soldiers threw open the gate and asked me where Oumar or any of his friends were.

"I haven't seen him today."

"I thought he lived here," one of the soldiers barked.

"Used to. Not for months."

The soldiers bolted through the yard and searched my house anyway. It didn't take them long.

My heart started racing. "Why are you looking for him? What's wrong?"

No response.

After they left, I opened the gate and looked down the sand road to see dozens of armored cars and military men questioning everyone who was out. I asked a neighbor what was going on. She asked someone else. No one seemed to know what was happening.

I slipped into my sandals and walked to the pumps where Oumar once watered the goats, thinking Mariama might have asked him to take care of them while he was home. As I stood there looking over the herders, a deep roar startled the camels and goats and they shied away from the trough, water dripping from their mouths. The nomads drawing the water from the well dropped their black buckets on the sand. The sound came not from a predator stalking their animals from the surrounding dunes but from above. We shaded our eyes against the sun. "Avions," airplanes, a shirtless schoolboy shouted, his friends jumping and waving their arms.

Oumar wasn't there. I started running. The women pounding millet along the road paused, the sudden sound and shadows of the planes interrupting the steady rhythm of their wooden pestles. Business at the market stopped mid-transaction as the traders turned from the piles of spices and silver bracelets and looked up at the planes. I kept running through the village looking for Oumar—thinking he would have already left Mariama's if he'd slept there—getting breakfast, buying tea, joking with his friends. When he saw me, he would tell me what was happening. Explain everything. I kept searching.

Along the sand roads in the village and scanning the dunes beyond, I saw Tuaregs stop and turn their faces toward the sky then hurry along when they saw the armored cars.

Clouds of dust from the vehicles hung in the air. Traders peered from their doorways unsure of why the military was there but knowing the gendarmes' thirst and hunger from such a journey. One man quickly rewrapped his turban and arranged some orange Fanta under damp burlap bags on a table in front of his shop. Oumar wasn't there, but a soldier got out of a car, opened a bottle with his teeth, and drank it straight down.

The ground filled with shadows. I shaded my eyes against the sun at what looked like clouds slowly floating to the ground. Skydivers, I thought. The feral dogs ran wild when paratroopers started dropping to the ground. My neighbors, the vendors, the herders, the nomads walking down the roads—no one knew anything. Everything was happening fast, the pace all wrong. Maybe Niger was at war and someone was invading.

I had to find Oumar. Maybe Frankie would know. I circled back to my house. Again, no one there. I ran across the road to the neighbor's house. The woman always at home and prepared, the one even Mariama went to see when there was no water. I clapped and then pounded on the door with my fists. When no one answered, I darted between the military vehicles to the shops where Frankie probably went, and where Oumar might be. From a short distance, I saw Frankie's familiar boubou and Mokao's lithe silhouette leaping in front of Frankie as if he were dancing for her. Others moving toward them as if to watch. Then I heard the rapid pop of firecrackers and saw the nomads along the row of shops fall to the ground. Everyone was suddenly running away, but I ran straight ahead to Frankie and Mokao, the soldiers shooting the Tuaregs. Everyone screaming.

As I sprinted toward Frankie and Mokao, time warped into slow motion, like running in a dream, a nightmare. I recognized the faces of the storeowners who'd sold me tea and laundry soap only the day before, inert on the ground. Mariama's husband, Abdullah, lay beside one of them, his eyes open, unblinking. Tala's husband. People here died young and often; the desert claimed them, but Nigerien soldiers murdering their own citizens point blank with machine guns. Beyond comprehension.

Mokao lay dead on top of Frankie, his fake Ray-Bans askew on his face, my tears blending with my breath against his cheek, the faint promise of rain on a slight breeze. I looked at Frankie's closed eyes, her bleeding shoulder wound. I couldn't tell if she was breathing. "Frankie?" I rolled Mokao off her body. "Frankie?" I tried to stanch her wound with her tagelmust. Applied pressure. Kissed her forehead, still warm. Her lips.

"Hey." A weak smile.

"Shit, Frankie. You're alive."

"Mokao?"

"I'm so sorry."

She reached for him, grasped his arm and held on. "Oumar?"

"Haven't found him yet."

"The short-cut to Agadez. Take the Scout."

First, I'd load Frankie, go home and consult *Where There is No Doctor*, the chapter on bullet wounds, then take the shortcut to Agadez. I glanced at the side of the Scout facing us, riddled with bullet holes from the spray of fire directed at the nomads. "Frankie. At least two tires are flat, but I can drive it home, get a better look at your wound. I'll pull it over and help you get in. How do you know the shortcut to Agadez?"

"I don't fuckin' work for Rothmans."

"I knew you were a spy."

She tried to laugh; her breathing changed, her voice quiet. "Listen. Roll Mokao back onto me."

"I can't leave you here like this."

"This wound is superficial. Someone is coming for me; go find Oumar."

I dragged Mokao on top of Frankie, placing his head on her wound for direct pressure then hesitated. Was it just a flesh wound? Was someone coming?

She opened her eyes and squinted up at me. "Fuckin' go."

I ran home, dipped a cup of water from the tukunya, trying not to slosh on the way back to Frankie. The area now abandoned of any life. Still. Any sounds of gunfire in the distance. Frankie's eyes remained closed as I lifted her head, wet her lips with the water. She opened her mouth and swallowed as I tipped the cup.

"Thank you," she whispered. "I'm just going to rest here with Mokao. Now fuckin' go find Oumar."

When I entered Mariama's encampment, the military had already been there. Mortars overturned, pestles strewn across the sand as if thrown midair, the coal in the brazier still smoldering, the teapot on its side still warm to the touch. "Mariama!" I forced myself to enter her tent. Ransacked, her possessions lay in disarray but otherwise empty. Mariama and little Izza weren't there. I entered the other tents one by one. Mariama's camp abandoned. No matriarchs, no children.

I ran back to my neighbor's house and clapped, then pushed open the door to find my neighbor and her son annihilated where they must have looked up in surprise when the soldiers burst into the yard. The woman dead beside her brazier and over-turned teapot, her little boy still holding a splinter of sugar.

"My God," I wailed to no one, imagining unarmed women and children such easy prey, and for what? It was savage. I knelt beside my neighbor and her young son dabbing my eyes so I could see to remove their gris-gris—protecting them from djinn but not the military—remembering that Mariama had said Allah didn't like talismans.

I was in that place outside of myself where I could see what was happening as if it were a dream or a nightmare that I would eventually wake from. Numb. I kept running.

More chaos and carnage at the refugee camp. I ran to Alhassane, the tea man, to ask him about Oumar, but those who were able had fled. Someone said a guard was accidently killed with his own gun at the protest. The protesters had run.

Oumar was not there when I returned home, so I left again. I didn't know how much time had passed, had lost any sense of it. The locals were saying the military occupied the wells, not poisoning them, but hiding nearby and waiting to shoot the people and their animals when thirst compelled them to go there.

"Who are they waiting for? The protesters?"

"The Kel-Tamasheq. Anyone who is a Kel-Tamasheq, Tuareg, is being burned alive, cut to pieces, hanged, or executed."

"That's, that can't be. For the accident at the gendarmerie?" I couldn't understand it.

"The Kel-Tamasheq are being looted and tortured because they are Kel-Tamasheq."

"The women are being raped," someone else said. "They are being exterminated and their corpses are being desecrated."

"No," I said, but as I ran through the town toward the school, I saw otherwise. The school was deserted. Maybe it had been evacuated, the teachers and students fleeing for their lives.

I saw naked old men being made to walk in front of military jeeps, forced to parade in front of everyone, the men who covered themselves to their eyes out of honor and respect. I looked away from them and glared at the soldiers who appeared drunk with power, beyond reason. When I looked up and saw the children, some of my students, dead in the branches having tried to hide in the few straggly trees on the route, I retched.

"Tuareg lover!" a soldier yelled, laughing.

I put my hand on a tree trunk for support and power, stood up, and continued home, trying to concentrate on where else Oumar might be, hoping he'd reached safety.

A car I didn't recognize was parked outside my yard. "Lark," someone said as I opened the gate.

"Oumar?" but the voice didn't match. It was Roy's, which might have surprised me but didn't.

"Thank God you're alive," he said. His voice sounded tinny and far away.

"We have to leave here," he said. "And find your friend, Oumar."

He took my face in his hands.

"Lark, I saw what happened."

"Tell me. You have to tell me! Everything."

He dragged over the string chairs. I sat, rigid. Roy was shaking, or it might have been me.

"Four refugees went to occupy the police station. Unarmed, as Ahmed said last night. When they voiced their protests, the guard dismissed them. A fight broke out. The guard pulled his gun and aimed it at Oumar, who tried to wrestle it from him in defense."

I stood back up. "Oumar was there?! Is he all right?"

"In the scuffle, the guard's gun fired, killing the guard. The protestors fled. I bolted after Oumar, but I lost him in the... mayhem."

"But he was okay," I said it just to hear again. "He and Nick rode camels here; Frankie thought they'd take the shortcut back to Agadez."

"Would he know the way?"

"The desert has no secrets from the Kel-Tamasheq."

"What does that mean?"

"Oumar knows the way."

"I know the way, too," Roy said. He pulled out a map with red penciled dashes marking the route, the coordinates. "We'll drive my car. I just overhauled this Mercedes. They're extremely reliable and it's fully serviced."

I was staring at my bloody hands as if they were someone else's.

"What do you think about waiting till morning?" he said. "It's already dark, and my navigating skills would be better in the light."

I walked past him into the house for water and then to the latrine to wash off the blood. My hand was shaking as I dipped the can into the bowl of water, and I started to cry, a deep shudder that moved through me like the low reverberations of a drum. The image of Frankie standing in my yard drinking water, so vivid. I couldn't wash the blood from my hands. I still saw it. Stained. Permanently stained. Did Frankie survive? Was she lying about someone coming for her? My mother, my friend, Mariama. Izza. Vanished. Were they okay? My students. Eddoua. Tala. My neighbors. I leaned against the banco wall and cried for them, for the mothers who lost their children, for all my mothers, all parents, for the children who lost their mothers, their parents, their friends, for those who survived. I cried for Patience. She hadn't come home. The water itself made me cry. Then I remembered Oumar. I washed the remaining blood and dust from my body, my face, my hair, my clothes, covered myself with a pagne, and stepped back into the yard. Roy was still standing in the same place. "In a car," I said, "we'll catch up to Oumar. I'll be able to see better in the day, too."

I handed Oumar's mat to Roy and stood there holding my own, my mind churning. Mariama, Izza, Mariama's husband, my students, Frankie, Mokao and hundreds of others killed, injured, or missing. How did President Saibou allow this to happen, the dark power of the army to overshadow his promise of peace? I dropped my mat on the sand and walked toward the gate.

"No," Roy said. "Don't go out, especially at night when no one can see clearly."

I opened the gate.

He talked faster. "You won't be able to do anything anyway. You're unarmed. You're an anasara, a Peace Corps volunteer."

"Frankie was shot, injured outside the shops. I have to make sure she got out."

"What if Oumar comes while you're gone?" Roy said. "I owe Frankie; I'll go."

Roy was right that I should stay home in case Oumar showed up. He would know I'd be worried about him and come to me if he could. If not, I would find him.

"I'll change into some jeans and a t-shirt and drive over. If she's still there, I'll bring her with me."

"If she's still there, she's dead, with Mokao."

I started sweeping the yard, not in an artful pattern but out of nervous energy and had nearly finished when I finally heard Roy's car purring then silent outside the gate.

"Not there," he said. "Frankie, Mokao, the Scout, all gone."

"Gone?" He could say anything, anything he thought I

wanted to hear. I chose to believe him. I needed to.

"Listen, Lark. Maybe we should go now too. Not cut across the desert in the dark but get out of here, away from your house. I don't think it's safe."

"Where would we go? Where is safe? If they wanted to kill us, they would have. If you want to go, go ahead. I'm staying here tonight in case Oumar shows up."

"Let's at least sleep in the car so we won't be so vulnerable out in the open yard. The protection from being inside the car will give us an edge if we need it."

I didn't think it mattered but didn't have the energy to argue with him. I lay in the back seat, windows cracked and looked at the thousands of stars visible in the square of the sunroof. I heard the automatic door lock and somehow eventually dozed.

Frankie was in the passenger seat admiring Mokao dressed in full regalia for the Geerewol and driving the Scout to the Cure de Salée, but it kept backfiring; they couldn't move.

I startled awake to the sound of distant gunshots and panicked at being imprisoned in a dark interior. I lay still, intentionally calming my breath, allowing my eyes to focus, adjusting to what? A vehicle. The inside of a car. Roy's light hair now visible from the front seat. I let myself out and entered my yard. Still empty of Oumar, Patience, life.

CHAPTER TWENTY-ONE
HOT SEASON, EN ROUTE FROM TCHIN-TABARADEN 1990

I filled my guerba and briefly considered taking the entire tukunya of water, but someone here would need it. I lit the lantern and searched the house for necessary supplies: some dates I wrapped in a scarf that doubled as head protection, my compass, teapot, Swiss army knife, the sleeping mats, and got into the car with Roy.

Seeing Roy sprawled across the seat, surreal. "Roy, wake up, time to go."

"What time is it?"

"I don't know. Time."

"It's still dark."

"Twilight. We'll be able to see in the bush, the desert. The ambient light from the stars, the moon. But drive by the shops first."

He disappeared into the latrine, taking... forever.

We drove by the empty shops where vendors and consumers alike still lay haphazard, their disarrayed cloth illuminated in the half-light.

Roy had spoken the truth. Neither Frankie's body entwined with Mokao's, nor her Scout were there. Unless Roy had moved them. It did take him awhile. "How did you find them?" A trick question.

"I said I didn't."

He still could have though, to let me hope.

We drove north out of Tchin-Tabaraden.

I glanced at Roy's profile, his pale hands on the steering wheel slightly curved as if strumming his guitar. It was as if we had stepped out of time and were driving across the past, though instead of grass and wildflowers there was only sand, both outside the window and inside myself. Heavy sand making it difficult to breathe. I stared out the passenger window as we passed the windscreen where I'd first stood on the edge of the Sahara, a person I barely remembered. It would be easy to spot Oumar in such a stark, horizontal landscape. Harder where the wind whipped the sand into dunes.

Roy flipped on the air conditioner.

I rolled down my window.

"Right," he said, "Too much contrast."

He turned it off and lowered his window. "I wonder how far ahead Oumar would be. They. He probably didn't go by himself."

It sounded odd, Roy saying Oumar's name. Pronouncing it correctly as if he knew him, as if he understood what that name meant.

After several kilometers of silence, Roy put my old favorite mixed tape into the cassette player: Stones, Clapton, Joan Armatrading, Pink Floyd, George Harrison. The me from before, and he'd added more Marley, audio clips from MLK and JFK.

I squeezed my eyes closed momentarily. Resumed my search. "Up ahead," I said, but as we reached the lone Tuareg, he lashed his camel with a switch, and it ran diagonally away from us. "Slow down. It's not Oumar, and there's no need to wear that man's camel down."

About the time Harrison started singing "Here Comes the Sun," for the third time, the cassette player started screwing up. I'd forgotten how annoying that was. Roy pressed eject, blew on the tape, and rapped it against his palm and reinserted, but it still sounded warped, wavy. When he tried other tapes with the same results, he turned on the radio instead. Static.

I passed him the guerba. "Only a little, we're only a few hours in."

"Where is everybody?"

"The Tuaregs are probably hiding when they hear a vehicle. In the draws, the valleys, the low spots. They don't want to be seen; the dunes provide cover." It made me feel better to know they were out there even if we couldn't see them. Maybe Oumar was watching us now, even if he recognized Roy's car, not knowing I was in it so sheltering in place. I shook the guerba at Roy. He briefly drank.

It was midafternoon when I saw three figures, silhouettes actually, against the glare. I pointed straight ahead with my chin. "See them?"

"Two camels, three people?" Roy sped up and then started thumping at the plastic panel over the odometer.

"What?"

"Something's up with the gauges. Nothing serious, the needles flicking a little. I'll check it in Agadez."

The closer we got to the figures, the further the figures moved away until they vanished completely on the rippling horizon. "Mirage," I said. I swallowed another drink of water and handed the guerba to Roy. He drank deeply.

The engine started missing as if it too were feeling the fatigue of afternoon, and Roy held his head at an angle as if to hear it more precisely like he did when tuning his guitar.

"That's odd," he said. "I'm pulling under that acacia to have a look. We should take a break anyway."

In the scant shade, he popped the hood and surveyed the

familiar territory. After blowing the film of dust off the engine, he reported that all the cables and wires were intact, still plenty of coolant in the radiator. He'd brought an extra jug of emergency water and extra petrol.

"Everything looks fine. Must be an electrical glitch." He left the hood ajar a couple of inches.

I'd gotten out to stretch my legs. The wind was blowing its hot breath, razing any exposed skin with sand. We each had another drink of water, ate the dates, drank again. "Oumar can't be much ahead of us," I said, leaning against the driver's side door.

Roy agreed.

"I'll drive now, though you'll have to navigate."

"No, I'm fine," Roy said, angling past me, sliding into the driver's seat, and turning the key. The engine groaned then made a series of clicks. "What? This is a brand-new battery," he mumbled to himself. He re-opened the hood.

I followed him. "Is the battery dead?"

"It can't be, but it sounds like it." He pulled a faded red shop rag from his pocket and dabbed at the beads of sweat trickling from his hairline. "You might as well relax in the shade. It may be a while."

"Here. Drink some water so you can think straight." I passed him the guerba. "I should have paid more attention to mechanics, so I could help."

He refilled the empty guerba and handed it back. "I've got this. Nothing the right tool won't fix, and I brought them all."

May was the peak of the hot season in Niger, and it was living up to it. I knew the best thing we could do in the situation was to conserve energy. I covered my body loosely with my pagne, squinting into the distance for any sign of movement, of Oumar.

It was evening before Roy discovered the cable to the alternator had been cut. The car had run fine at first, he explained, because it was running off the charged battery. The lethargic cassette player and jumping gauge needles were symptoms of its draining power. It was a clean cut so close to the battery that it was hidden, beneath, as if someone had purposely sliced it there to conceal it.

I finished his thought. "So that by the time it was discovered, it would be too late." I turned away from the car. "But it's not too late; we still have water."

"The window washer reservoir is filled with water that we can siphon if necessary, too."

"Do you have electrical tape?"

"Yeah, I could do a temporary repair on the cable, but the problem is there's no way to recharge the battery."

"Right." I looked into the distance. "It's too far to walk either back to Tchin-Tabaraden or ahead to Agadez, but there will be other Tuaregs coming this way to escape."

"And others in pursuit," Roy said. He moved the toolbox aside in the trunk and looked in the back seat. "Are we out of food?"

"Yeah, but water is the main thing. Thirst."

We unpacked the sleeping mats and stretched out next to each other under the tree, using the car as a windbreak. We both lay awake but quiet under a blanket of glittering stars, the moon glowing and familiar.

The second day, the sun rose red on the horizon turning the sand pink. I hiked a short way into the distance with my teapot and relieved myself. The landscape completely silent except for Roy and me, who kept looking at the same problem with the same incapacity to do anything about it, our movements like beating moth wings against the blinding light.

It was true that we still had water, but I knew that this might be how our lives ended. I didn't feel panic but a deep sense of calm, an opening up, a blossoming, an awareness not only of the depth of sky and the vast stretch of sand but of my life, the lives of everyone at once. Oumar would be incredulous that I would think I could help him survive in his own landscape. But I would try. I would see him again. In my time here, I'd made only a small contribution; the children of the nomads could speak, read, and write English. That could only potentially help them with their future, which was at best cloudy. Mine was much clearer, and the only one I had any control over. Roy and me against the landscape. Unless help arrived, the desert would win, of course. Oumar said it always does. This reckoning allowed me to see with more clarity, to let go of the past, the figments of my imagination, to see what was actually here. I felt all the scattered parts of myself align.

Walking back to the car, I contemplated further. If we were rescued, I still had to acknowledge that Roy had traveled to the other side of the world to reunite. Unless he'd been the one who'd cut the line. I squinted at him, his torso curled over the engine. That seemed too dark. He'd been reckless, careless, but never malicious. At that moment, I was incapable of feeling anything but love, and I surrendered to it. I would do everything possible to survive, but even if I didn't, I was in control of how my life played out, how our life together played out.

"Anything new?" I asked, the light glinting off the engine.

"To be honest, we're screwed unless someone shows up. "

"I know," I said. "And maybe someone will. Maybe Allah will will it." I opened the jug of emergency water for the radiator, drank just enough to wet my lips, moisten my mouth and offered it to Roy. Then I kissed him, one distortedly long kiss.

"Damn, Lark," he responded, kissing me back, in the slow-motion time of the desert.

It was afternoon before Roy spoke again. We were following the shade as it revolved around the car.

"When I saw you at the Cure de Salée, I thought it was too late. I thought you'd lost your mind."

"You were seeing Keats' chameleon quality."

"The ability to tolerate a loss of the self by trusting in the process of recreating oneself."

"A defense mechanism for preservation, for survival. And I wanted to hurt you."

"We damaged each other."

"Yes." I closed my eyes and massaged my temples.

"Headache?"

"Nothing some Tuareg tea wouldn't cure, if I'd thought to bring some."

"Maybe. It's also a sign of dehydration. The body loses water at a constant rate. We should drink the rest of the water now." He opened the jug and handed it to me.

We quit talking again, sharing nearly all of the extra water by evening when I asked him to remove my gris-gris.

He removed one, whispering and kissing the length of my neck in slow motion, then the other.

That night, we spent our conserved energy on each other, holding onto and blending so completely as to blur the edges of our physical bodies. There was a weakness, a heaving of whitecaps and weeping, a tickling of frail bones tumbling end over end in deepness, a rippling of bent elbows rounding point over point, a roving of toes through liquid sand, ribbons of us woven together, falling like feathers.

On the third day, I saw Oumar riding toward us on a camel packed with a goat's hide bulging with water. I stumbled through the sand calling to him. Roy came up from behind, locked his arms around me, and held me still.

"There's no one there," he said, his voice, or mine. He cut a hose and siphoned the water from the washer reservoir. "Drink this."

Later, when I'd watched for several minutes but heard no sound, I didn't mention Frankie's Scout either. We observed each other's reactions to gauge reality, to verify it. He grabbed the shovel from the trunk, as if he could dig to the water beneath its surface. I put my hand on his arm. He put the shovel back.

We quit talking except for practical purposes. It required too much energy and it began to be painful to form the dry words in our mouths. Our bodies became flushed, fatigued, feverish.

Our thirst became extreme. Once in the afternoon, I got up to relieve myself.

"Don't leave," Roy slurred.

"Piss," I whispered.

"Drink it."

Then we both heard a noise and looked up to see a lone plane crossing the otherwise empty desert sky. We waved our arms at it squinting into the bright pane of light until it disappeared. Had it seen us? A narrow, buzzing ribbon of hope looped around us for several hours.

Roy siphoned the motor oil into the jug. We drank it only when we couldn't stand our thirst anymore.

I knew we had cut our rate of water loss in half by resisting the urge to walk across the burning sand. We had stayed by the car and rested in as much shade as it offered and had protected our skin from the sun with light colored cloth. I knew we were using all the appropriate survival techniques in our situation and that it wasn't enough.

We stayed in place. We couldn't afford to waste the energy of raising our heart rates through stress. By late that afternoon, we quit speaking. I willed myself not to sweat, but if we did, we licked it off each other with thickening tongues.

Roy cut his wrist with his utility knife.

"No," I mouthed. My tongue stuck to the roof of my mouth, my jaw slack.

As the ruby liquid drew to the surface, he brought it to my mouth, moistening my lips with his blood. I cut my own wrist then and held it to Roy's lips.

I looked into his hazel eyes now glazed, his mouth stained with my blood. I pressed my lips against his and we breathed each other's breath. We leaned into each other, holding each other up. No tears. The wind blew the sand around us, a vast sea of dry whitecaps.

I could no longer distinguish between dream or reality, mirage or mass. Maybe Roy died. His body cracked and broken under my arm. I heard him want to call out to me, to leave my body and its torturous thirst. He seemed to look at my face, my physical self as it once was.

In the morning, the sand turned to snow. Because of Roy's blue coloring, I thought he was chilled and tried to cover him with my pagne. I scooped some snow up in my hand, tasting it on my tongue. It turned to grit in my mouth. I cut myself again and again, cradled Roy's head in my arm, urging him to drink, but my body was so dehydrated I couldn't bleed. I couldn't swallow.

A shadow hovered over his body then disappeared. I squinted up at the light and saw vultures cutting the sky into white pieces. I fell on Roy's body, hurtling soundless curses and waving my arms in weak, frantic spasms at the predators. They kept coming for him, so many of them, circling in so closely, I heard the dark flight feathers whistling.

Or was it voices woven together like the Tuareg women's intricate braids? Tala talking about escaping Tchin-Tabaraden, riding to Abalak to warn the nomads of the chaos, the carnage. To pick up supplies. Waiting for the moon to wane before fleeing. Less visible, less vulnerable.

Oumar confessing to cutting the cable to the alternator in Roy's car to discourage him from pursuing me. Wanting me to stay, marry Ahmed, become a part of the family. "If Roy was such a clever mechanic like everyone said, it would just slow him down, frustrate him. Anyone else wouldn't survive."

It's okay, Oumar. I love you, too. Do you hear me?

The sound of camel bells.

Oumar again. "Miss would try to find me. What if she went with Roy?"

Tala's voice. "Roy is the best mechanic in Agadez, maybe all of Niger. He can handle car trouble, especially if she is with him."

Frankie? Can you hear me? Did sound carry across the empty space of the desert like it did across water? Were these auditory hallucinations?

This is before the caravan of camels and donkeys crest the dune. Before Oumar's silhouette slumps against Ahmed's back, before Patience strains against the tether wrapped around Oumar's hand, before sunlight glints off the bells on Mariama's camel. Or is that their crystalline sound? Before the matriarchs walk alongside their camels and donkeys to let them rest, before Tala rises from the landscape itself.

Before they see Roy and me powdered with salt and sand. His badly burned arm lying stiffly across my torso. His opaque hazel eyes like glazed marbles, staring up at the bleached sky, his hair, mixed with the sand, nearly faded to white. Our burst lips stained like red lipstick. Before Tala gestures for Ahmed to keep the steady rhythmic pace so as not to waken Oumar. Before Mariama says, "What you don't need can kill you." After Patience jerks the tether from Oumar's wrist, runs, and touches her nose to my arm, and sits.

When Oumar says, "There she is!"

The entourage stopped, blocking the sun. I felt the release, the relief. Oumar pouring water between my lips, Mariama cradling my head in her lap, the smell of trees. Tala saying, "You're strong, Miss." Their eyes, deep pools. This is before someone lifts me up on Ahmed's camel. After Oumar says, "I have the seeds, Miss. I'm planting a sunflower here. Two, so it doesn't have to be alone."

The wind is blowing eddies of sand against the emptiness. Only the light, the sand, the intersecting planes of land and sky endure, the temporary remains of someone who has moved on, another crossing the distance.

GLOSSARY OF TAMASHEQ TERMS

Achai—tea

Adhou—wind

Ahlan wa sahlan—welcome

Akafar—Westerner (aka anasara)

Algheras—in peace

Akh—milk

Allah 'akbar—God is great

Alhamdulillah—praise be to God

Alaykum a salaam—and peace be upon you (Muslim greeting response)

Aman—water

Amanukal—Tuareg chief

Anasara—Western foreigner

Anebzeg—person who has lost touch with reality

Anzad (aka Imzad)—single-stringed traditional guitar usually played by women

Arabaz—Tuareg therapeutic massage

Asakalabo—hollowed-out calabash floating in a shallow tub of water, drum instrument

Asasmad—refrigerator

Assouf—longing

Autogare—bush taxi park

Ayat—verse from the Koran

Azawak—a dry basin covering what is today the northwestern Niger and parts of northeastern Mali and southern Algeria.

Babu bayan gida—no bathroom (Hausa)

Banco—mud

Bar L'Ombre des Plaisirs—The Shadow of Pleasures

Bismallah—with Allah's blessing

Cure de Salée—The Salt Cure (French), annual gathering of the nomads Tuareg and Wodaabé in the northern Niger town of Ingall. The celebration marks the end of the rainy season.

Djerma (aka Zarma; more broadly Songhai)—ethnic community based in Niger and Burkina Faso

Djinn (aka jinn)—supernatural creatures made of smokeless fire that can possess humans

Ehan—tent

Elem—skin

Espion—spy

Firiji—refrigerator (Hausa)

Foo-foh—Hello (Fulfulde greeting)

Fulfulde (aka Fula, Fulani, Peul)—language of the Fulani people

Fulani (aka Fula, Fulani, or Fulɓe)—one of the largest ethnic groups in the Sahel and West Africa, nomadic group of cattle-herders

Fura—millet porridge mixed with spices and milk

Geerewol—annual courtship ritual competition among the Wodaabé Fula people. Young men dress in elaborate ornamentation and make up compete through dancing and beauty contests to attract marriageable young women.

Gendarmes—armed police (French)

Gris-gris—amulet

Guerba—canteen usually made from goat hide

Hajji—a Muslim man who has made the pilgrimage to Mecca

Hufra—shallow hole or pit

Ifulan—Fulani and Wodaabé camps at the Geerewol festival

Iftar—nightly feast with family and friends during Ramadan
Iloudjan—camel
Ina ruwa—Where's your water? (Hausa, meaning: It's none of your business)
Ishumar—unemployed Tuaregs
Kaocen (ag Mohammed)—leader of the Tuareg insurrection in the Aïr Mountains in 1916
Kel Tamasheq—how Tuaregs refer to each other
Koobgal—arranged marriage
Kuka—stove (Hausa)
L'allah—in God's name, oh my God
L'horba—exile
Marabout—Muslim holy man
Méchoui—a whole goat or sheep splayed on crossed sticks and roasted over a fire
Nacala (aka warri, mancala, to move, Arabic)—ancient game played using small stones, beans, or seeds and rows of holes or pits
Pagne—traditional patterned cloth wrapped at the waist and worn like a long skirt
Piment—hot pepper Prosopis—mesquite plant, desert variety
Ramadan—the ninth month of the Islamic calendar, observed by Muslims worldwide as a month of fasting, prayer, reflection and community
Sahel—ecoclimatic and biogeographic region between the Sahara to the north and the Sudanian savanna to the south.
Salaam alaykum—Peace be upon you (Muslim greeting)
Savanna (aka Savannah)—ecological region or vegetation type that grows under hot, seasonally dry climatic condition
Sécheresse—drought (French)
La soudure—drought, literally "soldering" (French)
Sey jaango—See you later (Fulfulde language)
Tabaski (aka Eid al-Ada or Festival of Sacrifice)—Islamic holiday honoring the willingness of Ibrahim to sacrifice his firstborn son as an act of obedience and sacrifice to Allah. Tuaregs who observe it by sacrificing a goat or sheep and share a third of the meat with

those in need, a third as a pardon for any offenses to friends and relatives, and keeping a third for the family.

Tafoud—thirst

Tafouk—sun

Tagelmust (aka cheche)—cotton garment ten meters in length, used by Tuareg men as a veil and turban.

Takomért—Tuareg cheese

Tamasheq—spoken language of Tuaregs

Tanamert—thank you

Taxi de brousse—bush taxi

Teegal—a marriage of choice that occurs at the Geerewol, the annual courtship ritual competition among the Wodaabé Fula people.

Tekatkat—white blouses embellished with red thread patterns worn by Tuareg women for special occasions

Ténéré—desert, also solitude

Tindé—drum

Trou—shallow hole or pit

Tuareg (aka Touareg or Twareg)—An ethnic Berber people, traditionally nomadic pastoralists who live in the Sahara and Sahel in Algeria, Niger, Mali, and western Libya

Tukunya—clay vessel for storing water (Hausa)

Wodaabé (aka Mbororo or Bororo)—subgroup of the Fulani ethnic group, traditionally nomadic cattle-herders and traders in the Sahel

Warri (aka Nacala and Mancala)—ancient game played using small stones, beans, or seeds and rows of holes or pits

Welen—drought (Tamasheq)

NOTES

6. HOT SEASON, AGADEZ 1989

1. Communauté Financière d'Afrique, Financial Community of Afri

11. RAINY SEASON, CURE DE SALÉE, GEEREWOL, WORSO, IN GALL 1989

1. Kaocen ag Mohammed, leader of the Tuareg insurrection in the Aïr Mountains in 1916

SHORT LIST OF RESOURCES

Beckwith, Carol and Marion Van Offelen, *Nomads of Niger*

Bernus, Edmond, *Les Touaregs*

Dayak, Mano, *Je suis né avec du sable dans les yeux; Touareg, la tragedie*

Decalo, Samuel, *Historical Dictionary of Niger*

Fischer, Anja and Ines Kohl, *Tuareg Society within a Globalized World*

Glen, Simon, *Sahara Handbook*

The Holy Quran

Kisingani, E.F., *The Tuareg Rebellions in Mali and Niger*

Porch, Douglas, *The Conquest of the Sahara*

Seligman, Thomas and Kristyne Loughran, *Art of Being a Tuareg*

SHORT LIST OF RESOURCES

de Villiers, Marq and Sheila Hirtle, *Sahara*

ACKNOWLEDGMENTS

I would like to thank Mary Petiet, founder of Sea Crow Press, for her unwavering support, creativity, vision, and style and Eugenia Nordskog for her positivity and editorial insight. I so appreciate the invaluable role of the small press and the vision and aesthetics of Sea Crow in particular.

I owe a debt of gratitude for all those who read earlier drafts or met with me for research purposes when I was still trying to discover the story: Bill Myers, David Tangeman, Doug Penner, Raylene Hinz-Penner, Sara Jackson Miller, Royal Alvis, Tom Averill, the late Howard Faulkner, Alice Dewdney, Barbara Worley, Cheyenne Barron, Sierra Barron, Ruben Salamanca, Musa Wakhungu Olaka, Koutana Vanloon, and Abdullah Ag Lamida. Your insights and feedback were a crucial part of the process.

Thanks especially to my writing community friends/sisters, Louise Krug, Jennifer Pacioianu, and Raylene Hinz-Penner for their keen insights and incredible support. This book would not have happened without you.

Aimee Liu, Laura Moriarty, and Mark Sullivan, thank you, thank you for your generous support.

I would also like to thank Washburn University College of Arts and Sciences Dean Laura Stephenson, Vice President of Academic Affairs JuliAnn Mazachek, English Department Chair, Corey Zwikstra, the Academic Sabbatical Committee, and the

Washburn Board of Regents for granting me a sabbatical to write the initial draft. Thanks to Modern Languages Professor Courtney Sullivan for assistance with writing coherent letters in French to various African contacts.

Special gratitude for the enduring patience and love of my family, Greg Barron, Shawnee Barron, Cheyenne Barron, and Sierra Barron, Mary Lou Heckathorn, and Alice Barron, and the memory of Cliff Heckathorn, Jim Barron, Kevin Heckathorn, and Bodil Graae, my Danish mother and inspiration for Gaia Commune.

ABOUT THE AUTHOR

K.L. Barron is a writer of place: poetry and prose. She earned an MFA in fiction from Bennington College. Her prize-winning fiction, poetry, and creative non-fiction has been published in *New Letters*, *The Bennington Review*, *Little Balkans Review*, terrain.org, *ChickenBones* (Library of Congress), among others, and in several anthologies. She teaches writing and literature at Washburn University in Topeka, Kansas and lives and writes in the Flint Hills. This is her debut novel.

ABOUT THE PRESS

Sea Crow Press is committed to amplifying voices that might otherwise go unheard. In a rapidly changing world, we believe the small press plays an essential part in contemporary arts as a community forum, a cultural reservoir, and an agent of change. We are international with a focus on our New England roots.

Sea Crow Press is named for a flock of five talkative crows you can find anywhere on the beach between Scudder Lane and Bone Hill Road in Barnstable Village on Cape Cod.

According to Norse legend, one-eyed Odin sent two crows out into the world so they could return and tell him its stories. If you sit and listen to the sea crows in Barnstable as they fly and roost and chatter, it's an easy legend to believe.